BOOKS BY ALAN PATON

Cry, the Beloved Country

Ah, But Your Land Is Beautiful

Too Late the Phalarope

South Africa in Transition

Tales from a Troubled Land

Sponono

South African Tragedy

For You Departed

Apartheid and the Archbishop

Knocking on the Door

Towards the Mountain

Journey Continued

Ah, But Your Land Is Beautiful

ALAN PATON

SCRIBNER PAPERBACK FICTION
PUBLISHED BY SIMON & SCHUSTER

New York   London   Toronto   Sydney   Tokyo   Singapore

Scribner Paperback Fiction
Simon & Schuster Inc.
Rockefeller Center
1230 Avenue of the Americas
New York, NY 10020

First Scribner Paperback Fiction Edition 1996

SCRIBNER PAPERBACK FICTION *and design
are trademarks of Simon & Schuster Inc.*

Manufactured in the United States of America

1   3   5   7   9   10   8   6   4   2

Library of Congress Cataloging in Publication Data
Paton, Alan.
Ah, but your land is beautiful.
I. Title
PR9369.3P37A73   823   81-13547
ISBN: 0-684-82583-X   AACR2

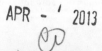

This book is dedicated to its first four readers:

Peter Brown of Pietermaritzburg, Natal
Abraham de Vries of Ladismith, Cape Province
Elliot Mngadi of Ladysmith, Natal
Pat Poovalingam of Durban, Natal

They were asked to read it
to prevent me from committing solecisms.

AUTHOR'S NOTE

This novel is set in South Africa in the years 1952 to 1958. It contains both real and fictitious characters. Of the real characters most are no longer alive. Some are actors in the novel, and these are Chief Albert Luthuli, Dr. Monty Naicker, Mr. Patrick Duncan, Advocate Molteno, and Archbishop Clayton. I have written no evil of them, because I had a high regard for them all. Other real characters appear, but they can hardly be described as actors.

Two real characters are Mrs. Helen Joseph and Archbishop Huddleston. They have both given me permission to introduce them, which is very trusting of them, they not having seen the script.

All the other characters are fictional. Some will be identified by those who lived so intensely in the years 1952-58, but I have not given them their real names, because I have not confined myself to the historical facts of their lives.

Of the events, some actually happened and some were invented.

CONTENTS

∞∞∞

PART ONE

The Defiance Campaign

Mr. Bodasingh stood in front of the big picture window in the big sitting-room of his big house in Reservoir Hills. The view is fantastic, and is admired by all their visitors. At night it can draw gasps of wonder, for you can see spread out below you the lights of the city of Durban, greatest port in the whole continent of Africa, and you can see the lights of ships riding out there in the Indian Ocean, awaiting their call to enter the harbour. For Durban Bay itself, though it is the busiest port in Africa, is a small affair compared with Sydney and San Francisco and Rio.

Mr. Bodasingh is very proud of this city, for he and his forebears helped to build it. In the broad sense he is a citizen of Durban, but in the legal sense he is not, for he has no vote and therefore no say in the government of the city. But he is not political. He has never joined the Congress, and has never made a speech except at weddings and directors' meetings and school functions. He is a rich man, although his great-grandfather came to Natal as a labourer in the 1860s and owned virtually nothing but a willing pair of hands and a mind whose real quality was revealed only in his descendants.

But he was not today thinking of the sweeping view before him or of the material success of the Bodasinghs. He was thinking of a much more personal matter, and it was clearly weighing heavily on his mind. As he looked again at his watch, his wife said to him,

– What time is it?

– Five minutes to ten.

They could both imagine the scene. Their daughter, Prem Bodasingh, their only child and the pride and joy of their lives, eighteen years of age, obedient and respectful to her parents and her elders, head-girl of Centenary High, would now be standing outside the doors of the Durban Municipal Reference Library, waiting for them to open on an event the like of which they had never opened on before in all their history. For above the doors it was clearly stated that the library was for *Whites Only — Blankes Alleen*. At ten o'clock their daughter would enter, take a book from the shelves, and sit down at a table to read. The young white girl at the inquiry desk would almost certainly go to tell her superior that a young Indian girl was sitting at a table in the library, and the superior, who would almost certainly be an elderly lady of learning and refinement, would go to the Indian girl and tell her that the library was for the use of whites only, and she would regret that she must ask her to leave. Their daughter will say that she knows that, and that she is there to defy the law, and that therefore she cannot leave. The superior will possibly be shocked at this, and she may possibly not be shocked at all, having heard all about the Defiance Campaign, and she will know that Indian and African people are sitting in white railway waiting-rooms, and on white benches in white parks, and are refusing to pay in their employers' takings to tellers who are designated to serve 'Non-Whites Only'. Therefore it is not surprising that sooner or later someone would challenge the colour bar at the Reference Library. The superior would then go to the Chief Librarian, and Mr. Bodasingh winced at this thought, for the Chief Librarian was a very nice man who had given a very nice address to the Reservoir Hills library group not long ago, and Mr. Bodasingh had been in the chair.

To go on imagining the scene now became very painful, for the Chief Librarian would leave his important work and go to the Reference Library and ask the Indian girl to leave. Then their daughter would say that she was there to defy the law and could not leave.

Now came the most painful part of all, for what would the Chief Librarian do? There was only one thing that he could do, and that was to call the police. Mr. Bodasingh could not hold back a kind of groan.

– M.K., what's the matter?

– You see, I have been imagining it all, and I have just got to the police.

– I think faster than you. I got to the police some time ago.

– I hope they send a senior man, perhaps with a daughter like Prem. These young white constables . . . Mr. Bodasingh shuddered.

– Then what happens, M.K., when the police come?

– They take her away and charge her. Then I'm not sure

where they will take her. But as soon as we know, our friend
Maharaj will go there at once.

– Someone is knocking at the door.

Mr. Bodasingh winced again, but soon realised that the
caller could not possibly be bringing news of their daughter.
It was his old friend Jay Perumal. Both of them were in their
early fifties, and had climbed up the ladder of success
together. Mr. Perumal clearly looked as though something
were on his mind also.

– Mrs. M.K., greetings. You both look troubled, and we
all understand it. We Perumals understand it especially well,
because we have troubles too.

– Your grandmother?

– Yes.

– So she agreed to carry on?

– Yes.

– Shame, said Mrs. Bodasingh. An old lady like that. How
old is she?

– She's ninety-two. But the reason why the Congress
wanted her is of course because she is the only one left of the
first ship from India. You remember, M.K., the s.s. *Truro*.
She was born on that voyage, so she is now as old as the
Indian people of South Africa.

Mr. Perumal spoke more vehemently.

– M.K., I blame Dr. Monty for this. And I blame him for
Prem too. The old lady should be sitting in her special chair
in the sun, instead of in the white waiting-room at Berea
Road. And Prem should be working hard for her Matriculation instead of sitting in the Reference Library. You see, the
old lady can't say no to Dr. Monty. She can't read and write,
and he is a doctor from Edinburgh. What is more, he looks
after her for nothing. He never sends an account. She thinks
he is a Mahatma.

– You're lucky, said Mrs. Bodasingh. She hasn't been
arrested. We don't expect to be so lucky.

– Her hair is as white as snow, and she wears a clean white
sari every day, said Mr. Perumal with some pride. So she
looks like, you know, some angel of purity. They have
warned her twice, but now they don't warn her any more.

Many of the white people greet her now when they come into the waiting-room.

He took out his wallet, and took out a picture from the wallet.

– You see what I mean. The white hair, the dark face, full of care you know, the white sari, what can they do to her? No, I don't mean full of care, she's not full of care, I mean her face is — what do they say? — careworn, eh? Her great-grandchildren think she is the most wonderful woman to have for a great-grandmother. The great-great-grand-children are too small.

– How many great-grandchildren are there?

– Oh, between forty and fifty, we don't count any more. Perhaps it's between fifty and sixty. They had big families then, not like us with three and four. M.K., you tell me why the Congress must use old people and children. Don't they have enough grown-up people to support them? At ninety-two your life should be finished — no, I don't mean finished, I mean, you remember, M.K. and Mrs. M.K., what they said about King George the Fifth, that his life was drawing peacefully to its end. Well, the old lady's life should be drawing peacefully to its end, but not in a railway station. She should be at home, in a chair, sitting in the sun.

Mr. Perumal paused a moment to pull himself together. Then he spoke with greater vehemence than ever.

– And your daughter Prem. The cleverest girl in Durban, they say, at any high school, white, black, or Indian. A wonderful future before her but what happens today? A week suspended. So she goes again and what happens then? Two weeks not suspended plus that week no longer sus-pended.

– Don't talk like that, said Mr. Bodasingh with pain.

– I *do* talk like that. This is not the time for nice talk, M.K.

– Who said she would go again?

– My daughter, Lutchmee.

Mrs. Bodasingh cried out.

– Why didn't Lutchmee go to the library too?

– She is not allowed to.

– Who won't allow her? You, the clever father?

– No, not me. Prem will not allow her. Prem will not allow any of the girls to do it. They must work for their examinations. Don't you know your own daughter? She says, Do it, and you do it. She says, Don't do it, and you don't do it. She will be like Mrs. Pandit.

Mr. Bodasingh looked the picture of misery, pride struggling with dread. But Mr. Perumal was now in full cry, and either ignored his friend's misery or did not see it.

– You do nothing for your daughter, M.K., and I do nothing for my grandmother. Your daughter is very important, M.K. Her life is just beginning, but the old lady's life is drawing peacefully to its end.

– You said just now, said Mrs. Bodasingh sharply, that it was *not* drawing peacefully to its end.

– I am getting mixed, Mrs. M.K. That is because I am ashamed. I do nothing for my grandmother. You ought to be ashamed too, M.K. You do nothing for your daughter. We are a disgrace to the Indian people.

– You are very clever, Jay. What do you say we do?

– We go to Dr. Monty. We say we object to the way Congress interferes in our private lives, and the way it puts heavy burdens on old women and children.

– M.K. won't go to see Dr. Monty, said Mrs. Bodasingh again sharply. He is afraid of him. You are all afraid of him, not just because of Congress, but because he went to Edinburgh.

– M.K., are you afraid of Dr. Monty?

– I don't say I am afraid of him. Look, Jay, I am not afraid of anyone in business, but Dr. Monty isn't in business. Outside business he's too clever for me.

The telephone rang and Mr. Bodasingh ran to it. He could hardly hold the receiver because his hands were trembling. Both his wife and Mr. Perumal listened for every word.

– Prem's arrested. She's in the Smith Street charge office. Bail is twenty pounds. I must go at once. Ring Maharaj and tell him to go there as soon as he can.

– M.K.!

Mr. Bodasingh turned to his wife.

– Yes.

– M.K., you mustn't pay bail.
– What, I mustn't pay bail? But I want my daughter.
– If you pay bail, you'll lose your daughter.
– Who told you that?
– She told me that.

Mr. Bodasingh looked at his wife, full of despair and frustration.

– God Almighty, he said, God Almighty. You remember, Kuniamma, when she was six years old, she would climb up on me and say, When I grow up, I'm going to marry you, daddy.

– I can pay bail and she would never know, said Mr. Perumal.

– You go and pay bail for your grandmother, Jay Perumal, said Mrs. Bodasingh. You look after your family and we'll look after ours.

– This is not a time for quarrelling, said Mr. Bodasingh. Kuniamma, I must go.

So Mr. M. K. Bodasingh, director of companies, chairman of philanthropies, welcome if somewhat over-flowery speaker at weddings, now rendered inarticulate by circumstance and weighed down by woe, departed for the Smith Street charge office to inform Mr. Maharaj that on no account was bail to be paid.

This girl Prem Bodasingh, the one who keeps going to the Durban Municipal Reference Library, is causing trouble in Pietermaritzburg also. Dr. William Johnson, Director of Education for the province of Natal, doesn't want to take punitive steps against her, but the Chairman of the Natal Executive, Mr. Harry Mainwaring, member of the great Natal family, says that he must.

– Do you mean to say, Director, that this girl can go on breaking the law with impunity?

– She is not doing it with impunity. She has been punished for it three times.

– And she goes on doing it. I may say I find it intolerable. So we are asking you to give her a warning, that if she does it again, all schools are closed to her.

– Mr. Chairman, I'm an educator, not a judge.

– Yes, I appreciate that, but you have the power in consultation with a school principal to expel a child from a school. You could call that a judicial function.

– Mr. Chairman, it's a power I use very sparingly, and then only in extreme cases, serious theft, or a bad sex scandal, or dangerous insubordination.

– You don't think it is dangerous insubordination to break the law of the country, openly and persistently?

Johnson did not answer immediately. He rested his chin on his hands, and looked intently at the blotter in front of him.

– You find that question difficult, said Mainwaring.

– Yes, indeed. Extremely difficult.

– I don't need to tell you, Director, that it is a very dangerous thing when an individual decides that a law is wrong, and then disobeys it. The whole fabric of law and order breaks down. You may only be going to sit in a reading-room from which the law debars you, but you are in fact challenging the authority of Government and the State.

Again Johnson said nothing. Mainwaring irritated him but he must not show it. Mainwaring was very conscious of belonging to one of the great Natal families. Although they had both been to the same exclusive school, Johnson could lay no claim to any kind of illustrious ancestry.

– Harrington came to see you about this, didn't he?

– Yes, he did.

– I happen to know this, not because I was snooping, but because he came to see me too. Thinks we would be doing a most un-British thing if we debar this girl from our schools. He makes me angry. He obviously doesn't know a thing about the history of British India. And he obviously didn't know that my grandfather was a Boer, my mother's father. Did you know that?

– Of course. I met him at your home in the Karkloof when we were schoolboys.

– I should have remembered that. Well, Harrington has some idea in his head that English-speaking South Africans know more about justice than Afrikaners. He looked a bit silly when I told him my grandfather was a Boer. He also has an idea that St. Michael's knows more about justice than all the other schools, except probably St. John's in Johannesburg and St. Andrew's in Grahamstown and Bishops in the Cape.

– I think I should make it quite clear, Mr. Chairman, that my reluctance to take action against this girl has nothing to do with British and Afrikaner ideas of justice. It's just that I cannot accept the idea of ending a girl's education because she goes to a white library. I know she's breaking the law, but such a penalty seems to me out of all proportion to the seriousness of the offence.

– So you don't think it is a serious offence to go on persistently breaking the law?

– From your viewpoint I can see that it is. That is partly because it's *your* authority that she is flouting. But there is another point of view, equally valid. She goes to the library, she dresses quietly, she doesn't carry a gun, she doesn't threaten anyone, she takes out a book and sits down to read. The only visible instruction is to be silent, and she is silent enough. But for this offence you would bring her education to an end.

– You are in fact refusing to debar her from the schools of the province.

– I think I intend to do so.

– You realise it is a grave decision?

– Yes.

– Why don't you refuse now?

– Because I have decided to go to Durban tomorrow to see the girl's principal, and then I shall go to see the girl herself.

– In prison?

– Yes.

– I can't stop you, Director, said Mainwaring angrily, but I disapprove totally. I don't think it part of your duties. There are fifty thousand Indian children in our schools, not to mention whites and Africans. And one gets herself into trouble and you must go rushing off to see her. If someone has to go and see her, why don't you send one of your inspectors?

– The province appointed me Director, and I am its

servant. But they mustn't tell me how my job must be done. And if they disapprove totally, they can get rid of me.

– Are you threatening us?

– No more than you are threatening me.

– I just don't understand you, Johnson. People like the Bodasinghs came to South Africa as coolies. The men earned something like ten or fourteen shillings a month and a free hut and rations. Today this girl's father is a rich man. This country gave him opportunities far greater than any he would find in India. In India he would still be a coolie. And yet his daughter has the impudence to complain of the laws of the country that made them rich. It makes me fume. Let me go before I really get angry. I still think that if this girl must be seen, you could send someone else to see her.

The Director rose as his superior left. If he had spoken his thoughts, Mainwaring would have been shocked, for the Director would have said, I won't send anyone else because I want to go myself, I want to see this Indian girl, this child of a powerless race, who has challenged the majesty of the Government and the State. I want to see what kind of girl she could be.

The Durban prison is no thing of beauty. From its ramparts one does not see the blue expanse of the Indian Ocean or the stately indigenous trees of the Berea. One sees instead a waste piece of land bounded on one side by the prison itself, and on the other sides by nondescript commercial buildings. The waste land has to some extent been hallowed because on Sunday afternoons people have been gathering there to pray for the well-being of those who have been sentenced for sitting in white waiting-rooms or on white benches in the public parks and gardens, or as in the case of this girl Prem Bodasingh, for going to the white reference room of the Durban Library.

The Superintendent met Johnson with a deference due to a Director of Education and with an authority proper to the Superintendent of a prison, who has the responsibility for the health and safe custody of a few hundred souls who have broken the laws of the land but not very grievously, because in that case they would have been sent to prisons much more formidable than this unimposing building on a piece of waste land in Durban.

– I've bent the rules for you, Director, as I am entitled to do on occasions. You can see the prisoner in a private room, and your conversation will not be listened to.

– Thank you, Superintendent.

The Director followed the Superintendent down a passage smelling of disinfectant, and into a room where a young Indian girl was sitting under guard. As they entered, the wardress said in a sharp voice, Stand up, and she and the girl stood up.

– This, Director, is prisoner Prem Bodasingh, who is at present serving a three-week sentence for contravening municipal bye-laws. Prisoner Bodasingh, this is Dr. Johnson, the Director of Education for Natal. Wardress Smith, you will not remain, but will take up your duties outside the door. You will see that no unauthorised person enters this room. You may sit down if you wish. Director, will you kindly tell Wardress Smith when your visit is ended, and I shall come to escort you. I must ask you not to move from this room unescorted.

He left the room and shut the door, and Johnson said to the girl, Sit down, Prem.

Prem Bodasingh, even in the shapeless prison dress that she was wearing, appeared to him as a creature of grace. She was slender and not very tall, and her features were what one might call aristocratic, although she was in fact the descendant of labourers. These labourers had been brought to Natal in 1860 to work on the sugar plantations, and some of their descendants had become teachers, professors, manufacturers, lawyers, doctors. Others still belonged to the very poor, and now regarded with respect those whose ancestors had been labourers like their own. All of them had once been called coolies, a word which with the passage of time has become a term of contempt, and is no longer used in polite society.

Prem not only had these aristocratic features, but her hands were aristocratic too, with fine tapered fingers. Her eyes were luminous, more like those of a young gazelle than a young revolutionary. She met his scrutiny with composure, without either boldness or embarrassment.

– Miss Ramsay sends her best wishes to you. She wants very much to have you back at school. She says that the school is not easy to control without you.

The girl gave a smile of pleasure, but she quickly suppressed it.

– Prem, you heard who I am, and you know why I am here, don't you?

– Yes, I know, sir. You are here because I have broken the law, and because some people want me to be expelled.

– I am here also for quite a different reason. Do you know what *in loco parentis* means?

– Yes, sir, I do.

– I have not come here to talk to you about breaking the law. I am not a policeman. I am a teacher, and I am filled with apprehension — you understand that? — I am filled with apprehension — that you may destroy your life.

She did not reply.

– You want to make the world better, and you are right to want that. But this particular world in which we live is not going to get better tomorrow. It may go on like this for ten, twenty, thirty years. Nobody knows. And you may have to live in it for those thirty years, doing what? Perhaps spending more and more of your life in prison, without matriculation, without university, without a career. You want to be a social worker, don't you?

– Yes, sir.

– Well, Prem, at this rate you will never be a social worker, unless of course you go to some other country. But it would be difficult for you to do that now. You would regard it as running away, is that not so?

– Yes, sir.

– You have to ask yourself, which is better, to serve your country and your people for thirty years as a social worker, or to go in and out of jail for thirty years. Prem, I don't want to stop you from breaking what you think is an unjust law. I want to stop you from damaging your whole life. Do you understand what I am saying?

– Yes, sir, I understand it.

– Do you understand that you may be damaging your whole life?

– I understand it.

– Are you willing to throw away education, knowledge, learning, for the sake of your cause?

She said to him in a low voice,

– Yes.

– But these are — what shall I say? — holy things.

She said with a spark of fire,

– The cause is holy too. And my promise. A promise is holy too.

– A promise to whom? To Congress?

– No. To God and myself.

– What was your promise, Prem?

She did not answer. He could see that his questions were painful to her. But having been brought up in the ways of obedience, she could hardly refuse to answer this great personage, this great white personage who was filled with apprehension that she might destroy her life.

He said to her gently,

– My child, what was your promise?

She bowed her head and said in a voice so low that he could barely hear her words,

– To the death.

– Who asked you for that?

– Nobody.

– Who heard your promise?

– Dr. Monty heard it.

– Dr. Monty Naicker?

– Yes.

– What did he say? Did he say you mustn't do that?

– No.

– What did he do?

She was silent again, till he said to her,

– Prem.

– He took out his handkerchief.

– And blew his nose?

He laughed, and the girl laughed too, the laugh transforming her face so that he thought her suddenly beautiful.

– There's one last question. What do your parents say?

– They want me to stop.

– And you are held back by your promise?

– Yes, sir.

– Well, you must think it all over carefully. I also would try to keep a promise. But I think it is possible to make too much of the sanctity of a promise. Is one entitled to hurt others? Is one even entitled to hurt oneself? Your life doesn't belong to you, Prem. It belongs to your parents and your school and your friends, and even to the country of what you call the unjust laws. I shall do everything I can to save you from total expulsion. But you must remember that I am only a servant of the Provincial Council. The final power is theirs. Goodbye, Prem.

She stood up and made him a kind of curtsey.

– If my parents were here they would thank you for your kindness.

William Johnson walked up the broad path that led to Dr. Monty's house and observed the garden with an appreciative eye. The house too was worth looking at, cool and wide-verandahed, and was situated in one of the beautiful residential streets of Durban. Dr. Monty's action in legally buying this house was known as 'penetration', and the majority of the white citizens objected strongly to the infiltration by Indians of what they regarded as their own areas. Their first attempts to stop this kind of thing had been unsuccessful, but now the Group Areas Act of the new Nationalist Government promised relief. Dr. Monty would no longer be able to live in a white group area, but would have to take himself and his family to an Indian group area, where they could speak their own language and cherish their own culture and pursue their own social, political, religious, and economic goals in peace, unhampered by the proximity of alien races. The Group Areas Act was indeed one of the cornerstones of the great edifice of separate coexistence, and it was welcomed

by the white citizens of Durban, of whom it was cynically
said that they voted United Party and thanked God for the
Nationalists.

Coming down the path to meet Johnson was Dr. Monty
himself, a well-built man of middle height, his white teeth
shining in a broad smile of welcome. Johnson had seen him
on the platform, humourless and uncompromising and
somewhat frightening, but the man coming to meet him was
friendly and benign.

– Dr. Johnson.

– I didn't think you'd see me, doctor.

– Why is that?

– Because the Department has forbidden its teachers to
take part in the Defiance Campaign.

Dr. Monty gave his famous chuckle, an endearing sound
which gave his hearers the assurance that he was human, an
impression they might not have got if they had heard him on
a public platform.

– The reason why I see you, Director, is because of what
you have done for our schools. The moment you rang, I had
no hesitation in deciding to see you. We are not fanatics,
Director. Come this way. We are going to have tea on the
verandah.

– It's a pleasant house, doctor.

No sooner had Johnson said this than he wished that he
could have recalled his words. Dr. Monty saw his embarrassment and smiled at it.

– It *is* a pleasant house. It's an oasis in the desert, but as you
know, it's to the desert we must go. While we are here, we
intend to enjoy it.

– And your neighbours?

– Many don't want us to go, and they come to tell us so.
It's handy to have a doctor next door. It has benefited them
more than once. But you didn't come here to talk to me
about the Group Areas Act.

– No, I didn't. I came to talk to you about Prem.

– You think I ought to stop her.

– I came to tell you that she weighs heavily on my mind,
and on my conscience too. You may have heard that she may

be debarred from all schools. I don't think that is likely. The Natal Executive Committee would have to find a new director, and I don't think they would be willing to go as far as that. That's not what worries me, doctor. It's the possibility that the Defiance Campaign may go on for many years. Prem has promised — to God and herself — that she will go on to the death. I am afraid that she may destroy her whole life. You know, don't you, that she won't allow any other girl in the school to join the campaign?

– Yes, I know that. I may tell you, Director, that I had nothing to do with persuading Prem to join the campaign. I did not even know her. And I certainly never expected that one of M.K. Bodasingh's family would join us. Now when a young girl like that, clever and beautiful, decides that this is what she wants to do, that this is the right thing for her to do, who am I to stop her?

– I see that. But you have a wisdom and a knowledge that are denied to her. She is serving an ideal of universal justice, and I am proud that our schools have produced such a girl. But she also owes a duty to herself. Did you know she wanted to be a social worker?

– Yes, I knew.

– And you know that if the campaign goes on for many years, and if she believes herself to be bound by this overwhelming promise made at the age of seventeen or eighteen, she will never become a social worker?

– Yes, I know that too.

– Don't you also stand to her *in loco parentis?* Her own parents are powerless, as you know. But you have a great influence over her. Do you believe that she is serving the cause better now than she possibly could in later years? Have you any reason to believe that?

– You don't understand, Director, that this is going to be our life from now on. Some of us have to be destroyed now so that freedom can come to others later. We have come to realise this only in the past few years. I am talking about Indians especially. We made big speeches about freedom, but we didn't suffer. Now many of us are ready to suffer, just as Prem is ready.

— But she is only a child.

— We were all children once. What am I to say to her, Director? Shall I say to her, You must go on living a normal life but in ten years' time I shall call on you to suffer? Couldn't we all do that? Couldn't I finish building my new clinic first, and then go out and suffer? Couldn't Lutuli first get his shop on its feet and then go out and suffer? Wouldn't it be easier for me to suffer if I could leave my partners to run a new clinic while I join the struggle? Couldn't Lutuli suffer better if his shop were giving security to his wife and family? And couldn't the girl Prem suffer better if she first qualified as a social worker? You don't change the world that way, Director.

Johnson knew that he was looking at a world different from his own, a world that he would never enter. He would proceed honourably to his pension, and would receive many praises. He and his wife would retire, in Pietermaritzburg or on the South Coast, where if he wished he could play golf for another ten years, and perhaps after that play bowls for another ten. He could read his newspapers and all the books that he had never had the time to read. He could sit on his verandah and look at the blue waters of the Indian Ocean, and the ships on their way to Australia and the Far East, and read about the protest marches of the Lutulis and the Montys. But destiny, or history, or something else, had made it a world which he could not enter.

— The Suppression of Communism Act has left only one way open to us, Director. If you resist the laws, long enough, militantly enough, you will be silenced, you will be shut off from the world of people, of pleasure, of travel, even of education. That will happen to Lutuli soon, and it will happen to me.

The smiling Dr. Monty was gone, the other Monty was speaking, and it was evident to Johnson that under the even tenor of the words there was an almost ungovernable passion, here in the quietness of this residential street.

— The girl is beautiful, Director, and I hear she is clever too. But she has something more than beauty and cleverness, she has the courage to oppose injustice, and she has the courage to oppose the unjust laws that can silence the brave and take away the houses and the shops of decent law-abiding people, because of an accident of birth over which they had no control. But the girl is destined to suffer, Director, unless she betrays the cause that she believes in. When she came to see me I could have wept to see her courage, and her beauty. But stop her? There are some things that can't be done.

Johnson stood up.

– I did my best. I wanted to save the girl.

– It does you credit, Director. That's why we respect you and are thankful that you are in charge of our schools.

He chuckled. The benign Dr. Monty was back again.

– Politics is not the only thing in our world. There are other things too, pride in our schools and our children. And in our houses and gardens. But in the last resort, politics is the most important of them all. That sounds terrible, Director, but it isn't, because for us politics means justice.

. . . I think, my dear aunt, that you are overestimating the importance of the Defiance Campaign. I can tell you in the strictest confidence that the Government is considering steps which will bring it to a decisive end. The unnatural alliance between Chief Lutuli of the African Congress and Dr. Naicker of the Indian Congress will be ended too. It is certain that Lutuli will be ordered to choose between his chieftainship and his presidency of the Congress. Whichever he chooses it will be the end of him.

I can also tell you that the Cabinet is angry about Africans and Indians 'cooperating' in the campaign. You will remember that only a few years ago, in 1949 to be exact, the Zulus went after the Indians because of some trouble between a Zulu boy and an Indian shopkeeper. More than 140 people lost their lives, more than half of them being Zulus, most of them killed by the police to stop them killing Indians. There was a malicious slander that the Government was encouraging the riots; on the contrary the whole intention of apartheid is to prevent them by the policy of peaceful coexistence. It is

a well-known scientific fact that racial mixing leads inevitably to racial conflict. Therefore no good can come out of
this 'cooperation'.

The determination of the Government has been increased
by the news that Patrick Duncan has resigned his post as
judicial commissioner in the British Colonial Service in Basutoland in order to join the campaign. You will remember that
Duncan's father, when he was Governor-General, refused in
1939 to grant General Hertzog's request to dissolve Parliament after he had been defeated by thirteen votes on the
decision to declare war on Germany. Instead Duncan asked
Smuts to form a new government, and that is why the name
of Duncan is held in low esteem by all true Afrikaners. My
Minister has ordered the head of Security to give him a full
report on Duncan. The young man will pay heavily for his
treachery.

My Minister finds one feature of the campaign extremely
insolent. These Indians who have been to prison have taken
to wearing the white Gandhi cap, a ridiculous headgear that
perches on the top of the head like those paper hats that
people wear at Christmas. Most of the Indians wearing them
would now be sleeping on the pavements of Calcutta had
their forefathers not come to South Africa as labourers last
century. Our Durban Nationalists find this insolence quite
intolerable, and have sent a deputation to the Minister asking
him to consider a twelve-months' sentence for the wearing of
such a cap. He was willing, but Dr. Malan said he would not
make himself ridiculous by punishing people for wearing a
particular kind of cap. I can tell you that the Minister was
deeply offended by this remark.

However, I can promise you that an important step will
soon be taken. The punishments for sitting in white waiting-
rooms and in white libraries are so light that it is no hardship
to go to jail for a week every few months. More than eight
thousand people have done it so far and they are clogging up
the jails. They think it is a kind of joke but in fact they are
defying the Government and Parliament. Most shocking of
all, they are defying the State, which all Christians believe to
be ordained by God. Was it not Paul himself who wrote that

rulers are not a terror to the good but only to the evildoers? It is true that Peter wrote that we must obey God rather than men, but he had clearly not grasped the point that those men who became rulers were in fact ordained by God. This difference of opinion has caused much trouble among the wavering kind of Christians, and has also been seized upon by those who hate any kind of authority. It has also been exploited by the communists, who are the champions of civil liberties until they come to power, after which they destroy them all. It can also be pointed out that Paul was a scholar, while Peter (through no fault of his own, I hasten to point out) was only a fisherman. Now the Afrikaner has a profound respect for scholars, but he can hardly be expected to have the same respect for fishermen, most of whom are coloured men. Some of these coloured men still have the old Cape vote to send white M.P.s to the white Parliament, but this anomaly will soon be removed, for while it is the aim of the National Party to give civil and political rights to every man and woman in South Africa, they must achieve these rights as members of their own groups, each enjoying sovereign powers in its own sphere. This is the political doctrine of separate coexistence, a doctrine which has no parallel in any other country of the world. In any case Peter can hardly be expected to enjoy the full confidence of Afrikaners; he founded the Roman Catholic Church, which Scripture has likened to a harlot sitting on seven mountains.

You must not allow to enter your mind any thought that the Government is frightened of the Defiance Campaign. Our Prime Minister bears a name that is revered only second to that of Paul Kruger. My own Minister believes that it is his sacred duty to be a terror to evildoers. Even more unshakable than they — if I may say so without disloyalty — is the Minister of Native Affairs, our revered Dr. Hendrik, who is regarded by many as the supreme architect of the doctrine of separate coexistence. They are three great men, three of the greatest in the history of Afrikanerdom, and they are implacably determined to destroy the Defiance Campaign. They will destroy it not by the killing of the protesters, as Stalin would have done (some say Hitler also, but this allegation has been put forward mainly by Jews and liberals, and can therefore be regarded with scepticism), but by the use of the powers given to them by Parliament. My Minister says that after forty years of the spineless rule of Botha, Hertzog, and Smuts, it is the Malan Government that has given teeth to democracy. And they mustn't cry if they get bitten, he says.

I have just come from the Minister. I have never seen him so angry about anything as he is about Duncan. He expressed his anger to me in forcible language.

'Tell me, Van Onselen, how can a white man do a thing like that? How he can join forces with Indians and Africans against his own people, I just cannot understand. I sit here at my desk and I try to understand it, but I just cannot do so.'

The Minister is waiting impatiently for the Security report on Duncan. There may be something in it that would enable him to destroy Duncan. But whatever the case, he wants to know exactly what kind of man Duncan is.

As for me, my dear aunt, I continue to live my own, what some people would call, cloistered life. I enjoy my work, I like my Minister, I read *Die Transvaler* and the *Star*, and of course I have my table tennis. I must modestly confess that I am a bit of a champion. Dear old Sophie gives me my breakfast, and stays for a couple of hours. I cannot say that I like living alone. I think of my mother every day. But life has not been unkind to me.

The mountain kingdom of Lesotho, called Basutoland by its British administrators, is austere and beautiful. The nation itself was the creation of the great Moshweshwe, the ruler who sent his enemies gifts after he had trounced them in battle. He gathered together the remnants scattered by the Mfecane, the dispersion of the tribes caused by the rise to power of Shaka, who also created a nation, and sent clan after clan fleeing over the Drakensberg. Those who fled from Shaka in their turn scattered the tribes of the interior, and it was Moshweshwe who made the remnants into a new nation, the Basuto. This new nation in its turn could have been scattered by the all-conquering Boers, but in 1868 the

British took the Basuto under their protection, so that they became, in Moshweshwe's words, 'the lice in the Queen's blanket'.

Patrick Duncan served the Basuto well in his capacity as a judicial commissioner. He was renowned for his courtesy, which was considered remarkable for a white person who had been born in South Africa, but then of course he had been educated at Winchester College, where manners makyth man. He was intelligent but his greatest gift was his vitality. Out of his bluest of blue eyes shot flames that consumed any cruelty or cant within burning distance, and he had the ruddiest cheeks in the world, giving him the appearance of abounding health. He was a man of passionate beliefs, and had a veneration for Mahatma Gandhi. He believed with all his heart that *satyagraha*, the soul-force, the power of truth, was able to topple empires.

But his heart was not in the mountain kingdom. It was in the country where he was born. Great events were happening there, noble, stirring events from which his position as a British administrator excluded him. He was passionately stirred by the daily stories of men and women going to prison in protest against unjust laws. There was dear old Manilal, son of the Mahatma, sitting on park benches marked *For Whites Only*. There was this eighteen-year-old girl Prem Bodasingh who had now gone to prison for the third time in protest against the segregation of the libraries. And now the exciting news that Chief Lutuli had refused to obey the order of the formidable Dr. Hendrik to resign either his chieftainship or his presidency of the Natal branch of the African Congress. So Dr. Hendrik had deposed him from the chieftainship, and Lutuli, no longer chief, but always to be called the Chief, issued a statement of intention that will be remembered as long as any words spoken in South Africa are remembered.

Who will deny that thirty years of my life have been spent knocking in vain, patiently, moderately and modestly at a closed and barred door? . . .

As for myself, with a full sense of responsibility and a clear conviction, I decided to remain in the struggle for extending democratic rights and responsibilities to all sections of the South African community. I have embraced the non-violent passive resistance technique in fighting for freedom because I am convinced it is the only non-revolutionary, legitimate and humane way that could be used by people denied, as we are, effective constitutional means to further aspirations.

The wisdom or foolishness of this decision I place in the hands of the Almighty.

What the future has in store for me I do not know. It might be ridicule, imprisonment, concentration camp, flogging, banishment and even death. I only pray to the Almighty to strengthen my resolve so that none of these grim possibilities may deter me from striving, for the sake of the good name of our beloved country, the Union of South Africa, to make it a true democracy and a true union in form and spirit of all the communities of the land.

My only painful concern at times is that of the welfare of my family, but I try even in this regard, in a spirit of trust and surrender to God's will as I see it, to say: God will provide.

It is inevitable that in working for Freedom some individuals and some families must take the lead and suffer: The Road to Freedom is via the Cross.

Mayibuye! Afrika! Afrika! Afrika!

The effect of Lutuli's statement on Patrick Duncan was tremendous. He decided that he could no longer remain in Basutoland. He would join the Defiance Campaign, and that meant he would have to resign from the Colonial Service. This burning desire to be *doing* something, something difficult and noble, the desire that had come to torment him more and more, would at last be satisfied. South Africa was approaching the greatest crisis in its history, and white South Africans must choose whether change was to come with or without violence. It was his duty to persuade them that there was yet time to make change peacefully. It was a task of which his father the Governor-General would have approved. Why should God not use him as the instrument, now that he was ready and willing? And if that made him famous, that would not be unacceptable. Like his friend Trevor Huddleston he would not object to being famous, provided the fame was earned by the doing of something good. In fact he would go to Johannesburg as soon as he could, to see Huddleston. He would go to Durban to see Lutuli and Manilal. He might even meet the girl Prem Bodasingh. It was a new world that was opening up to him. He was more happy, more confident than he had ever been in his life. He would not need to pretend any more. He would not need to pretend to believe in justice while he accepted unjust laws. He would not need to keep silent out of considerations of expediency. He felt within himself, not only intense emotions, but a new sense of power. Might he not be the man that God was looking for?

You must hurry up, Patrick Duncan, if you are going to save South Africa. Black people are rioting in Port Elizabeth and East London and Johannesburg and Kimberley. Forty have been killed and hundreds injured, some of them innocent, a white man going to the office, a black woman going to the shop. Moroka and Njongwe and Lutuli watch the riots with anxious eyes. They are not warriors; two of them are doctors and the third is a teacher. Violence and bloodshed are painful to them, but most painful of all to them is the violence done in East London to Sister Aidan, herself a servant of *satyagraha*.

Sister Aidan, whose professional name was Dr. Elsie Quinlan, and who had devoted her life to the care of the black sick of East London, while driving her car encountered an angry mob in the location. They had been holding a prayer-meeting, which had been ordered to disperse by the police, on the grounds that the meeting was not religious. Stones had been thrown by members of the mob, and shots fired by the police. Neither her record of devotion nor her Sister's habit could save her. Her car was overturned and a man opened the door and struck her on the head. The Sister fell on her side and put her hands together in prayer. The man who had struck her lit a match and threw it into the petrol that was running out of the tank. The heat was so intense that none of those who hoped to rescue her could come anywhere near.

When the flames had died down a woman from the crowd cut a piece of flesh from the body of the nun and ate it, saying that it would give her strength. Her example was followed by others. One woman who was ordered by others to eat refused to do so, reminding them that this woman had been a servant of their people. When threatened she took a piece of flesh, and wrapped it in a piece of paper, saying that she would eat it at home, but when she reached the privacy of her house she buried it in the earth of her tiny garden.

Dr. Moroka, the national president of the Congress, condemned the violence on behalf of the African people. He blamed the police for causing the riots, and called for a full inquiry. Prayers were said in many churches for the repose of the soul of Sister Aidan. These services were marked not by anger at her death but by thanks for her life, and prayers for peace.

Of course it is said, and how could it not be, that the Defiance Campaign is responsible for her death. And of course it is said, and how could it not be, that the real causes of her death are the laws of apartheid, and the poverty, and the frustrations, and the belief that the white rulers of South Africa know only one language, and that is the language of violence. It is the language they speak, and therefore it is the language in which they must be spoken to. It is not a campaign of protest, it is a war, and therefore everything white must be destroyed, even the sisters and their hospitals and their clinics and their schools.

It is this hatred that fills lovers of peace with despair. When Sister Aidan saw the mob, did she know she was looking at hatred, perhaps even for the first time in her life? Or did she not know it till she put her hands together?

Ah, but your land is beautiful. That's what they say, the visitors, the Scandinavians and the Germans and the British and the Americans. They go to see the Cape that is the fairest in the whole circumference of the earth, and Groot Constantia and the vineyards. They travel over the plains of the Karoo, bounded everywhere by distant mountains. They go down over the great wall of the Drakensberg, into the green hills and valleys of Natal. And if they are fortunate, they take the journey from Johannesburg to Zululand and pass through some of the richest maizelands in the world.

Some visitors are more inquisitive than others. They poke their noses — one is sorry one cannot use nicer language — into District Six and Orlando and New Brighton. They even go to the courts, to see Mrs. Katlana fined ten pounds for going to church without her reference book, and to see Mr. Tsaoeli fined ten pounds for sitting on the roadside outside his employer's house without his reference book. He told the police that the book was in his quarters, and he could get it in a minute, but the police said that they were not interested. These things are very unfortunate, but surely when South Africans visit Stockholm or Washington, they don't go poking their noses into the courts.

Ah, but the land is beautiful. It is the land where Sister Aidan met her unspeakable death, and fourteen-year-old Johnnie Reynders hanged himself in his bedroom because the white high school turned him away, although his brothers and sisters had been there before him. It is also the land where white fisherman Koos Karelse of Knysna jumped overboard to save the life of black fisherman James Mapikela; the black life was saved and the white life was lost.

There is talk of another land too, where the tears have been wiped from every eye, and there is no more death, neither sorrow, nor crying, nor any more pain, because all those things have passed away. But here in the land that is so beautiful, they have not passed away.

Mr. Harry Mainwaring, the Chairman of the Natal Executive, and member of the great Natal family, has been dealt a terrible blow. His son Hugh, a product of St. Michael's like his father before him, has conveyed to his parents the most shocking news. He has decided to go to Johannesburg to join Patrick Duncan and others in an illegal entry into the black location at Germiston. In other words he is going to join the Defiance Campaign.

What makes the matter worse is that the eminent Pietermaritzburg legal firm of Montgomery, Royston, and Macfarlane has just agreed to accept young Hugh as an articled clerk, and when they hear this news they will certainly withdraw the offer.

– You know that, don't you?

– Yes, dad, I know it. I went to see Mr. Montgomery about it and he told me that he regretted that they would withdraw the offer.

– Well, you know what *I* think about it, don't you?

– Yes, dad, I know.

– It is with the utmost difficulty that I bring myself to speak to you. You have no regard for your parents' feelings, nor for my standing in Natal. You make me ashamed to go to the Provincial Buildings or to the Club. I'm a governor of St. Michael's, but you make me ashamed to go there too. I blame this damned National Union of Students for this. Ever since you joined it you've gone farther and farther left. And when you became the national president, you made speeches that I am ashamed to remember. I tried to be understanding about it, different generations, enthusiasm of the young, et cetera, et cetera. But this is the last straw for me. I cannot feel any pride in a son who plans deliberately to break the laws of the country. Now there's one thing you must understand. If you go through with this, then on your return I'd be glad if you would find other accommodation.

What is so painful for Harry Mainwaring is a gift for the press. What could be more dramatic than a protest led by the son of a Governor-General, accompanied by the son of a Mahatma? It is probably unique in history. And now it is to be joined by the son of a provincial chairman. What is more, Duncan is on crutches, having broken his leg in a car accident caused by his being on the wrong side of the road. But that will not deter him, because after the violence in East London and Port Elizabeth he is anxious to demonstrate the power of *satyagraha.* It was this that finally persuaded Manilal to join him, because the son of the Mahatma does not like the word *defiance.*

The protest has been made still more dramatic by the fact that the Governor-General has issued a proclamation under the Native Administration Act which prescribes a maximum of three years' imprisonment or a fine of three hundred pounds for any person who incites any African to break any law, or who holds a meeting of Africans without authority. But this does not deter Duncan either. He was going to save a country from violence and destruction. The wisdom or foolishness of his action he must leave in the hands of the Almighty.

In the event the protest went off quietly. Duncan on his crutches, to which he had tied yellow, green and black ribbons, the colours of the African Congress, led about thirty-eight people through the gate of Germiston location. There were plenty of policemen, but they made no attempt to prevent the entry. In a few minutes the protesters were lost in an excited crowd of at least a thousand people. Duncan called for a chair and he stood on it to say a few words in English, followed by some words in Sotho.

– Today South African people of all kinds have come among you. They have come with love for you and with peace. We have not come to make trouble. I ask you on the long road that lies ahead not to make trouble but to do what you have to do with love.

He then gave the freedom cry in Zulu, *Mayibuye! Afrika! Afrika! Afrika! Afrika!* This was taken up by the crowd, after which Duncan gave them a few words in Afrikaans as well, *Julle vryheid kom! Julle vryheid kom deur die Kongres.* Your freedom is coming through the Congress!

Duncan then led his party back to the gate, where they were all arrested.

Mayibuye! Afrika! Afrika! Afrika! That means, Come back, Africa! Come back, Africa, to those from whom it was stolen, by the British and the Germans and the French and

the Belgians and the Portuguese. But it also means, Let this
country return; to those from whom it was stolen, by the
Dutch and the British and the Afrikaner, by the Voortrekkers
and the colonists of Natal.

Have you heard Lutuli speak? He can coo like a dove and
he can roar like a lion, he can call out for the return of Africa
in that great resounding voice that can fill a black hearer with
hope and a white hearer with fear, even one who wishes him
and his cause well.

Can white hopes and black hopes be realised together, in
this southern land to which both white and black have given
their devotion? Who knows the answer to that question?

But at this moment there's no need to worry any more
about Prem Bodasingh and the old lady Perumal. Prem can
go back to school, and the old lady can go back to her seat in
the sun. The congresses have called off the Defiance Campaign.

The reason for that is that Parliament has passed the
Criminal Law Amendment Act, which now makes it a
serious offence to break any law however trivial, if it is
broken *by way of protest*. For this offence a person may be
fined three hundred pounds or go to jail for three years or
receive ten lashes or any two of these. It is even more serious
to incite any other person to break any law by way of protest.
For this a person may be fined five hundred pounds or go to
jail for five years or receive ten lashes, or any two of these.

The congresses have decided either that the people cannot
be expected to pay such penalties or that they will be
unwilling to do so.

The return of Africa must be for a while postponed.

. . . You will remember that I wrote to you in the strictest
confidence that the Minister was considering what steps to
take to bring the Defiance Campaign to an end. Well, of
course you now know that they have been taken and the
campaign is at an end. People like Lutuli and Dr. Monty
Naicker talk very big, but the idea of paying up five hundred
pounds or going to prison for five years has brought their big

talk to an end. The liberal press has made a great deal of the ten lashes, but never mentions the humane provision that lashes will not be inflicted on any person over fifty. I can tell you that it was the Prime Minister who insisted on this.

The provision would benefit both Lutuli and Naicker, but not Patrick Duncan. I think we shall not hear much more from this gentleman. He has quite lost his credibility. He was sentenced to one hundred pounds or one hundred days, and after twenty days he decided to pay the fine. He told the London *Observer* that his book business was falling to pieces, and that he and his wife and children depended on it. He should surely have thought of that before deciding to break the law.

Others say that his leg was troubling him badly. It is sufficient to quote the Minister's caustic remark that the young man must learn not to kick against the pricks.

There are yet others who say that Duncan the great defier just couldn't stand up to being in prison. He is what you might call a clean-living man, in a narrow sense of course, and it was exceedingly painful for him to hear the incessant filth and obscenity that poured out of the mouths of his fellow prisoners. He was also unprepared for their brutality. Perhaps he had hoped to raise the tone of prison behaviour and make it something like that of Winchester College, but he found that he was nobody, that no one respected him because of his 'protest against unjust laws', and that his particular part of the prison was ruled by an eighteen-year-old gangster who is reputed to have killed, even at that early age, a fellow prisoner who questioned his rule. Duncan's views on racial equality absolutely disgusted his fellow prisoners, and it is reassuring to find among our white prisoners such sound views on racial identity and racial separation.

The Minister was extremely annoyed when the State Prosecutor withdrew the charge of incitement. He is satisfied that Duncan meant to incite. He quoted to me Duncan's words: 'I ask you on the long road that lies ahead, not to make trouble but to do what you have to do with love.' He asked what Duncan meant by the words 'do what you have to do'. He regards them as hypocritically ambiguous, defiance masquerading as non-violence. He is also very dissatisfied with the sentence imposed by the court. I think you will find that the magistrate in question will not go very far in his profession.

It seems to me, my dear aunt, that years of peace now lie before South Africa. With the Prime Minister at the helm, with Dr. Hendrik to plan the course, and with our Minister to deal with any attempt at mutiny, I do not see what can go wrong with the ship of State. The communists are on the run, and any preaching of racial equality will in future be regarded as an attempt to further the aims of communism. Our Minister is emphatic about that. Our Security Police are going to be greatly strengthened, and it is the aim of General Smit to know every subversive thought in the country, and to know every person who harbours such thoughts. I do not mind saying that I would not like to get into his bad books. He is, in a good way of course, a man without mercy.

I tell you in confidence that the Prime Minister will retire soon. His obvious successor is Dr. Hendrik, but for reasons of sentiment the caucus is likely to choose Johannes Gerhardus Strijdom, the Lion of the North, who will receive his reward for refusing to join the Hertzog–Smuts alliance twenty years ago. He is one of the few leading Nationalists who is not afraid to say that he believes in white supremacy.

But you must watch Dr. Hendrik. He is the intellectual giant of the Cabinet. It is he who will make the blueprint for the future. In truth he does not need to compete for the premiership. He is in a way the big man of the Cabinet already.

I predict that his Department of Native Affairs will become the most powerful department of all. This year all Native schools will be handed over to him. He is determined to destroy the missionary hold over the Native schools by the non-Calvinist churches. He maintains that Native Education is first and foremost an instrument of policy, and only thereafter an educational affair.

The future of our country is bright.

PART TWO

The Cleft Stick

Mr. Wilberforce Sibusiso Nhlapo, headmaster of the J. H. Hofmeyr High School at Ingogo, sat with his wife in the sitting-room of his house and listened with pain and resentment to the noise coming from the house of his senior Science master, Mr. Jonathan Dlamini. He knew that his younger members of staff were celebrating the election of Lutuli. After Lutuli had refused to resign either from Congress or from the chieftainship, he had been deposed by Dr. Hendrik and had immediately become the darling of Congress and the black people. He had been president of the Natal branch of the Congress, but now by acclamation they had made him the national president. Thus he replaced Dr. Moroka who had committed the unforgivable offence of engaging separate legal defence for himself when he had been charged with others for taking part in the Defiance Campaign.

Mr. Nhlapo had a plain duty towards the Education Department to go to Dlamini's house and stop the party, for according to regulation no political function could be held on school property. But how was one to prove that Dlamini's party was political? In any event, whether the party was political or not, the headmaster could have done nothing more foolish than to interfere with it in any way. If he had tried to do so, the school would have been plagued with a series of strikes, not against him of course, but against the food, the peeling paint, the poverty of the library, even against the inefficiency of some teacher who had been invited but had not attended the celebratory meeting.

If that had happened, the white inspectors would have come to find out what was going on, and they would have found nothing. They would never have found out that the strikes stemmed from the meeting in Dlamini's house. They would have tested the food and would have conceded that it could have been better. They would have seen the peeling paint and they would have acknowledged the poverty of the library. They would have admitted that the teacher was in fact inefficient, and had long been a thorn in the Department's side. But they would never have discovered that the whole thing was a demonstration for Lutuli and against the headmaster. They would certainly have interviewed Dlamini and his friends but they would have come up against an impenetrable wall. Then they would inevitably have come to the conclusion that there was something lacking in the control of the school, and therefore that there was something wrong with the headmaster. And if that happened, Dlamini and his friends would have scored a victory.

It was a melancholy conclusion, but fully justified, that the police would have arrived at the truth far sooner. The police could set out to terrify a child, but an inspector could not. The police could also have terrified some of Dlamini's friends, and the truth would have come out. They would not have been able to terrify Dlamini himself, partly because he was an intensely proud man, and partly because with his qualifications he could easily have had a job in the world of industry. They could have terrified Mazibuko in three minutes. They would simply have said to him, Did your mother obtain a permit to leave Eshowe and to come here and live with you?

Mr. Nhlapo would not easily forget this night of the celebratory meeting. There was a great deal of noise, of singing and laughter, and one could occasionally, when the wind changed, hear the sound of a speech. It was one of those meetings where there prevails an extraordinary mood compounded of frustration, defiance, and joy. They would go round and round Dlamini's dining-room table, holding their thumbs aloft and singing *Sizomlandela Lutuli*, We shall follow Lutuli. They would be lost to the outside world, intent on their song, totally unselfconscious, certainly with no concern lest they looked undignified or ridiculous. Mrs. Sithole, who weighed close on three hundred pounds, and had long since lost the figure of a dancer, would go round and round the table, with the sweat pouring off her cheeks and staining her clothes, and with that rapt expression that transformed the faces of the admirers of Lutuli.

Someone would make a speech, Dlamini of course, and most surely Mkhize the Zulu master, who might have become headmaster when Mr. Nhlapo was appointed, and would now probably finish his teaching days as a master at the J. H. Hofmeyr High School. Dlamini's speech would be bitter and forthright, but Mkhize was a planter of barbs.

He would call them all to attention, and they would wait expectantly for his witticisms. He might start off full of melancholy, and tell them what a great and tragic day it was, great because Lutuli was now their leader, tragic because some of the foremost educational figures were not present. My English is very poor, would say Mkhize, whose English was very good. These foremost figures are not present. Is that because they could not be present, or because they would not be present, or perhaps because they thought they should not be present?

Those who understood these nuances would be seized by fits of laughter, and those who did not understand would be seized just the same. For the barb was directed against Mr. Nhlapo and his assistant headmaster, Mr. Stephen Koza. Mr. Nhlapo could see the gathering in imagination, the bitter Dlamini and the bitterly witty Mkhize. He could see those whose enjoyment of Lutuli's election was unalloyed, and he could see those who were afraid, because they knew that they were attending a meeting of a kind forbidden by the Education Department on any school property.

The noise from Dlamini's house filled Mr. Nhlapo with resentment and pain. He had been excluded from the celebration. His pain was increased by the knowledge that if he had been invited he would not have gone. How could he have gone? He was the senior African headmaster in the Education Department, and his pension day was drawing closer. How could he attend a meeting of a kind forbidden by the Department? And for this loyalty he must pay this painful price of being treated as an outcast and a traitor to his people, and of sitting in his own house and listening to the noise of their defiance and joy, and of the speeches that would contain open attacks and barbed innuendos. All through his teaching life he had enjoyed the confidence of his pupils and colleagues, and in these later years much respect. It was when he came to the J. H. Hofmeyr High School that he had met the first two men who had ever treated him with contempt.

His wife looked up from her knitting, and said,

– There's someone coming. I think it's Koza. I'll let him in.

– Good evening, Koza. Come and sit down. You're up late.

– The hostels are restless tonight, headmaster. They have all heard about Lutuli. And they can hear the noise of Dlamini's party. Some of them asked me why they cannot celebrate.

Mr. Nhlapo steeled himself to hear the worst. He was in that state of mind where one wants to hear no more and yet one wants to hear it all.

– Who asked you, Koza?

– Malinga and some of his prefects. And Constance Mtshali for the girls. They want to know why no announcement has been made.

– And what did you say?

– I said Lutuli's election was a political matter, and that we did not make political announcements.

– And what did they say?

– They did not agree. They said it was a national event, and should be announced.

– Are they now in bed?

– Yes. I did not force them. I thought it would not be wise.

Mr. Nhlapo digested this news in silence. He would have remained silent if Koza had not said,

– Headmaster.

– Yes.

– I had to make them a promise.

– What did you promise?

– I promised to bring their request to you. I thought it wise to do so. I said I could not promise what you would do, but I would certainly bring their request to you. I thought it wise to go further. I told them I would bring their request to you this very night. Headmaster, I must also tell you that on the way here I met Mbele. He left the party early because his wife is not well. You know he is friendly to us. He told me the staff are sending a deputation to you tomorrow.

– What for?

– Headmaster, it is very difficult.

Mr. Nhlapo roused himself from his depression, and showed a touch of anger.

– Yes, I know it is difficult, Koza. But I am not a child. I did not get where I am by shutting my ears to difficulties. What do they want?

– They want you to change the name of the school.

– They want to call it the Albert Lutuli School, I suppose.

– No, they want to call it the Chief Albert Lutuli School.

– Indeed?

– Dlamini quoted the old saying, A chief is a chief because of the people. He is not a chief because of the government. Therefore Lutuli is still a chief.

– Tomorrow will be a hard day, Koza. You must meet me in my office half-an-hour before school starts. And when you come, bring good advice.

– I'll be there, and I'll try to bring good advice.

– I am lucky to have you, Koza.

– Headmaster.

– Yes.

– I must tell you one thing more. That man hates you.

Mr. Nhlapo nodded heavily.

– Yes, I know.

When Koza had gone, Mrs. Nhlapo said to her husband,

– Father, you must pull yourself together. You have sat here the whole evening and you have not spoken a word. I know things are difficult, but you told Koza you have not got where you are by shutting your ears to difficulties. You think too much about this Dlamini. It is not like you to be afraid of a man like that.

– I'm not afraid of him.

– All right, you are not afraid of him, but you think too much about him. You are not firm enough with him. I know that man. If you are not firm with him, he will spoil your school, he will spoil your teachers, he will spoil your children. Why don't you ask Inspector Anderson to move him away?

– Do you know how difficult it is to get a Science teacher? And a good one like Dlamini?

– All right, keep him. But what is more important, your Science results or your school? I do not like to see you like this. It is not your true nature. You have one of the best schools in Natal. Look at the troubles some of your friends have had. Majola's whole school was burned down. And Zondi still cannot walk after that attack.

– Mother, you're right, I must pull myself together. I shall announce to the school tomorrow that Lutuli has been elected. They can shout and clap if they want to. And I'll tell the deputation I do not decide the names of schools. However, if the members of the deputation put down their suggestions on paper and sign their names, I shall send it to the Department.

Mrs. Nhlapo gave a little cry of delight.

– That's the way to talk, Father. They won't do it.

– They make me angry. It was J. H. Hofmeyr who every year while he was Minister increased the amount for African education. And every year he was opposed by the men who are governing us now. They called him a *kafferboetie*. I don't mind a school being called the Albert Lutuli School, but they must not take Hofmeyr's name away in order to do it. Mother, I am going to Newcastle after school tomorrow.

– To see Robert?

He smiled at her intuition.

– Yes, to see Robert.

– That's a good thing to do. He's the right man to see in a time like this. Tell him from me that I had a husband who was a jolly laughing man, but I have lost him. Robert must help me to get him back again.

– Mr. Mainwaring, you remember the last congress of the National Union of South African Students, what you call NUSAS. The congress was held in July 1953.

– Yes, I remember it.

– You were in the chair, were you not?

– Yes.

– Your congress passed a resolution congratulating a person whom you called Chief Lutuli, on being elected national president of the African Congress.

– Yes.

– You knew, I suppose, that Lutuli was no longer a chief, that he had been deposed by the Minister of Native Affairs.

– Yes.

– Then why did you congratulate him as Chief Lutuli?

– Because many people call him that.

– You mean many people of your kind, liberals, communists, Congress members, disaffected people, people with subversive views.

– NUSAS does not hold subversive views. We hold strong views, very often anti-apartheid views, but we do not advocate what you call subversion, by which I suppose you mean the willingness to overthrow the Government by violence.

– Yet you continue to address as Chief a man who has been deposed by lawful authority. You are in fact doing something which in terms of the Native Code is now unlawful. You don't call that subversive?

– It was not meant to be subversive.

Lieutenant van der Spuy looked at his notes. That may have been a signal to his superior, for Captain du Plooy took over.

– Mr. Mainwaring, we are not interested in what you meant or did not mean to be subversive. We are interested only in what our legal advisers think to be subversive. They are of opinion that it is for example subversive for a students' organisation to continue to give a man a title which has been taken away from him by a Minister who ultimately derives his power from Parliament. It is in fact contempt of Parliament, which is a serious offence indeed. The penalties are heavy, and could be crippling for you and your organisation, even though you receive such generous help from people outside South Africa who have no loyalty to this country whatsoever, and some of whom have said that their aim is to bring our lawful authorities to their knees. Have you, or any of your associates, ever used this expression: to bring the Government to its knees?

– It has been used, yes.

– Has it been used by you?

– No.

– By whom then?

– Must I answer that question?

– At the moment, no. But I must warn you, Mr. Mainwaring, that we have not come here to play games with you. We regard your union as dangerous, and we can advise the Minister to use his powers to bring its life to an end. Would you like to see that happen while you are its president, and have presumably been given the responsibility of guiding its fortunes?

– No.

Here Lieutenant van der Spuy intervened.

– Can I suggest, Captain, that we let Mr. Mainwaring rest for a few minutes? He is very young, and he is clearly disturbed . . .

– So he ought to be disturbed. Mr. Mainwaring, what do you mean exactly by the expression: to bring the Government to its knees?

– It's a strong expression. Students use strong expressions. It means, to make the Government change its course.

– Does it not mean, to make it capitulate? To make it make way for another government?

– Yes, it could be that.

– And will you tell me, said the Captain in a hard voice, a voice as hard as the eyes that never left Hugh Mainwaring's face, how you could make this Government capitulate except by force of arms, that is by armed revolution?

– That was never intended.

– Then what was intended?

– To use the powers of reason, of persuasion, to arouse public opinion, to make the Government change course.

– And how does a government change course when it is on its knees?

– I admit it is too strong an expression.

– Just now you admitted it was strong. Now you admit it was too strong. What you really mean is it should not be used. Did this same congress of yours condemn the proposed new Bantu Education Act that will transfer all Native

Education to the Department of Native Affairs?

– Yes.

– Did one of your speakers say that it was an education designed to prepare black children for slavery?

– Yes.

– Did you call him to order, and ask him to withdraw the expression?

– No.

– Why not?

– It was a student debate. Such things happen frequently in student debate. If you were to examine Hansard, captain, you would find that the same kind of language is used in Parliament.

– Parliament is privileged, Mr. Mainwaring, but NUSAS is not. When you say that the Minister of Education has designed an education which will prepare black children for slavery you are gravely defaming the Minister. But what is more you are asserting that the Minister proposes to revive an institution which is forbidden in international law. Do you realise that?

– The word was used in an exaggerated sense.

– Like the words: on their knees?

– Yes.

– So that every time a student uses subversive language in NUSAS you as president will claim that it was not meant in a literal sense, only an exaggerated or symbolic sense. Like poetry, I suppose.

– Captain, can't we let Mr. Mainwaring have a few minutes off? Your questions are upsetting him, so that perhaps he is not thinking too clearly.

– I'll soon be finished with him. Mr. Mainwaring, what were your movements on the eighteenth day of September 1953?

– I can't remember.

– Do you keep a diary?

– Yes.

– Where is it?

– My secretary has it.

– Will you get it, please?

– . . . Well, Mr. Mainwaring, can you tell me now what your movements were?

– I went to Ladysmith in the afternoon.

– To a speech contest?

– Yes.

– With two Indian girls?

– Yes.

– Miss Prem Bodasingh and Miss Lutchmee Perumal?

– Yes.

– The elder girl was in jail last year, three times I believe.

– Yes.

– The contest finished at ten-thirty p.m., and Miss Perumal stayed with friends in Ladysmith, while you and the older girl set off back to Durban?

– Yes.

– Where you arrived at ten o'clock the following morning?

– Yes.

– What did you do between ten-thirty p.m. and ten o'clock the next morning?

– I am sorry, captain, I have tried to be civil with you, but what authority have you to ask me such questions?

– As a matter of fact, Mr. Mainwaring, I don't have any authority at all unless I suspect a crime to have been committed. And when a young white man and an Indian girl take twelve hours to travel from Ladysmith to Durban, then I am fully justified in suspecting a crime to have been committed.

– What sort of crime?

– Under the Immorality Act of 1927 as amended in 1950.

– She is not that kind of girl.

– And you are not that kind of man. We've heard all that before. The police caught a white man and a black woman in the bush at Umhlanga Rocks a few days ago. They had taken off some of their clothes because the night was so hot. And what were they talking about? Music. And why did they go into the bush? Because of what people might say, of course. All right, say I don't have any authority. But I have the authority to go to the Minister of Justice and tell him that you are leading NUSAS into subversion, and that you ought to be banned from public life for five years. He could ban you from the university too. Therefore it would be advisable for you to tell me your movements between ten-thirty p.m. on the eighteenth and ten a.m. on the nineteenth. And if you still refuse to tell me, I have no doubt that Miss Bodasingh will tell me.

– I'll tell you. We got to Pietermaritzburg after midnight, and went to stay with friends in Scottsville.

– At 127 Carmichael Road. Name of Harper.

– Yes.

– And you slept in separate rooms?

– Yes.

– That's very satisfactory. As a matter of fact I did not suspect a crime to have been committed. But I want you to know that everything you do is known to us. At this congress did a black member from Fort Hare move that NUSAS should persuade all Native teachers and pupils to boycott the schools of the Bantu Education Department?

– Yes.

– Did you pull him up?

– No.

– You allowed a debate?

– Yes.

– During which the speeches were highly inflammatory?

– Some yes. Others no. Many pointed out the foolishness of such a step, especially if the Minister expelled all who took part in the boycott.

– The mover was Thomas Mafolo, of Bloemfontein?

– Yes.

– You had better warn Thomas Mafolo, Mr. Mainwaring. Another speech like that, and that's the end of his education. And you had better be careful yourself. Your father is the Chairman of the Provincial Executive, not so?

– Yes.

– I have thought several times of going to see him, to ask him to warn you.

– I don't think it would help, captain. He doesn't speak to me.

– Because you went into Germiston location with Patrick Duncan?

– Yes.

– Mr. Mainwaring, you had better be very careful about what you are doing. You are on a dangerous course. You probably do not know it, but the communists are using NUSAS to further their own ends. Last year you were the president, and no doubt you thought you were running the organisation, but you were only their tool. In fact they put you into the presidency, a nice high-up liberal who'd been to St. Michael's and whose father was Chairman of the Provincial Executive. I suppose they thought that we would then leave you alone. But we won't leave you alone, Mr. Mainwaring. If it's necessary we'll smash you and your career and your reputation and your organisation. I want you to be in no doubt about that. Good day.

Lieutenant van der Spuy allowed his superior to go ahead, and then he smiled at Hugh Mainwaring.

– Be careful, old chap. It's not worth it.

A nice chap, Lieutenant van der Spuy.

. . . I can tell you that the take-over of all Native schools by Dr. Hendrik and his Department of Native Affairs has gone off splendidly. They will come under a new Department of Bantu Education. Dr. Hendrik has been making speeches that can only be described as magnificent. They will endure as long as Afrikanerdom endures. Sometimes his imagery is breathtaking. He said that the missionaries showed black children the green pastures in which they would never graze.

He has of course been bitterly attacked by the non-Afrikaner churches. Archbishop Clayton of Cape Town has said that African education will now become the instrument of a white political party, and that this is a Nazi technique. A certain Reverend C. W. L. Skey has declared that the Government is following communist practice. And the chief trouble-maker, the glib-tongued Father Huddleston, has called it 'education for servitude'.

Dr. Hendrik exposed their fallacies with a skill and a logic that we lesser mortals can only admire. He quoted them all to show that it was 'highly desirable that their hold on Native education should disappear'. After that what could they say? The Archbishop and Huddleston don't know a word of Afrikaans. They came to South Africa knowing nothing of our customs and traditions, and then had the impudence to criticise. The Archbishop has a great head, and is reputed to have a great intellect, but he cannot stand up to Dr. Hendrik. They dislike each other intensely, that is if a great man like Dr. Hendrik could be said to *dislike* a man of lesser stature.

Of course Lutuli and the Congress are making trouble. They urged a boycott of the schools, and seven thousand children stayed away in protest. Dr. Hendrik reacted magnificently. He ordered that not one of these children should ever be allowed in a school again. That was the end of the boycott.

I can tell you in confidence that Dr. Hendrik is now urging the Cabinet to create a Department of Coloured Education and a Department of Indian Education. The first would fall under a yet-to-be-created Department of Coloured Affairs and the second under a Department of Indian Affairs. The whole magnificent plan of Separate Coexistence is taking shape under our very eyes. The Cabinet, with one or two exceptions, are under the spell of Dr. Hendrik. He may not be the Prime Minister, but it is he who is at the helm of the ship of State. The future is bright indeed.

I think I told you that Welthagen was due to retire. Well, he has gone and I have a new superior, Dr. Jan Woltemade Fischer, B.A., B.Ed., LL.B, Ph.D. He is said to be the most brilliant student that our university here has ever produced. He was making a fortune at the Senior Bar, but the Minister asked him to join the Department. The Civil Service Commission objected but the Minister is not a man to be opposed. Dr. Fischer is in his middle thirties, and it seems clear that he is destined to go very far indeed.

Dr. Fischer is said to be, after the Prime Minister and Dr. Hendrik, the most compelling public speaker in the country. He is highly regarded in church circles, not only for his theological knowledge, but for his unshakable principles in all matters of sex and race. But his strongest card is his membership of the Broederbond, and he is regarded as one of the most promising of its younger members, which means that he will certainly reach high office .

It can, I think, be safely said that soon every key position in South Africa will be held by a Broederbonder. When the Broederbond was founded, its intention was that the Broeders should rule South Africa. That is nearly the case. The Prime Minister, my own Minister, and Dr. Hendrik are all Broeders. I was never asked to become one, and that is why I am now junior to a man ten years younger than myself. Naturally I feel rather bitter and, I must confess to you, a bit second-class. I did have hopes of getting the post myself. My superior has on his desk a rectangular piece of polished wood which reads, Dr. Jan Woltemade Fischer, B.A., B.Ed., LL.B., Ph.D., which I think vulgar. Sometimes I toy with the idea of asking for a transfer to Dr. Hendrik's department. That is where the future lies.

I am sorry, my dear aunt, that I have allowed these personal matters to intrude upon what I try to make a factual and reliable account of what goes on behind the scenes. I must try to think less of my private affairs, and more about my duty to Afrikanerdom. It troubles me greatly that I do not feel attracted to a man who is a one hundred per cent Afrikaner. I have to confess a deep secret, that if you are not a member of the Broederbond you are not an Afrikaner in the fullest sense of the word. This may not matter if you are a farmer or a doctor or a mining man. But if you are a member of the Civil Service it matters a great deal.

Yes, my dear aunt, you are quite right. I should not have compared Peter with Paul, and I should not have compared fishermen with scholars. I did it because I was angry about the Defiance Campaign, and I went too far. Sorry, dear Aunt Trina.

— Robert, I am in deep trouble
  — Is it Dlamini?
  — Yes, it is Dlamini. But the deep trouble is in me. I am losing my jolliness, Robert.
  — Have you tried to get Dlamini transferred?

– Yes, I have tried. Inspector Anderson says it is impossible. He says that the J. H. Hofmeyr High School is one of the most important of African schools, and that this is largely due to the excellence of its Science ánd Mathematics.

– Can't Dlamini swap places with another first-class Science master?

– The inspector says that the Department has no other Science teacher of his calibre. He says I should think myself lucky to have such good teachers in both Science and Maths. He says no other high school is as lucky.

– Why does Dlamini have this hatred for you?

– I don't think he hates me for personal reasons. He hates me because I am a moderate, because I don't believe that things will change tomorrow. I am the good boy, Robert. I am not a revolutionary.

– What is he? A Marxist?

– I don't think so. I think he is a black national-socialist of an extreme kind. He does not communicate with any white person. He does not communicate with me except on formal matters. If I go to him and say, I've had a letter from Matthew Zondi's sponsor, and he wants to know how the boy is doing in Science, then Dlamini will tell me. He will say, The boy is excellent in Chemistry, with so-much per cent. But Dlamini is also talking a silent language and he is saying to me, Why don't you give a lead to your people? Whom do you follow, our black leaders or the white Director of Education? If he says that the boy is equally good in Physics, then he is also saying to me, Why are you losing hold of your school? Because for you it is not a school for the black nation, it is a school for the white Director of Education. He is saying to me, You are a white man's stooge, you are selling out your nation.

– Don't you just imagine all this, Wilberforce? Aren't you, as we say, at your wit's end?

– Yes, of course I imagine it all. Did you not hear me say that it is a silent language that he talks? Of course I am at my wit's end. Why do you think I came to see you? Last time I came to see you was when the children wanted an announcement of Lutuli's election, and the staff deputation wanted me to ask the Department to change the name of the school. You gave me great courage, Robert. I was afraid to meet them. I thought, now they like this bitter Science master, not their jolly headmaster any more. I thought, now Lutuli, who has no enmity towards me, and who was a warm friend to me in his teaching days, has destroyed my life's work in a moment. You said to me that I was not in fear of real things but of things I had created in my own imagination. It gave me courage to hear that, which is very strange, because I knew it already. I imagine the worst, I fear the worst, and this often prevents me from facing trouble immediately, and if you don't do that it can grow bigger because you are not doing anything. You shut yourself off, Robert, you don't want to hear anything. You are like a horse in — what do you say?

   — In blinkers.

   — Yes, in blinkers. I am very ashamed of this weakness.

   — It is a weakness many of us have.

   — Well, I went to face the children. You know we allow quiet talking in our assembly until the headmaster comes in. Then there is absolute silence. When I came in on that day, there was absolute silence. My heart was lifted up by that small thing. I said, Members of the school, I understand that some of you have a grievance against me because I did not announce the election of Chief Lutuli to the national presidency of Congress. I do not wish you to have a grievance against me. But it is not the custom of this school to make such announcements. We did not announce the previous election of Dr. Moroka. Nevertheless I announce this morning that Chief Albert Lutuli, who was deprived of his chieftainship by the Minister of Native Affairs, but will always be known as the Chief, has been elected by acclamation the national president of Congress. Then the children clapped and some gave the sign of the Congress and some called *Mayibuye* but very self-consciously. It was all very orderly. I said, John Malinga and Constance Mtshali, is there anything you wish to say? The head boy and the head girl exchanged a few words, and then John said to me, Headmaster, we are satisfied. Then there was more clapping, this time for me, I suppose. I said to the school, I shall call you together again soon to talk to you about the new Bantu Education Act and how it will affect all of you and all our schools. Let us close the assembly by singing *Nkosi Sikelel' iAfrika*. When the children had gone, the staff, most of them I would say, gathered round me. I was the headmaster again, not some frightened man. I could see the relief in their faces. Koza said to me, Headmaster, you are a clever man. I said to him, Koza, I have a man who gives me good advice. I love that man, Robert.

Nhlapo sat in silence, recalling the past, and Mansfield did not like to recall him to the present. But Nhlapo recalled himself.

– Robert, it's all gone, the happiness has gone, the fear has returned. The jolly laughing man has gone. I ask myself if he will ever come back again. Dlamini is dividing my school in two. On one side there are those who want to pass their examinations, who want to become doctors and lawyers and teachers, who respect their headmaster, who indeed respect all older persons, which, as you well know, Robert, is our ancient custom. On the other side are those who think only of liberation, of equality, of the universal suffrage, of freedom tomorrow. They do not say so to me, they also speak the silent language. I have one outstanding boy, Nathaniel Kuzwayo, whose father was dismissed by the Transvaal Education Department because he spoke out against the new Bantu Education Act. He is a tall, bitter boy, a great admirer of Dlamini. He also speaks the silent language. When I speak to him about the way his work is falling off, he speaks to me in the silent language, he says, Why have you not been dismissed too? Is it because you have not spoken out against the new Bantu Education Act? Why do you not speak out? Is it because you are afraid? This is the boy, Robert, who said to me in open class, Why should we study in days like these? Who wants a certificate in days like these? It makes me angry, Robert, that his Science marks do not fall off, they are as high as ever.

Nhlapo's voice rose in protest.

– Dlamini led a deputation to me, Robert. They asked me to resign my post as a protest against the Bantu Education

Act. I refused. I said I had a boy and a girl at university. If I resigned, they would have to leave. I could not do that to them. Do you know that Dlamini can say the most cruel things without raising his voice, without any sign of anger. I think it is a gift some of us have learned during centuries of conquest. It is in the first place a way of talking to white people, and of raising their blood to boiling point, so that they reveal some ugliness that was concealed behind their greetings and their smiles. But it is also a way of talking to your black superiors as well. I have had to suffer under it. But up till now I have kept myself in order.

— Wilberforce, you must get rid of Dlamini.

— How?

— I shall have to think. I can't see you go on like this. This man is not really a Lutuli man. Lutuli wants to change things, not destroy them. Dlamini is only using Lutuli to destroy you, and sooner or later he will want to destroy Lutuli too. I'll go to Pietermaritzburg to see the Director. I know he no longer controls African schools, but he can perhaps advise us. You can't keep this man. Elizabeth is right, he is spoiling your school.

— Robert, I have something more to tell you.

— Yes.

— Somebody tried to kill me. Last Wednesday night, in that little dark avenue that runs to my house.

— Are you certain of this?

— I have the instrument. I didn't bring it to show you. That would have been unsuitable. It is an assegai.

— It was thrown at you?

— It was thrown at my back. If it had got me I would have been dead. But by the grace of God, by a miracle, Robert, it struck the space between my body and my right arm. It tore the cloth of my jacket, but it did not touch my flesh.

— Does Elizabeth know?

— I could not hide it. There was this long tear in my jacket. How could you explain such a thing except by telling the truth? In any case I have never lied to her, not once in our married life.

— And beyond what you tell me, you know nothing.

– Nothing. The assegai fell on the ground, and I could see what it was. I turned round at once, and in the dark I saw the figure of a man. It could not have been a woman, the assegai was too heavy and its force was too great. It was my imagination no doubt — you know, Robert, the strength of my imagination — but the man seemed to be dressed as a warrior, one of Shaka's warriors.

– Then you were lucky that he didn't use the short stabbing spear.

– Yes, I was lucky. But my luck didn't fill me with joy. Who wants to kill me at this time of my life? As far as I know, Robert, I have never hurt anyone in my whole life. I've caned a few naughty boys, but I have tried never to hurt a boy or a girl in their pride. I must go now, but I shall tell you one good thing that came out of all this. I have had a joint letter from my boy and girl at university. They both thanked God that I was not hurt. They had also heard that I would not resign because of the Bantu Education Act. They said they knew I had done it for them. They said that the whole university is torn in two between those who want to boycott all education, and those who want to continue their studies. But they themselves — my son and daughter — were torn in two inside themselves. Half of them wanted a father who would resign, and half of them wanted a father who cared about their education. It seems to us black people, Robert, that everything is falling apart.

– You mustn't think that only black people feel that. I feel it too, very strongly. Apartheid is driving us apart. That's what it's meant to do, isn't it? It's not only that the centre cannot hold. It's being torn to pieces. If it isn't put together again, the whole country will fall apart. Your children will be fighting my children, Wilberforce.

– Do not speak like that, Robert. I must go now. You know me better than ever. Full of fears, some real, some not. Not without courage though very low at the moment. Imagination much too powerful. Does not lie to his wife. Has two children, both torn in two, want their father to be brave but also want him to be fatherly. Just like their father who wants them to be brave but also wants them to get their degrees. Robert, whatever goes wrong, Elizabeth and I will never forget you.

Mansfield accompanied his friend to his car, and watched him drive away up the street on his way back to the J. H. Hofmeyr High School. He thought with a wry smile of Nhlapo's summing up of his character, for it was also the summing up of his own. People didn't know that. They saw him as the confident headmaster of the Newcastle High School. He had no Dlamini on his staff, and no boy like Nathaniel Kuzwayo. He had no disciplinary troubles with the boys, largely because he had played cricket for South Africa, and none with the girls because he was tall and fair and had blue eyes, and had an amiable weakness for girls anyway.

He and Nhlapo were lucky in their wives. Elizabeth Nhlapo was no docile Zulu woman, and would upbraid her husband in unmistakable language if she thought it necessary — if she thought, for example, that people were trading on his good nature. Naomi Mansfield was also a woman of strong character, but she would upbraid her husband in a more subtle and less spectacular manner. Both of them agonised a great deal over the way in which their son and daughter were growing up knowing nothing of the children who were separated from them by barriers of language and race and colour, but most of all by their segregated schooling. Mansfield and Nhlapo had arranged more than one inter-school visit. Their schools had debated against each other; the boys had played cricket, and the girls hockey. But the resistance of the white parents of Newcastle, and some of the members of the cricket and hockey teams, was painful to both the Mansfields.

– . . . I don't mind my boy learning Zulu at school, Mr. Mansfield, but I don't want him playing cricket against black boys. And he doesn't really want to play either. He volunteered to play only because you asked him, and he thinks you're a hell of a good chap. He says they can't play anyway, and you have to bowl slowly and bat slowly too. He's a decent lad, and he doesn't think it's treating them fairly to play down to them. He says the cleverer ones can easily see through it.

– . . . I admire you very much for doing it, Mr. Mansfield. And my daughter Janet thought it was wonderful. She wants to ask two of the girls for the weekend and, although we've never done anything like that before, my husband and I have decided to do it. He said to me, Do you realise that although we have lived forty years in this country with black people we've never had one in our house?

– . . . I know you believe in what you are doing, Mr. Mansfield, but you're a hundred years before your time. I have been approached by many parents, and by other people too, who object very strongly to racial mixing, and I, as the member of the Natal Provincial Council for this constituency, intend to raise this matter first with the Provincial Executive. Between you and me, this could do great harm to the United Party, because this constituency isn't one of the safe ones, and I can't allow that.

After his talk with the member of the Provincial Council for Newcastle, Mr. Barend Coetzee, a powerful figure in northern Natal, Mansfield realised that he had entered deep waters. He admitted to himself, but not to his wife, that he was afraid. He had opened a door for Janet Armstrong and her parents, who would for the first time in forty years have a black guest in the house, but he had angered many others. His wife had told him of the disgust that his racial experiments had aroused, not only among members of her tennis club, but also among members of the Women's Anglican Guild. None of these women had expressed their disgust to her, but they had to some of her friends.

The hardest blow of all was dealt to him by his own Director, Dr. William Johnson, who issued a circular to all headmasters and headmistresses under his authority, stating that it was not the policy of the Department to encourage racially mixed school functions. Mansfield was both friend and admirer of his Director, and he decided to go down to Pietermaritzburg to see him.

– Robert, I couldn't do anything else. I'm sure you've heard all about the girl Prem Bodasingh. Well, to put it plainly, I won that battle, and now I can't afford to fight another. I wouldn't win it anyway. The Administrator-in-Executive Committee instructed me to forbid racially mixed functions.

– But Bill, the Administrator said to Rotary in Pinetown, only a few weeks ago, that he was shocked by the ignorance of children in white schools, of the languages and cultures of other children, and he advocated the introduction of special studies to remedy the situation.

– That's true, and Miss Moberly of the Girls' High School immediately arranged a hockey match with the Indian Girls' High. As soon as the Executive Committee heard about it they ordered me to cancel it. Then Professor John Durant of the University of Natal wrote a scathing letter to the *Natal Witness*, and said the Administrator wanted to teach children how to swim without letting them go into the water. I tell you, Robert, I was ashamed, of myself, and the Administrator, and of the Executive Committee. But the fact is that the Natal Director of Education can't change the racial policies of the Government. If I had tried to do so, then this time they would have fired me. I was willing to be dismissed over Prem Bodasingh, because to prevent her from going to any school again would have been, in my calendar, a gravely immoral act. But I can't feel the same about preventing mixed games. Do you see my point?

– Yes, I see your point. You're in a cleft stick, Bill, and I'm in a cleft stick, and your damned Administrator-in-Executive Committee is in a cleft stick, and we can all be forgiven because we were all born in a cleft stick. It fills me with despair for the future. We all live in the same country, yet we allow our children to grow up in total ignorance of their future fellow South Africans, and I'm telling you, Bill, that if they don't play with each other today, then they're going to kill each other tomorrow. I'm reaching the end of the road. I'm feeling more and more strongly that I must give up my job, and go out and try to do something about it.

– Robert, you can't do that. In a couple of years Jenkins retires and Maritzburg College will be yours. You always wanted that, didn't you?

– Yes, I did want it, but I don't want it any more. What

would I do there? Teach another generation of boys to uphold the mores of the Administrator-in-Executive Committee? Teach another generation not to look at the truth about their own country? It would be an act of criminal negligence on my part, and I won't do it.

– You are of course implying — or shall I say that you are implicitly saying — that I as Director am also criminally negligent.

– Look here, Bill, I haven't come all the way from Newcastle to insult my boss. And I didn't come here to say that. Yet I can't deny that there is an implication, not only for you but for all of us.

– Then there's no point in talking further. I was appointed as Director, and I'll do the job as I think best. Now I'm sorry, but . . .

– I shan't waste any more of your precious time. But I must congratulate you and the Executive on saving Newcastle for the United Party.

So he went, leaving Johnson subdued and angry. It was all very well for Robert Mansfield to take a brave stand; after all his mother had left him a tidy sum of money. Cleft stick? Yes, he *was* in a cleft stick, and we were all in cleft sticks, but not all of us had the money to get out of them.

Just suppose he had refused to forbid the white schools to play the others. This time he would have been dismissed. If the Administrator-in-Executive had changed its decision, which was highly improbable, indeed impossible, the Government would have intervened. No province of the Union of South Africa could defy the laws of the country.

The chances were that he would have been dismissed without pension, and he would have had nothing to live on. A dismissed Director of Education is not a likely candidate for re-employment. How pleased he had felt when the Administrator-in-Executive had dropped the matter of Prem Bodasingh. And a bit proud too, he had to confess. But the feeling of pride had gone. He knew perfectly well that the Administrator's speech to Rotary and his order to cancel the hockey game were mutually contradictory actions, but he had to carry out the order. He thought with bitter self-criticism that his pension was now safe, just as Newcastle was safe for the United Party. At that particular moment, after his unpleasant encounter with Mansfield, he recalled with distaste that he had spoken, half-jokingly it is true, of his anticipation of ten years of golf followed by ten years of bowls.

– A note for you, Director, from Mr. Mansfield.

Bill, sorry for my remark about Newcastle, I understand your position, but I don't want to stay any longer in mine. Robert.

It was typical Robert.

The resignation of Mr. Robert Mansfield from the headmastership of the high school has come as a shock to the people of Newcastle, pleasant to some, unpleasant to others. The parents are more or less divided into two equal parties, the one totally opposed to the headmaster's racial experiments, the other not necessarily all in favour, but unanimous in their high opinion of his headmastership. The majority of those white citizens who are not parents are glad to see him go. They do not all agree with Mr. Barend Coetzee, who had told Mansfield that he was a hundred years before his time; some of them reckon that his time will never come at all, that the Government, and especially the powerful Dr. Hendrik, have a master plan for the total separation of the races, not for a hundred years but for ever.

The school itself is not so sharply divided. There are a few boys and girls who are glad to see him go, and most of these are the sons and daughters of parents who find the racial experiments abhorrent. But most of the boys are full of regret to lose a headmaster who has played cricket for South Africa, and as for the girls, many of them have been in love with him in schoolgirl fashion, which is not altogether surprising, for he is a very handsome man.

And what has he resigned for? The newspapers have asked him of course, but he has refused to tell them until the day after he leaves the service of the Education Department. This gives credence to the rumour that he is going into politics, and that he is going to join the new Liberal Party. The party has attracted a fair number of whites who would call themselves liberals, including the redoubtable Margaret Ballinger, one of the three white members of Parliament elected by those black voters who in 1936 were removed from the common roll. In return for their removal they were given three white M.P.s, and the black voters of Cape Eastern chose Margaret Ballinger to represent them. She is one of the finest brains in the House, and has energy to match her intelligence. The Liberal Party considers itself lucky and privileged to have got her.

The Liberal Party has had a contemptuous reception from the ruling National Party. Indeed some Nationalists are implacably hostile, and want it to be made a criminal offence to oppose the policies of separate coexistence. They regard the establishment of a nonracial party as a flagrant defiance of the powers-that-be. Most other white South Africans are hostile also, because, while they reject certain forms of racial discrimination, they really cannot approve of cooperating with other races to fight it. The African Congress, and still more the Indian Congress, accuse the new party of undermining the Congress front. Most hostile of all is the white Congress, which is strongly Marxist, and regards concern about civil rights as almost irrelevant in a war situation. Their hostility is understandable, because the Liberal Party has expressed its condemnation of all forms of totalitarianism, including communism and fascism.

– I understand what you are doing, Robert, and I admire you for it, but I am desolated all the same. You know it is my weakness to lean on you, and whom shall I lean on now?

– I thought of you a great deal before I did it. I had to ask myself which was more important. You and I have tried to bring our schools and our children closer together, but now our attempts have been forbidden by both our departments. What was more important, for me to stay here to comfort you, or to go out and fight on a national platform for the things we believe in?

– You don't need to explain it to me, Robert. But Elizabeth and I are going to miss you and Naomi . . . sorely.

– But at least you haven't got Dlamini to contend with. Tell me, why did he resign?

– He didn't tell me, but I assumed it was because he refused to teach under Bantu Education. The Security Police wanted to know too.

– So they've been to see you.

– For two days running. They searched Dlamini's house from top to bottom. They asked me why he resigned. I said I had heard that he had been offered a job as an industrial chemist in Durban. But they didn't believe me. They asked me his views of Bantu Education, and what he thought of Dr. Hendrik. I told them that he didn't approve of Bantu Education, but that I had never heard him speak about Dr. Hendrik. Then they wanted to know why he disapproved of Bantu Education, and I said it was his opinion that it was an inferior education, and furthermore that the insistence on home language as the medium of instruction up to Standard Six simply meant that no black child could ever become a scientist or a mathematician. Then they asked me if I agreed with him, and I said that this was the opinion of the majority of black teachers of Science and Mathematics, and that I agreed with them. Then the black man took over, Sergeant Magwaza was his name, and asked if I was ashamed of the Zulu language. Robert, I nearly laughed, but I decided not to. I said no, I was very proud of it, and I wanted all my pupils to speak it well and to write poems and stories in it, but it was not the language of Science and Mathematics, no more than English is the language of cattle and grass and herbs. Then this black fellow asked me what I thought of Dr. Hendrik and I told him that my opinion was my own, and that in any case I was not a great talker about other people.

– Good for you, Wilberforce. How did they take that?

– Not well at all. The white fellow said to me that where the security of the State was concerned, no one's opinions belonged to himself, and that it was the duty of the S.P. to know everyone's opinions, and that it was the duty of every person to let the S.P. know what his opinions were. I wanted to say he was talking rubbish, but I thought I had better not. I just said I did not believe that. I believed that every man and woman had a right to privacy, just so long as they were not using their privacy to break the law. This white fellow said to me that a court of law might decide that my views were subversive, and that I had better be careful. I said the big trouble was that the court of law was no longer allowed to judge such matters. It was decided by the Minister of Justice acting on the advice of the S.P. The white fellow was now getting angry, and he asked me whether Dlamini and a number of staff members had celebrated the election of Lutuli as national president of Congress. I said they had had a party, yes, but I was not invited so I did not know what they were celebrating. Then Sergeant Magwaza said they had proof that I knew perfectly well what they were celebrating. I thought to myself, only my wife and my vice-principal could have given them proof, and neither of them would. But then I thought of someone else. That's what happens, Robert, you begin to trust nobody. I remembered that on his way to report to me about the hostels, Koza had met Mbele coming away early from the party, and Mbele had told him that the staff was sending a deputation to me the next day to ask me to change the name of the school. Koza and I have always regarded Mbele as on our side, but then one begins to doubt. So I said to Magwaza, What is your proof? He said it was not their custom to bring the proof, and that made me think again of Mbele. The white fellow asked me if I had announced to the school that Lutuli had been elected and I said yes. I had done it because the school was restless. He wanted to know if I had called him Chief Lutuli, and I said yes. He asked if I knew that he was no longer a chief, and I said yes. Why then did I call him a chief? Was I trying to belittle Dr. Hendrik in the eyes of the school? Had some of the boys and girls called out *Mayibuye*? Yes. Did I know what this meant? Yes. I was now almost at the end of my patience. You have never had this experience, Robert, of being interrogated by two hard and determined and limited men, who have sold themselves body and soul to this terrible machine that has no mercy. I regard these men as my inferiors, but I must sit for hours and be questioned by them. The white fellow I understand. He is defending his people and his language and his power and his children. The black one I do not understand at all. I want to say to him, Come and see me one day because I want to understand why you take a job like this. Then they get up to go, and the white man says to me, Nhlapo — not Mr. Nhlapo, not Headmaster, just Nhlapo — watch your step, we know everything that goes on here. Then they drive away and I think immediately of Dlamini, and I feel pity for him, because they'll get him one day, that's for sure.

Robert Mansfield, because he could speak and write Zulu, had quite a standing in the African community of Newcastle and the district. He was also known to be friendly with Mr. Nhlapo the headmaster of the J. H. Hofmeyr High School, not the kind of friendliness where a white man writes a letter to a black man and starts it off with the word Greetings, but the kind where the white man and his wife call the black man and his wife by their first names, and visit them often. Now Mr. Nhlapo was held in very high respect by the black people of the district, and if he and his wife could go to the house of the white headmaster for dinner, then the white headmaster and his wife must be human beings, they must have the quality of *ubuntu*, which is the quality of humaneness, the quality of human beings when they are at their brightest and best.

Mind you, the fact must be faced that many black people don't think white people have any *ubuntu* at all. They think the laws show this clearly, the law for example that does not give teacher Mr. Mazibuko the human right to have his widowed mother to come to live with him, because her home is in Eshowe, and her son is in Newcastle, and he is in Newcastle only because he is a teacher, and teachers are not subject to the stringent regulations that control the movements of African people into other areas. Or it would be truer to say, the Bantu Education Department is not subject to these regulations. However, the widowed mothers of teachers *are* subject to them. Black people are at a complete loss to understand how this can be, because such laws were unknown in their societies. But they do not protest, except to one another. Indeed to whom else could they protest?

But one must also face the fact that many white people don't think that the black people have the quality of humaneness either. Black people are cruel and merciless and will rise up tomorrow and kill everybody, as they killed Sister Aidan in East London. These white people have not heard of Mrs. Theresa Ganyile of that same city, who hid Inspector Pieter de Vries in her bedroom when he was in danger of his life, but luckily the angry mob went down another street, otherwise she would have been in danger of her life also. Or maybe these white people have heard of Mrs. Ganyile, but she is the exception that proves the rule of their fears.

Will these people ever overcome their fears of one another? Well, that's a big problem, and it exercises the minds of Robert and Naomi Mansfield, so much so that he has given up his job to join the Liberal Party, and she, after her initial shock, is supporting him.

There is one thing more. This white headmaster has more than once taken his boys and girls up to Ingogo to play cricket and hockey against Mr. Nhlapo's boys and girls. Then the Department of Education forbade him to do it any more, and he has resigned. Nevertheless his knowledge of the black world is still limited, but he is shortly to have it considerably extended.

– Mr. Mansfield, a Mr. Emmanuel Nene to see you.

– Mr. Nene? Who is he?

– He says he is the messenger of the court. But his visit is private, and if you would like him to come after school he would willingly do so.

– No, no, let him come now.

Mr. Nene was not a big man, but he had a fine big moustache. He wore riding breeches and short leggings halfway to the knees, and he carried in his hand a magnificent hat with Texan and South American connections. He appeared to be in his early thirties and he advanced on

Mansfield with a confident smile, holding out his hand with every confidence that such an action would not be regarded as presumption by the headmaster.

– Mr. Nene. Sit down.

Mr. Nene sat down and surveyed the office with his confident smile.

– Call me Emmanuel. That is what my father called me. It means, but you probably know, God with us. As far as I am concerned, my father was right, for God has been with me. And I am coming here today to hope that he will be with you also.

– So you are not here as messenger of the court?

Mr. Nene's eyes widened at such ignorance, and he smiled too at it, but very tolerantly.

– I do not go to white people as messenger of the court, Mr. Mansfield. I go to black people, not coloured people or Indian people or white people.

His eyes widened again as he prepared to instruct the headmaster in the intricacies of his profession.

– Could I come here to your office and tell you that you must be at D Court at nine o'clock tomorrow morning? Oh no, I could not do that. Or could I come to your house and take away your car because you have not yet obeyed the decision of the court to pay a fine of twenty pounds? Oh no, I could not do that. But I can go to Headmaster Nhlapo and tell him to be at the court.

Mr. Nene laughed with amusement at what he had to tell next.

– I was once sent by mistake to Mr. Ebrahim, the big merchant with the big house and the big car. He did not like being summonsed by an African messenger who had only enough money to buy a motorcycle. Now in Mr. Ebrahim's car he can roll down the windows if he is hot, and he can roll them up if he is cold. But there are no windows on my motorcycle, only fresh air. So he complained, and they sent him a white messenger.

– Then tell me, Mr. Nene, I mean Emmanuel, why have you come to see me?

– I'll tell you that. I've come to see a man who resigns his job because he does not wish to obey an order that will prevent the children of his school from playing against the children of Mr. Nhlapo's school. I want to see what this man looks like. We are not used to seeing such people.

– It is not quite true that I resigned because of that order. I resigned because I think it is time to go out and fight everything that separates people from one another, and especially people of one colour and one race from people of another colour and race.

– I am not foolish, Mr. Mansfield. You must not think, because I have this big hat and wear these riding trousers and ride round on a motorcycle, that I am foolish.

Mr. Nene laughs cheerfully at such a proposition.

– Perhaps you think I am foolish because I work for a government that sends white men to summons white men and black men to summons black men. Perhaps then you would be right. But I understand very well that you have not resigned just over a game of football. And I want to see what you look like for a special reason.

– Well, how do I look? Like a knight in shining armour?

– Like a what?

– A knight. K-n-i-g-h-t.

– Oh yes, a man on a horse.

– Yes, and his armour is shining because he is going out to do brave deeds.

Mr. Nene was suddenly serious, but even when he was serious, he smiled his innocent smile.

– Yes, you look like a knight in shining armour. But you are going to get wounded. Do you know that?

– I expect that may happen.

– Well, you expect correctly. In my work I see a lot of white people. They talk freely in front of me because in a way I am not there. They do not like what you are doing. They did not like what you were doing before, but when the Director of Education said no more games, they thought you would stop, and they wanted you to stop, because you are a good cricketer and a good headmaster. But you don't stop and so they are forced to do something they do not like to do at all, they are forced to say that a good cricket player is not always a good South African.

Mr. Nene smiled deprecatingly and smoothed his moustache.

– Now you know that rugby and cricket are the white man's religion, and it is a terrible thing when you find out that a man who is good in your religion is against the colour bar. Because rugby and cricket and the colour bar are really the same thing. That's why the All Blacks leave the Maoris at home when they come to play the Springboks. That's why no black man has ever been allowed into a white cricket club, and no black man has ever become a Springbok. Am I right?

– Your language is picturesque, Emmanuel. When you say that rugby and cricket and the colour bar are really the same thing, then I understand what you are saying, but I don't say it like that.

Mr. Nene acknowledged the criticism cheerfully.

– I *am* picturesque.

Mansfield laughed.

– I said your language is picturesque, but you are quite right, you are picturesque too. What is the special reason that made you come to see me?

– I understand that you are resigning to join the Liberal Party.

– I am not saying till I have left the service.

– But you must tell me. It is important to me to know. It might change my life.

– Yes, I am going to join the Liberal Party.

– I am thinking of the same thing.

– You're going to wear the shining armour too?

– Yes. And I'm going to get wounded also. Not only by the Government, but by my own people as well. Just like you. Some of them will say, Why don't you stay with your own people? Why don't you join the Congress? Why get mixed up with these white people, who are rich while you are poor? — There's your bell, so I must go.

– I must go too. Thank you for your visit. You must come to visit us. My wife will be glad to meet you.

Mr. Nene rose, and looked cheerfully around him.

– I don't worry about the wounds. When I go up there, which is my intention, the Big Judge will say to me, Where

are your wounds? and if I say I haven't any, he will say, Was
there nothing to fight for? I couldn't face that question.

Mr. Nene left his aura in the headmaster's office. Mansfield, who was sometimes troubled by the magnitude of his
decision, felt a burst of hope for the future. He felt that he
had experienced an *nhlanhla*, a sudden stroke of fortune, in
the strange person of a messenger of the court, a small man
with a big hat and a big moustache. He had in fact had an
encounter with the light. It was not the kind of thing to
expect in Newcastle.

. . . I am glad that you follow the political news with such
assiduity. Every good Afrikaner Nationalist should do so,
for ignorance is a poor weapon in these mighty days. There is
no doubt that you are watching the birth of a new society
which will one day command the admiration of a world that
is at the moment so hostile to us. I served under the Smuts
Government as you know, but I can assure you that there
was never in his Cabinet any evidence of the single-
mindedness and the devotion to one's people, combined with
such high intelligence, that you find in the Malan Cabinet.
Smuts and Hofmeyr had intelligence, it is true, but Smuts
was an internationalist and Hofmeyr a liberal, so that neither
of them understood the nature or the power of Afrikaner
Nationalism. Smuts called himself an Afrikaner, and indeed
he was one until the Treaty of Vereeniging, after which he
became the handyman of the British Empire. Hofmeyr was
never an Afrikaner at all; he went to an English church, an
English school, and an English university.

It has been said of our Cabinet by Dr. Johan de Villiers,
who as you know is one of the most penetrating of Afrikaner
observers, that never in history have so few legislated so
thoroughly and devotedly for so many divergent peoples,
nor ever before in history have rulers shown such a high
sense of purpose or such idealism; that never have so few
drawn such sharply critical attention. But, says Dr. de
Villiers, the critics did not understand that the manifest
harshnesses, the patent injustices, were all the necessary

results of a most rational, most passionate, most radical will
to restructure the world according to a vision of justice, all
with a view to lasting peace, progress and prosperity.

I know that you have at times been anxious about the
harshnesses and the injustices, and so have I, though perhaps
not so keenly as you. Therefore it is encouraging to have this
reassurance from a learned man that they are merely the
results of the radical will to restructure our world according
to a vision of justice. And it is even more encouraging to
know that this learned man sees the end as lasting peace,
progress, and prosperity.

The English press is making a great fuss about Dr. Malan's
attempt to get the coloured voters of the Cape on to a
separate roll. His legal advisers told him that he could do this
by simple majority, because South Africa had become a
sovereign state by the Statute of Westminster of 1931. He
followed their advice, but the Act was struck down by the
Appellate Court in Bloemfontein. The court held the view
that Parliament was still bound by the clause entrenched at
the time the Union of South Africa was created, which laid
down that the Cape coloured and African franchises could be
altered only by a two-thirds majority of both Houses of
Parliament sitting together.

In April 1952 Parliament legislated to make itself a High
Court superior to the Appellate Court, and then reinstated
the Act. But in November the Appellate Court struck that
down also. How was Dr. Malan to get his two-thirds
majority? There was only one answer to that. He must
enlarge the Senate in such a way that he would get his
majority, and he must enlarge the Appellate Court so that he
would be sure of a favourable decision.

But Dr. Malan did not do it. Was the step too radical for
him? Was he getting too old? Perhaps both. It is almost
certain that he will resign at the end of the year, and make
way — this is almost certain too — for Mr. Johannes
Gerhardus Strijdom, the Lion of the North, who is determined to get rid of the coloured vote altogether.

I can tell you in confidence that my Minister is developing
a kind of hatred of the Appellate Court. I watch him with

fascination because he has great difficulty in not spitting when the court is mentioned. He purses up his lips in preparation for spitting, then he restrains himself, and un-purses them. I have watched him carefully, and do not think he is merely play-acting. I think he wants to spit, but restrains himself because he does not think it would be proper for the Minister of Justice to spit in his office.

The name of Judge Olivier is particularly offensive to him, because he suspects that it was the judge who influenced the court to strike down the two previous Acts. I am prepared to prophesy that Judge Olivier will never become Chief Justice, a post for which he is clearly in line. Olivier is a revered name in South Africa, and the Minister says that the judge is dragging it through the mud.

I have a little game and this is the *most confidential* thing I have ever told you. When the work is getting too much for me, and when the Minister is perhaps making unreasonable demands on me, I slip in some innocent remark about Judge Olivier just for the pleasure of watching the Minister control his desire to spit. He has no suspicions of me, because he thinks I am the perfect subordinate.

As for my immediate boss, Dr. Jan Woltemade Fischer, B.A., B.Ed., LL.B., Ph.D., I must confess to you that I dislike him more and more. He treats me arrogantly and does not hide the fact that he thinks I am a person of no consequence. As I told you before, if you are not a Broeder-bonder you have little hope of promotion to a responsible post. It is a terrible thing to have doubts of the Broederbond. It is the brain of the National Party, it is the brain of Afrikanerdom. The question is often asked, Who controls the country, the Cabinet or the Broederbond? But it isn't a real question. Nearly every member of the Cabinet is a Broederbonder. Where does his first loyalty lie, to the Cabinet, or the party, or the Broederbond, or the *volk*? It is a question almost impossible to answer. I can only answer for myself. My first loyalty is to the party and the *volk*. My other first loyalty — of a different order altogether — is to God and Church. It is only this intense feeling of loyalty to God and nation that helps me to avoid bitterness and jealousy.

You ask me about the Liberal Party. My Minister and his colleague Dr. Hendrik, and our future Prime Minister as well, have two quite incompatible attitudes towards it. The one is of contempt, for a party of woolly-minded, liberalistic, sentimental do-gooders, who have no idea of the fire they are playing with. The other is an attitude of intense anger, that while the great restructuring of our society is taking shape, the great plan of which Dr. de Villiers has written, there should actually be people who are trying to obstruct it. There is considerable demand in the National Party that the Liberal Party should be banned under the Suppression of Communism Act, and that open political opposition to the policy of separate coexistence should be made a criminal offence. The great objection to such steps is of course the Prime Minister himself, whose authority while he remains in office is unchallengeable. He is still a democrat at heart, and does not favour the silencing of opposition, except of course that of the communists.

I must tell you finally that my Minister has had a traumatic experience. One of his boyhood friends was Cornelius Berg, and their friendship was strengthened when in the thirties they both supported Dr. Malan's tiny party against the United Party giant led by General Hertzog and General Smuts. Cornelius Berg died before he could witness the eventual triumph of Dr. Malan, and it was my Minister, who was then a practising lawyer, who took over the education of his friend's three sons, and saw them all through the university. The Minister and his wife had to change their style of living to do this, but they did it cheerfully for the sake of Afrikanerdom. These three sons, Jan, Frederik, and Izak, all young men in their twenties, have just announced publicly that they have joined the Liberal Party.

I shall write again soon, my dearest aunt.

It must not be thought that people are flocking to join the Liberal Party. The three young men of the Berg family are not a portent that Afrikanerdom is flocking to the party. The action of these three young men is an inexplicable phenomenon. They are not Anglicised, although they speak English well. They have the support of their mother in their decision.

Their action must be regarded as courageous. It is not an easy thing to proclaim yourself a liberal in Pretoria, the seat of Government, the home of Cabinet Ministers and the Civil Service, the stronghold of the Army and the Air Force, the seat of the intensely Nationalist University of Pretoria, and of course, the capital of the old Transvaal Republic and its famous president, Stephanus Johannes Paulus Kruger, whose top-hatted statue dominates the Kerkplein, the Church Square.

It is hard to describe the detestation in which the words *liberal, liberalism,* and *liberalist* are held in white Pretoria. Liberalism denotes moral looseness and degeneracy. White liberals are people who will hop into bed with blacks at the drop of a hat. Language, culture, pride, the sense of personal identity, mean nothing to them. Mongrelisation and bastard-isation are not for them national calamities but triumphs of love and justice. They are anti-Afrikaner, and this has made the action of the Berg brothers more incomprehensible and more reprehensible than ever. Surely only the lowest types of humanity associate with people who look down upon them. It goes without saying that these liberals condemn utterly the policies of separate coexistence. They say that the policies are cruel and heartless, and that the policy-makers are indifferent to the sufferings of the people for whom they were devised. Furthermore, the Liberal Party has no Christian foundation. It does not open its congresses with prayer, nor does its constitution acknowledge the sovereignty of Almighty God. It has no firm faith or belief, and welcomes Christians, Jews, Hindus, Muslims, agnostics, and atheists into its ranks. Its very formlessness and shapelessness and degeneracy are in total contrast to the discipline and order of the National Party.

The Berg brothers accept none of this. How they became emancipated — if that is the word — from the rigidity of their father's beliefs is beyond understanding. All three brothers attended a meeting of the Liberal Party in the

Coetzee Hall in Pretoria, and were in danger, if not of their lives, then of bodily injury. Students of the University of Pretoria were there in force to see the three outstanding renegades of their own institution. They were in an ugly mood. All of them were the sons and daughters of upright citizens, upholders of law and order, obedient to authority, industrious in their studies. But the sight of the renegades transformed them. Their faces were contorted by hatred, their voices were uncontrolled and raucous, they brandished knobthorn sticks, they cried out in outraged protest against the supreme apostasy, and who could wonder at it, for were they not witnessing the abomination of abominations, the sight of Afrikaners who conspire with men and women of other races and colours to challenge all those things that are held most dear in Afrikanerdom, who in the words of Holy Writ have committed whoredom with the daughters of Moab? Many of these students were well versed in Holy Writ, some indeed were theologicals who would devote their lives to the service of the Lord of Peace and his Church. The very fact that they could come here with heavy sticks and contorted faces was a measure of their abhorrence of those who flouted the holy laws of separation.

Jan Berg tried to speak, but no one could hear what he was saying. The chanting and the shouting went on without ceasing. Then suddenly all was silent. A commanding figure had risen and the students fell silent. He spoke in Afrikaans, and gave his name, Paulus Malan Pretorius, Paulus for the great President of the Transvaal, Malan for the great Malan the Prime Minister, and Pretorius for the great Pretorius, the founder of the city. He was loudly cheered.

– Mr. Berg, I have some questions for you.

Here the chairwoman stood up and said in Afrikaans,

– The time for questions will come later.

Mr. Pretorius replied,

– The time for questions will come now, or it will never come at all.

The chairwoman conferred for a moment with Jan Berg, and announced that the time for questions would come now.

– Mr. Berg, are you an Afrikaner?

– Yes.

– And are you proud of it?

– I am not ashamed of it, but I am not proud of it, for in fact I had nothing to do with it.

Here a few students sniggered, to the annoyance of Mr. Pretorius, for one does not make or approve pornographic jokes about Afrikaner birth. However, the students, seeing the displeasure of their leader, sniggered no more.

– So you are not proud of being an Afrikaner?

– No.

– And you have the impudence to say that in Pretoria?

– I say it, yes. But it is an honest statement.

– Mr. Berg, you have children.

– Yes.

– A daughter?

– Yes.

– When she grows up, will you allow her to marry a kaffir?

– If the law is then what it is now, she will not be able to marry any person who is not white.

– Let me ask the question in another way. If the law permitted it, would you approve of her marrying a kaffir — I beg your pardon — a person who is not white?

– If that were her choice, yes.

Mr. Pretorius addressed his students.

– You hear that, Afrikaners. He would allow his daughter to marry a kaffir. You are listening to the scum of the Afrikaner nation, the liberalistic scum that we have allowed to breed, the liberalistic scum that we have allowed into our own university. Look at the three of them, sons of a proud Afrikaner, Cornelius Berg, who followed Dr. Malan into the wilderness in 1934. What do you do with such scum?

The ban on silence was over. The shouting was deafening, and student marshals had to hold back those who wanted to rush the stage. People tried to leave the hall but the students would not allow them to do so. Members of the Liberal Party, with their distinctive green, black, and white rosettes, tried to look brave, but many of them were frightened, never having encountered the threat of violence before. Now and

then amidst the shouting they could distinguish the word
moor, to kill.

— Audrey, have you sent for the police?

— Fifteen minutes ago.

— Well, close the meeting.

The chairwoman stood up, but Mr. Pretorius held up his
hand for silence and addressed her in English.

— Sit down, lady. When this meeting is to be closed, we
will close it. Ladies and gentlemen, and people of other races,
no one is to leave this hall until we allow it. Mr. Berg!

— Yes.

— Who gave you this hall?

— The trustees.

— What are their names?

— I don't know their names.

— Whom did you deal with?

— A Mr. van Deventer.

— Then Mr. van Deventer must learn that this hall must
never be given again to scum like yourselves.

Mr. Pretorius raised his hand, and two of the large
imposing windows of the Coetzee Hall were shattered by
missiles thrown from outside the building.

— Two is enough. But if ever this hall is let out again to
liberalistic filth like yourselves, the whole place will be
destroyed. Mr. Berg!

— Yes.

— You were intending to have a kaffir speaker tonight?

— You mean an African speaker?

— Oh, I beg your pardon. Yes, I do.

— Yes, we did mean to have an African speaker.

— Is that him on the platform?

— Yes.

— We want him.

— What do you want him for?

— We want to take him with us. We want to teach him not
to come to Pretoria again. We want to teach him not to
appear again on the same platform with white speakers.

— We cannot agree to that.

This was the signal for the student marshals to rush

forward up the two aisles of the hall, followed by their
fellows with their weapons and their cries. The people on the
platform formed a protective ring round their fellow member, Jo Dube from Durban, and the chairwoman was thrust
into the ring too. And indeed it might have gone badly for all
those on the platform, had it not been for the dramatic entry
of the police through a door at the back of the stage, headed
by an imposing-looking officer of great height. The police
immediately interposed themselves between the people on
the stage and the students advancing up the aisles. The officer
held up his hand, Mr. Pretorius held up his hand, and the hall
was suddenly silent.

– Captain van Niekerk of the South African Police. With
the powers conferred on me under the Riotous Assemblies
Act as amended in 1946, I declare this meeting closed. I
propose to close it in this fashion. Students of the university,
I order you to leave the hall and I order you not to congregate
in small or large groups anywhere in the vicinity of the hall.
In fact I advise you to return to the university, or to your
lodgings wherever they may be. You will have ten minutes
to do this, and any student in the hall or its vicinity after that
time will be taken into custody. When that time has expired,
I shall order all members of the public who are not members
of the organisation to leave the hall and to disperse as quickly
as possible. When the operation is completed, I shall super-
vise the dispersal of members of the organisation. Any
members of the organisation who have no transport can wait
outside the hall, and transport will be provided for them.
They will have to travel in the police vans, but that is better
than travelling in an ambulance. I want no violence here
tonight. Anyone attempting it will have to bear the full
consequences of such action. Students, I order you to leave
the hall and not to remain in its vicinity. You have ten
minutes to do this.

It must have been some fifteen minutes later that Captain
van Niekerk turned his attention to the members of the
Liberal Party.

– You can think yourselves lucky that the police came
when they did. Otherwise some of you might have been

dead. Certainly some of you would have been injured. I am not a politician. I do not even belong to any party. But you people are playing with dynamite. Don't do it again.

– Do you mean, captain, that we are not entitled to hold a public meeting and put forward the policies of our party?

– You are fully entitled to do so unless the police are of the opinion that your meeting will lead to public disorder. You can see for yourselves. If you decided to hold a meeting next week in this hall, do you think the police would allow it? I know this city, Mr. Berg, and you ought to know it too. I know the students of this university, and you certainly ought to know them too. You saw how they dispersed quietly when ordered to do so by lawful authority. But when they see a meeting of this kind, and black people on the platform, they lose control of themselves, they become capable of extreme violence. Your meetings may go off peaceably in Durban and Cape Town, but they are like dynamite in Pretoria. Now please disperse. If anyone has no transport, report to the officer in charge outside.

Obedient also to lawful authority, the members of the Liberal Party dispersed quietly. Some were seething with indignation, and some were determined to have another meeting as soon as possible. But many were subdued. They had not seen hate before.

Mr. Robert Mansfield
Member of the Liberal Party

How are your black dolly girls? Do you like the fuzzy hair, is it very exciting? Does it get left on the pillow? Has your wife by any chance seen it? And how does your wife like to be poked by the same stick that has been poking the black dolly girls? Tell me, are they hotter than the white dollies?

How low can you sink? I am a white woman and proud of it, and if you were my husband I would shoot you dead and be proud of it. How you can sit on the platform with all that smell, I don't understand.

I read your speech at Mooi River. I knew that place when I

was young. Why didn't the white farmers string you up? Or castrate you, cut out your stick that pokes the black fuzzies?

At Mooi River you said you were a Christian. Do not let the name of Christ be spoken again by your filthy lips, that kisses those black tits and kisses the black twats.

You are a disgrace to Christianity.

Proud White Christian Woman

There was no address, but it had been posted in Durban. It was to prove the forerunner of many others.

Mr. Robert Mansfield   6 November 1954
Natal Regional Office
Liberal Party

This is a letter of warning to you. It should be taken very seriously. We note that you have accepted the chairmanship of the Natal region of the Liberal Party. We regard your party as anti-Christian, and anti-White South African, and we have taken the decision that all the regional chairmen of the party, and all those who are foolish enough to become their successors, should be eliminated.

Do you know the meaning of the word *eliminated*, Mr. Mansfield? It has the same meaning as it had in Germany under the great Führer Adolf Hitler. He decided to exterminate the Jews and he would have succeeded if the capitalist–Jewish–British–American money power had not 'won' the war, and delivered the Christian world into the hands of the communists. That is what you are trying to do, but we are going to stop you.

We give you fourteen days from the date of this letter to resign the chairmanship of the Natal region of the Liberal Party. You will announce your resignation in one Durban and one Pietermaritzburg newspaper. We have decided that you may give any reason you wish for your resignation. If you do not obey this order, you will be eliminated. We advise you to take this warning seriously. If you do not do so, we have solemnly pledged ourselves to kill you, in the most sacred of all causes, of Christianity itself.

We naturally do not sign our names. But we sign ourselves
The Preservation of White South Africa League

It's a big day at Ethembeni, a kind of field day for the younger members of the Liberal Party, combining picnic and politics. These young people have come from Pietermaritzburg and Durban to learn all about the 'blackspots', and Ethembeni is one of the most famous of them all. A blackspot is a piece of land surrounded by white farms, and its very existence is offensive to the Government, which has announced a tremendous plan to remove all black landowners in the blackspots to their own 'traditional black areas'. It was the British colonies of the Cape and Natal which allowed black people to purchase land in the 'traditional white areas'. There are about seventy or eighty blackspots in Natal alone, and they have been a continual and intolerable reminder of the days when Afrikaners suffered under alien British rule.

That is Emmanuel Nene who is speaking, the small man with the big hat and the big smile and the big moustache. It is hard to know what he is smiling about, for he is at the crossroads of his life, having recently joined the Liberal Party, and having made powerful enemies who will break him if they can. Perhaps he is smiling because the party has opened new doors to him, into the hearts of young people of all kinds. No one listens to him more intently than the young Indian members, whose parents have been afraid of the Zulu people since the riots of 1949, and have imparted their fear to their children.

– My father lived in Natal, but he worked in Johannesburg. He was a head clerk on the Crown Mines, and he was a very respected man. He and his friends worked in the towns, in Johannesburg and Benoni and Springs and such places, and some in your home towns of Durban and Pietermaritzburg. But they wanted a place of their own. They did not want to live under a chief but under their own council. They wanted a place where they could leave their wives and children in safety, a place to' which they themselves could return

whenever they were able. They called this place Ethembeni.
That means, the place of hope. Do you know that no person
has ever been killed at Ethembeni? No woman or girl has
ever been raped. We are not angels, you must not think that.
Sometimes we drink too much, sometimes we fight, sometimes we look — well, this is difficult for me to say —
sometimes we look at people we should not look at, but we
do not kill and rape.

– Well, I will not tell you all the details. But my father and
his friends had some good luck. They were able to buy a
white farm called 'Waterval'. There were forty-eight of
them, and they put all their money together. The farm was
cut up and each man got a title deed for his land. I cannot
show you these title deeds. They are too precious, so we keep
them in the bank. This happened in 1905, and since 1905 we
have believed that no one in the world could take our land
from us. Some of our men served in the first World War and
some in the second. That was because we felt we must defend
our land.

– This place Ethembeni has been our paradise. Look at the
grass, you will not find grass like that in any of the Reserves.
Look at our cattle, you will not find cattle like that, you will
not even find milk for your children. You see the mountains.
You call them the Drakensberg, we call them Khahlamba.
Two streams from the mountains flow through Ethembeni.
The water is cold and clear, we can drink it, and the children
can play in it. The police do not come here. They can catch
you without your pass in Newcastle, but they do not come
here. There are two schools, and one day we hope to have a
high school of our own.

– Now let me tell you what has happened to us. When my
father and his friends bought this farm, they bought it
lawfully. But in 1913 the white Parliament passed the
Natives Land Act, which meant that no black man could ever
again buy any land except in the Reserves, and that he could
almost never do, because the land in the Reserves is owned in
community by the chief and the tribe, and cannot be sold to
any private person. However, the Land Act did not affect our
title deeds. We thought we were safe. But we were safe only

till 1936, when the white Parliament passed the Native Trust and Land Act, which gave the Government power to take away the title deeds from what they now called the black-spots. This place Ethembeni, where they do not murder or rape, became a blackspot, and a blackspot is a blot on the white countryside.

— Now although the Government had this power it did not use it. But in 1948 the Nationalist Party came to power, with its policy of the complete separation of the races. Blackspots became offensive. It was the British who had allowed them to happen, but now the Afrikaners would put everything right. Our title deeds would be taken away, and we would be given plots of land, one-sixth of an acre, and on each plot there would be a hut, made of aluminium, so they tell me. There would be no cattle there, no milk for your children. You could not keep a cow, you could not even have a garden on such a piece of land.

— We could not believe it. Do you know what we called the title deed? We called it the white man's word, and now it was to be taken away. We did not understand it. We did not understand how a big man who lives in a big house in Pretoria can take away our small houses from us. We try to understand it but we cannot. Not one of us in Ethembeni would take away a house from a man.

— I showed you the house where Mrs. Doris Majola lives. She is more than seventy years old. She has six acres where she keeps two cows and grows mealies and beans and pumpkins. She is not rich but she lives a comfortable life such as we like our old women to live. But the Minister with the big house in Pretoria says she is living in a blackspot, and she must go to the aluminium hut where she can have no cows nor milk nor garden. We do not understand how such a man can be so cruel. It's not only white people, you understand. Sergeant Magwaza of the Security Police went to Mrs. Majola and offered her ten pounds for her two cows, and when she said she would not sell them he said it did not matter, because he would get them for nothing on the day they took her away. He also warned her against the Liberal Party, and especially against the local chairman Mr. Emmanuel Nene, but she laughed at him and asked why she would be afraid of a child that she had brought into the world with her own hands.

Mr. Emmanuel Nene laughed at that, and opened his eyes wide in wonder that a policeman could warn Mrs. Majola against a man who from his birth had been to her like a child.

– And now you see that fine house there. That is the home of the present speaker. It was built with bricks made by Mr. Reuben Majola, son of the late Mr. Joseph Majola who made the bricks for my father. Let me close my eyes a moment. Now I can see my father coming out of the door of his own house. He is wearing a suit and a tie, because he never came out of that door without a suit and tie. He was a very proper man, and very strict, oh yes. But his Christian name was Philemon, which means one who is affectionate, and he was always affectionate to us. Now let us go to my house, where my wife is waiting to give us tea.

The landowners of the seventy or eighty blackspots in Natal have formed the Natal African Landowners Association, NALA for short. They have approached Mr. Emmanuel Nene, messenger of the court, to become their full-time organiser, but they cannot offer him as much money as he made when he was the messenger of the court. But after he had talked to his wife he took the job. He said it was an order, and it had to be obeyed. If you asked him where the order came from he would say it came from high up, very high up, and if you looked puzzled, he would say in a bashful kind of way that it came from the Big Judge. You must not think that all the members of the party talk like that. Emmanuel is an exception. When he told a party of visitors that the order came from the Big Judge, they did not laugh at him, not even the younger ones. The Security Police have been swift to act against NALA. They have visited every blackspot in Natal and warned landowners not to join it, because the communists are behind it. They say that the Government regards it as a subversive organisation, and it may be banned any minute. The Government may even ban some of the members, who, if they were confined to places like Ethembeni, would lose their jobs. Sergeant Magwaza has been to see Mrs. Majola, and has warned her against joining NALA, and has warned her that it is even dangerous for her if Emmanuel Nene is seen visiting her house. When he was leaving her, she asked him to take a message for her to Emmanuel, and he, thinking that his warning had been successful, said he would be pleased to do so.

– Tell him, she said, to come soon to my house and bring me a paper for joining.

Magwaza, they say, left her house with a face as black as thunder, and they wonder what will happen to her, for it is dangerous to taunt the Security Police. Some say it is actually safer to plot for revolution. And Magwaza grew angrier still when after his warning only two of the landowners would not join NALA. One worked in the Magistrate's Court in Newcastle, and the other for the Department of Bantu Affairs. Neither of them was ostracised by the community, for if they had joined they would have lost their jobs, and their tolerant neighbours did not wish that to happen to them. But Sergeant Magwaza had to feel the sharp edge of the white lieutenant's tongue for his failure to halt the spread of communism at Ethembeni.

Emmanuel Nene never tires of pointing out that the word NALA, the acronym of the Natal African Landowners Association, is also a word in Zulu, and means an abundance of food and a good harvest. It is his hope, and the hope of all the landowners, that the seed sown by NALA will also lead to a good harvest. He points out too that *nala* also means a beast with red spots and white spots, but to the Government it means only a blackspot, an intolerable thing in a white man's country.

It has come as a relief to the leaders of the Liberal Party that Chief Lutuli has given his blessing to NALA, many of whose members are also members of the party. The fact has to be faced that neither the Chief nor Dr. Monty Naicker welcomed the launching of the Liberal Party. Nor did the white

Congress or the coloured Congress. Margaret Ballinger came all the way from Cape Town for the first meeting of the party in Durban, and she and Robert Mansfield were given a rough time by two of Dr. Naicker's lieutenants, the lawyer J. N. Ismail and the doctor K. B. Ram. Mr. Ismail said that the party was drawing away strength from the congresses and weakening the forces of liberation. The party thought its nonracial ideals were very noble, but the congresses had cherished such ideals for many years.

It is said that Dr. Monty Naicker was very displeased when the young students Prem Bodasingh and Lutchmee Perumal joined the Liberal Party instead of the Congress. Dr. Ram referred to them both by name at the Ballinger meeting, and said that they were traitors to the cause. They had been misled by sweet words of people like Mr. Robert Mansfield, who thought he was a hero because he had given up his teaching career. But many other people had sacrificed jobs and careers long before Mr. Mansfield and his party had been heard of.

In fact it was a bitter evening, and it was a lesson to some members of the party that to sally forth with goodwill does not necessarily get you anywhere in politics.

. . . I understand your concern about the Bantu woman Doris Majola. Your concern is naturally made greater by the fact that you have known her since childhood. But I'm afraid it would not help to speak to my Minister. He objects strongly to trying to influence his fellow Ministers, and he would rebuke me if I spoke to him. Why don't you go directly to the Minister of Lands? You are well known for your generous gifts to the party over the last twenty years, and you would get a good hearing.

Yet what could the Minister do? This place Ethembeni is to be deproclaimed, and all its present inhabitants are to be housed at Odakeni. All their goods will be transported free, and they will be paid compensation for their houses and their land, and even for crops that they will not be able to reap. It is true that they cannot take their cattle with them, and I understand that you feel deeply about this. But it would be quite unrealistic to expect the Government to find sufficient land to make this possible. It would also be impossible for the Minister to leave this woman at Ethembeni. For one thing she would be quite alone there. For another the houses are going to be demolished, and the place will again become the farm 'Waterval'. She would then be living in the middle of a white farm. I am sure you realise that such a thing could not be contemplated.

You say that this woman has spoken to you about the 'white man's honour', and this also troubles you. But the white men who allowed black men to buy the farm 'Waterval' were not Afrikaners. They were the British, and they knew very well our strong views on racial separateness. They ignored our views because they had just taken our country from us. The officials who are supervising the resettlement should make it clear to the inhabitants that the Afrikaners never gave any word of honour in the matter.

You must not distress yourself so much. The new South Africa cannot be built without suffering. You cannot dismantle a system which the Afrikaner finds totally alien, and build it anew, without hurting someone. Let me remind you of the words of Dr. de Villiers, who said that our critics did not understand that the manifold harshnesses, the patent injustices, were all the necessary results of a most rational, most passionate, most radical will to restructure the world according to a vision of justice, all with a view to lasting peace, progress, and prosperity. When you are in doubt, keep these words before you. You will note that Dr. de Villiers does not mince his words. What is going to happen to this woman Majola appears to be a patent injustice, but the result will be that her children, or shall we say her grandchildren, will live in a just society. She cannot really expect more than that.

I am sorry to write to you again about Dr. Fischer. At times I am troubled about myself. My feelings of dislike have grown into something like hatred. That's a hard thing for a Christian to put down on paper. I have to go into his office very often and I am sure that he must sense my hatred; or perhaps he does not, because he might think that my feelings for him were of no consequence. He is in that office because he is a Broederbonder, and I am not because I am not. If he laughs or smiles, it is to the Minister, not to me. I find his face grim and forbidding. You must pray for me, my dear aunt. I do not really like to be a vessel of hate.

There is a possibility that the Government may be approached by members of the Kerk to prevent white householders from letting black people use their garages for holding services of worship on Sunday afternoons. I realise that this might result in one of the 'manifold harshnesses'. But the singing is very loud, and so is the preaching, and after the services the people hang about the streets and laugh and talk loudly as Bantu people do. There is great trouble and heart-searching among members of our Kerk. Some are deeply distressed that black Christians have no place to worship in our white suburbs, and that white Christians can call the singing and preaching a public nuisance. Others maintain that if the doctrines of racial purity and separate coexistence are infringed in this respect, then the process of erosion has begun, and that it will continue until we reach a state of total integration in which all God-given identities are lost.

Some members of the Kerk have launched a movement to make all white church buildings available for black services on Sunday afternoons. But others declare that the noise will be greater and the nuisance worse because the congregations will be bigger than in the garages. A special meeting was held in Pretorius Hall to discuss the whole matter, and one of the speakers was Dr. Fischer, who is held in tremendous regard in the circles of our Kerk. I went especially to hear him. He has a cold manner of speaking that I do not like. I have heard Dr. Malan and he always made me feel proud to be an Afrikaner. He stirred a kind of warmth inside me. Dr. Fischer devoted no time to consideration of the duty of Afrikaner Christians to black Christians, and especially black Christians who belonged to our black sister Kerk. He stressed law and order and the undesirability of public nuisances. He knew — and he made it clear that he was in a position to know — that some people went to these garage churches to show their defiance and that behind them were other people, the communists, who if they came to power would destroy all the churches in the land. He mentioned the many churches in the Bantu townships, and admitted that they were far away, but he as a child had ridden twelve miles in his parents' horse-carriage to get to church in Ohrigstad, and twelve miles back again. But his great theme was the Divine blessing of racial identity and racial separateness, and this was something to be treasured at all cost. It was as much a gift to black people as it was to white, and white Christians should help black Christians to treasure it. Dr. Fischer's command of Afrikaans is so magnificent, and his reputation for learning so great, that he left his audience overwhelmed.

Indeed perhaps nothing more would have been said if a woman, who looked rather like you, my dearest aunt, had not stood up to tell us that she was one of those who had lent her garage for black services because black people were not allowed the use of the Kerk itself. What is happening to us Afrikaners, she asked, when the sound of the praise of our God has become an offence to us? What has happened to us when our black fellow Christians must worship in our garages because we will not let them worship in our churches? She had listened with great attention to Dr. Fischer, and she wanted to tell him that we denied the use of our church buildings to black people, not because of any desire to help them to cherish their racial identity, but because of the hardness and coldness of our hearts. Such speeches made her fear for the future of the Afrikaner. Then she sat down, leaving the audience silent and confused.

I think I must stop now. I am also a bit subdued and confused. I think a great deal about those words, Let not your heart be troubled: you believe in God, believe also in me. But it is hard nevertheless. I do not have your simplicity, nor that of the woman who spoke to us. When I listen to Dr. Malan, I have no doubts at all, but he seldom speaks in public today. When I listen to Dr. Fischer, I too fear for our future. Surely we Afrikaners have not grown hard and cold of heart.

PART THREE

Come Back, Africa

Mr. M. K. Bodasingh is standing in front of his big picture window in the big house in Reservoir Hills, and before and below is the fantastic view of the city of Durban and the Indian Ocean. But today it brings him no pleasure, nor does it appear to bring pleasure to his friend Jay Perumal. They are in fact in a gloomy mood.

– They had no right, M.K., to call out our girls in public like that. If they want to join this Liberal Party that is their business. But to call them traitors! I will not stand for that.

– I myself am sorry that Prem joined the party, but I cannot control her decisions. I used to think I could, but when she joined the Defiance Campaign, I knew that my days were over. She is nearly twenty, Jay, and you can see that she is a young woman. It is very hard to accept it, but I know it must be done. Do you know that when my father used to come into the room, it was like a judge coming into the court? It was like that not only for the girls, but for the boys too. But those days are gone. You must understand me, Jay, we are not ashamed of our daughter. My own sisters lived for simple pleasures, and to get good men for their husbands. But Prem is in love with justice.

Mr. Bodasingh laughed hollowly at his own wit. Mrs. Bodasingh said sharply,

– And she is in love with the Mainwaring boy too.

Mr. Perumal could not conceal his curiosity.

– Who is this boy, Mrs. M.K.?

– You are not well informed, Jay. His father Mr. Henry Mainwaring is the Chairman of the Provincial Executive. I tell you, we are moving in very high society, Jay, and I'm surprised you do not know it, because this boy is also a friend of your daughter Lutchmee. They are always together. I remember you said in this very room that you do nothing for your grandmother. Now I see that you do nothing for your daughter either.

– You shouldn't say that, Mrs. M.K., I said that about my grandmother because I was very troubled. It is all right if I say it, but you should not say it.

– You two quarrel too much, said Mr. Bodasingh. I have told you many times that there is already too much quarrelling in the world, and that we should bring peace.

– I am not quarrelling, said Mr. Perumal, and if I want to quarrel I don't want to quarrel with your wife. Mrs. M.K., tell me more about this boy Mainwaring. What does he do?

– That's a good question, Jay. He was going to be a lawyer, but now the firm won't take him because he went into the Germiston location with Patrick Duncan. He was the head of all the students — what do they call it? — NUSAS, that's it. And Prem was only a young student, and she thought he was wonderful. Then he joined the Liberal Party and so she joined it.

Mr. Bodasingh interrupted sharply.

– That's not true. She joined it because she believed in it. All our children are going multiracial or nonracial or whatever you call it.

– It's not all our children, said Mrs. Bodasingh. Some of Prem's friends have left her. Some have left her because they don't want any politics at all, and some because they think she should have joined the Congress. Some of them want to get out of NUSAS and start an Indian Students' Association.

– And what did she feel about having her name called out in public? Was she frightened?

– No, she was not frightened. She simply did not like it. But she did not like the Defiance Campaign either. That is what she had to do, and so she did it. Her father says she's in love with justice. She's in love with duty too. And of course with this boy Mainwaring.

– Aren't you frightened about that, Mrs. M.K?

Mrs. Bodasingh shrugged her shoulders.

– I would have been more frightened if I had not spent those years in London. And there the caste distinctions seemed quite stupid. Not only the caste distinctions, but also the race distinctions. I remember Zubie Bayat of Boksburg. She fell in love with a German student, and they married and went to live in Munich. Under Hitler's eyes, so to speak. She must have hated it. Then came the war and they were never heard of again. After the war the Bayats went to Germany, but the German family could tell them nothing either. Zubie and her husband were taken away by Hitler's police, but what happened to them no one knows. It was, and still is, the great tragedy of the Bayat family. And an English student wanted to marry me, and if I had married him, I would have been Lady So-and-so today. But my luck, if you call it that — here Mrs. Bodasingh gave what is called a hollow laugh — my luck was quite different. Do you know why I didn't marry the Englishman, Jay Perumal? Because I was mad. I wanted to get back to Durban, to the hotels where I wouldn't be allowed to eat, and the beaches where I wouldn't be allowed to swim. How mad can one be? In any case it doesn't help to be frightened. These young people have got caught up in the Liberal Party, and they go about together, and some of them fall in love with each other. And of course forbidden fruit tastes better. Young Indian girls are beautiful, Jay. I was beautiful once too. That's why M.K. wanted to marry me, though the Naidoos didn't want me to marry one of the Bodasinghs. They said the Bodasinghs thought only about money. But I was headstrong, and I persuaded my father, and we got married. M. K. was a clever young man, and we got rich, just like you. And yet we produce daughters like Prem and Lutchmee, who just don't care about being rich at all. But you can't help worrying. The Security Police watch them all the time. They stop the cars to see if the tyres are worn, or to see whether they might be carrying dagga or for some other silly reason, but they are looking to see if their clothing is disarranged.

– To see if what?

– Jay, you are very simple. They are looking at their clothing to see if they have been up to mischief. But in any case they want to arrest them under the Immorality Act. They will be found not guilty, but their families will have been frightened out of their wits. And the name of the Liberal Party will have been smeared. Think of the big white Chairman of the Provincial Executive. His voice will tremble when he is making a big speech. Think of the big business-men, Jay Perumal and M.K. Bodasingh. They will need to cover up their faces when they go to the bank.

– Wife, your tongue is too sharp.

– You have known that for a long time. It is time for you

two to wake up. Your daughters are going into a new world, and you can't stop them. They join this Liberal Party and they mix with all sorts of young people. So you must not be surprised if your daughter falls in love with a smart white boy who was head of all the students.

– Who told you she was in love? Did she?

– No, she did not tell me. She does not need to tell me. I can see her shining eyes. Her eyes shine just like yours used to shine when you wanted to marry one of the clever Naidoo girls.

– What is the matter with you today?

– Nothing is the matter with me. Have you told Jay who came to see you today?

– No.

– Well, tell him. It's only fair. They will probably go to see Jay tomorrow.

– Who was it, M.K.?

– I'll tell you. It was the great Dr. K. Ram, the one who insulted our girls at the meeting. I thought how can he have the impudence to come to see me. He said he had come to ask me for a contribution to the liberation fund of the Congress. He said Dr. Monty was sure I would make a contribution. So I looked in my book and I saw it was six months since I made a contribution. It was a hundred pounds, and I said yes, I would give the fund a hundred pounds. He said to me, A hundred pounds? for the liberation struggle? I said yes. He said to me, Only a hundred pounds? don't you believe in the liberation struggle? I said to him, Yes, I believe in the struggle, I support the struggle.

– You don't believe in the struggle, said Mrs. Bodasingh, you support it, but you don't believe in it. You don't want to be liberated, nor does Jay want to be liberated. Why can't you be honest? You'd much rather be governed by Dr. Malan than by Chief Lutuli and Dr. Monty. And did you ask Dr. Ram why he insulted our girls at the meeting?

– He said he didn't insult them. He said politics was a hard game, and if they entered politics, they must expect hard words. I asked him, Words like *traitor*? He admitted it was a hard word. I said our girls were not traitors, they had never belonged to the Congress so how could they be traitors? I was giving one hundred pounds to the liberation fund, I was doing it for Dr. Monty, but I would not give any more until Dr. Ram had apologised to our girls.

– I'm proud of you, said Mrs. Bodasingh.

M.K. surveyed her with some asperity.

– I suppose you are proud of my courage. That's what comes of marrying one of the Naidoo girls.

Mrs. Bodasingh laughed immoderately, spurring her husband to greater asperity.

– I haven't seen any sign of the Naidoo girls wanting to be liberated. As for your professor of whom you are so proud, he goes round the world from one conference to another, talking about making drinking-water from sewage, but does he ever say a word about liberation?

– I think I shall make some tea. Would you like some tea, Jay? It always helps to calm M.K. down.

She left the room gaily, and they could hear her laughing her way down the passage.

– Sometimes, said Mr. Bodasingh, it's as though the devil gets into her. Your wife is not like that, Jay.

– My wife is a saint, said Mr. Perumal complacently. I am married to a saint. You are not.

– You mean she is not a saint today.

– You can't be a saint one day, and not a saint the next. You are a saint all the time. My wife has her own shrine. She is a praying woman. I know it hurts her that I am not a praying man. I don't mind praying in public, M.K., at a wedding or a funeral, but I don't go for praying in private. She is what they call dutiful, M.K. I wish she would sometimes — how do you say it? — yes, I wish she would answer back. You know we have been married for more than twenty years, and she has never once answered back.

Mr. Perumal looked at his friend more complacently than ever.

– You must cheer up, M.K. It is not all — what do you say? — it is not all roses to be married to a saint. You ought to be thankful in some ways. I tell you one thing you can be thankful for. It is very hard to have a good party in the house of a saint.

Their laughter was brought to an end by the return of Mrs. Bodasingh.

— What is all this talk about saints?

— I was talking about Shintamoney, Mrs. M.K., I was saying she is a saint.

— He was also saying, said Mr. Bodasingh with some relish, that you are not a saint.

— A very interesting conversation. I'll tell you one thing about yourself, Jay Perumal. You come here and eat our food and drink our tea, and you can't say boo to a goose, but as soon as I go out of the room you come to life, even if in a stupid way. And I'll tell you both another thing. You ought to be proud of your daughters. In this mad and cruel country they are sensible and full of care for others. You mustn't think I want either of them to be like our professor who can make drinking-water from sewage. You forgot to mention, M.K., that in this very room he was boasting that he could also make samoosas from the same substance. It was a disgusting conversation. I can assure you that the Naidoo girls think that he is the greatest bore in the world. Now, Jay Perumal, you can come and fetch your own tea. There are no women saints in this house.

The party is experiencing a kind of minor boom. Its most illustrious recruit is Manilal Gandhi, son of the Mahatma, and no other party in South Africa has recruited the son of a Mahatma. In Cape Town, besides having the two Ballingers as members, the party has recruited the redoubtable Donald Molteno, who is thought by many to have the finest legal brain in South Africa, and Leo Marquard, the founder of NUSAS, the first man to open the eyes of the students, and many others, and to persuade them to look at the truth about their own country.

In Johannesburg John Parker, one of the leading games-masters in the Transvaal, has resigned from the teaching profession because the Transvaal Education Department has banned all sporting relationships between white students and others. He has joined too, and has proposed that the party should work for the exclusion of all South African teams from international sport. He has torn the party in two, for while the more militant members support him, the more conservative ones, although they have denounced the colour bar unequivocally, never contemplated working for the exclusion of South Africa from world sport. That is going too far and too fast, for sport is the country's religion. White South Africa, with its small population, has distinguished itself in world cricket and world rugby. The more timid members of the party are also anti-Parker. He will bring down the rage of white South Africa on them and, while they will endure ridicule, they are afraid of rage.

It was John Parker who challenged the conservative and the timid at the Cape Town conference. Was the party against the colour bar or was it not? If it was, then it must oppose South Africa's participation in world sport. Did they think they could oppose the colour bar on platforms and keep quiet about it on the sports fields? Did they think the duty of the party was to proclaim noble principles and to funk doing anything about them?

It looks as though John Parker is going to be a stormy petrel in the party. The trouble is that he wants people to *do* something. It is very uncomfortable to be with him in a national committee meeting. Noble speeches mean absolutely nothing to him. He stands up at the end of a noble speech, he acknowledges its nobility, then he wants to know what the speaker suggests should be done.

Donald Molteno is rising to his feet. Brains against fire. Sheer cold intellect against unbridled idealism.

– Mr. Chairman, I shan't keep you long. A client is coming to see me in ten minutes, and I must say I am looking forward to seeing him and getting away from this evangelistic zeal which is going to kill the party dead if it goes on much longer. We are talking of fighting an election in Sea Point. It is probably one of the most favourable constituencies from our point of view, fairly affluent people with guilty consciences, a high percentage of Jewish voters, and a large number of retired business and professional men. There is probably a higher percentage of voters opposed to racial discrimination than anywhere else in South Africa. There are thirteen thousand voters on the roll, and if eight thousand of them go to the poll, the party might get two thousand votes, which would be nothing to be ashamed of. Then we announce, or worse still our opponents announce, that the party has given Mr. John Parker the job of getting South Africa excluded from world sport. What would be the result of this lofty ethical statement? I should imagine that at the least we would lose the support of one thousand of our hoped-for votes. If at the same time the party were to announce that it would press for the opening of the white beaches and the white swimming-baths and the white tennis courts at Sea Point to people of all races, I should imagine that we would lose another five hundred votes, and the remaining five hundred who would vote for us would be those who no longer swim or play tennis. Of course this may go down quite well in Johannesburg, and I should expect rather less well in Durban, but in Cape Town it won't go down at all. We in the Cape want the party to win the election in Sea Point, and the rest of the country has so far supported us, but if the national committee takes a decision of this kind, the party will lose a great many of its members here. Now tonight Mr. Robert Mansfield, the Natal chairman, is going to speak to a meeting, which I think will be a big one, in the Cape Town City Hall. I want to ask him a question. Is he going to tell the meeting that the party has decided to launch a campaign, or is contemplating launching it, to throw South Africa out of world sport?

– I couldn't do that, Mr. Chairman, until the party has taken such a decision. I certainly would not tell the meeting of any steps that we were merely contemplating.

– Well, I sincerely hope that the party won't do anything so foolish as to take such a decision. I have to go now, but I must warn you that if you take such a course, and you announce it tonight, then you will be dealing a deathblow to the party in the Cape.

– Donald, I don't understand you, said Emmanuel Nene.

You joined the party because you were against racial discrimination, but you don't want us to oppose it in Sea Point.

– You must make up your minds. If you want to fight white elections and get white voters, then you mustn't take away white pleasures and arouse white fears. The trouble with you, Emmanuel, is that you think the Liberal Party is a church.

Emmanuel greeted this with a smile of approval.

– You are a clever man, Donald, because you are right. The party is my church. Well, perhaps not quite right, because I have my other church where I learn what is right, but in this church I try to *do* what is right. You force me to agree, the party is also my church. But you must please not tell my minister.

Molteno picked up his briefcase.

– You're a nice chap, Emmanuel. You understand religion and ethics very well, I am sure, but you don't understand politics at all. Mr. Chairman, excuse me.

Die Burger is one of the three (or four or five, it depends on your politics) leading newspapers in South Africa. It was founded in 1916, and its first editor was no less a person than the great Dr. Malan. Thirty-two years later he became the Prime Minister. When a new organisation like the Liberal Party holds its first meeting in Cape Town, the first thing you do the next morning is to rush for the newspapers, with curiosity, hope, apprehension, even dread, to see what these powerful men have to say about you.

Robert Mansfield forced himself to go first to *Die Burger*, and he recoiled when he saw its leading editorial which was titled *'n Gevaarlike Party*, A Dangerous Party. The editorial declared that the speech of the national chairman bordered on treason. It took a grave view of his statement that the Suppression of Communism Act, supposedly designed to defend a properly elected government against revolution and subversion, was in fact designed primarily to perpetuate the rule of the National Party.

– There may be some of you, said Molteno, who think it is

a matter of no importance if *Die Burger* brands us a dangerous party, and says that the main speech last night bordered on treason. We in the Cape do not take that view. We may not agree with the politics of the paper, but it is regarded as a responsible newspaper, and we quite frankly do not like being branded as dangerous and treasonous. As I have said before, such speeches may go down well in Johannesburg and Durban, but they are not acceptable in Cape Town. Last night I got the impression, and I was not the only one to get it, that the speech was directed largely at the coloured members of the audience. Their applause was certainly vociferous. We all acknowledge that the coloured people have grievances, but certainly we in the Cape do not want to exploit coloured anger, or black anger, or any other kind of anger. For three hundred years the coloured people have lived in peace with their white neighbours, and while we want to protest with them against the laws that govern them, we do not like this continual emphasis on the iniquities of white people. I was aware last evening of an undertone of anger in the applause, and I didn't like it. I am making these remarks now because we shall soon be passing on to the business of electing a new national chairman. We must not elect any person who will frighten away the more conservative members of the party. We must in fact elect someone who has the confidence of both the conservatives and the evangelicals. I shall make my nomination in due course. For one thing I am very grateful, that we did not make the gross political error of announcing that we would work to have South Africa thrown out of world sport.

Molteno has the power of subduing the evangelicals of the party. The trouble is that it would be a heavy blow if he left it. The party is so young, so small, so weak, that its more responsible members would go to great lengths to avoid a break between the evangelicals and the conservatives. The evangelicals give it its fire, but the conservatives give it its respectability. If Molteno were to leave it, the Ballingers would go too, and who could imagine a Liberal Party without Margaret Ballinger?

Even Parker has had to calm down. He wanted to blast

Molteno for attaching such importance to *Die Burger*'s use of the word *treason*. If the party was going to run for cover every time it was accused of treason, it would spend all its time running. Parker is one of those who is prepared to face Molteno's departure. He is in fact of the opinion that the party will never get anywhere so long as Molteno is in it. But he has been persuaded to keep his opinions to himself.

The party decided to let John Parker pursue his programme of rallying world opinion against the colour bar in sport, but not to adopt a policy of world exclusion. It elected as its new chairman Philip Drummond of Pietermaritzburg, proposed by Molteno, respected by both conservatives and evangelicals, with private means, a proficiency in Zulu, and an ironic way of speaking that concealed qualities of quite another order.

So Molteno declared a truce with the party.

Mr. Robert Mansfield
Member of the Liberal Party

I have read about your speech in Cape Town. So you are against the Immorality Act. That's nothing to wonder about, because every time you poke your black dolly girls, you must be afraid of getting caught. What do they say? Caught in the act, ha! ha! I can see it, you and your dolly girl pawing at each other like two animals, breathing, panting, stinking of sex and sweat.

I bet you wake up at night and can imagine it all. How can you imagine such filth? You call yourself a Christian. How can you imagine such things? And that fuzzy hair, above and below.

Has your wife found any hair on the pillow yet? Or has she got her own black lover? You would both stoop to anything, I am sure.

Do you still talk about your Christianity? And how you have these black friends because you are a Christian. Ha! ha! I bet you don't tell about the black dollies. So pure you are, aren't you? you dirty white shit, you disgrace to the white race. What made you sink so low?

    Proud White Christian Woman

Mr. Robert Mansfield   20 November 1954
Natal Regional Office
The Liberal Party

On 6 November we wrote to you giving you fourteen days to resign the chairmanship of the Natal region of the Liberal Party. You were required to announce your resignation in one Durban and one Pietermaritzburg newspaper. This you have not done and we therefore conclude that you have not resigned. We shall therefore carry out our decision that you should be eliminated.

    Your elimination will be carried out at a time and in a manner to be now decided. That this will be deemed to be a criminal act, we are well aware, but the alternative is the continued existence of what we regard to be an anti-Christian and anti-White South African organisation. For us there is no choice in the matter.

    We sign ourselves

    The Preservation of White South Africa League

– And this editorial really upset you?

– Philip, it did. It was the first time my name had ever been in an editorial. Of course in my cricketing days I was often in the paper and the references were usually complimentary. But to be accused of making a speech bordering on treason, that had never happened to me before. I felt ill, Philip. As the Americans say, I was sick to my stomach.

– We'll have to get used to it, Robert. Parker is quite right. What we are doing is going to be called treason, and if we are frightened by it, we might as well give up now. It's not nice, I know. I don't like it either. But what else must we do? Shut our mouths for the rest of our lives? Must we let them do what they like to Emmanuel and his landowners, and shut up about it?

– Philip, you don't have to argue with me. I'm telling you this because I thought you should know the kind of man you asked to be Natal chairman. I don't like being frightened by an editorial. But when Molteno spoke to me about it he was actually trembling. It wasn't either anger or fear. It was as though he was appalled at the enormity of it, that our party should be named dangerous by so great an authority as *Die Burger*. If an intelligent man like Molteno reacts like that, what about all the intelligent people outside the party? I'll admit to you that the reaction of some of the members of the Newcastle Anglican Guild to my sports experiments really shook me. I can tell you that it has been a revelation to me that my first real experience of what you might call neighbourly love was to be in a political party, and not in my own church. It has been a revelation to me to find that people I had always thought of as my friends have grown decidedly cool towards me.

– There's also a funny side to it. My Uncle William is chairman of the Royal Club, but he also regards himself as my guardian, and he's fond of me. He just cannot understand how his nephew has got so worked up about the colour bar. He says to me, Philip my boy, we've had a colour bar for generations and no one in our family ever got worked up about it. He has an inordinate respect for old Judge Culpepper, and the judge said to him, The trouble is, Drummond, your nephew doesn't understand tradition, that's bad enough, but he doesn't understand evolutionary change either, and that's extraordinary for someone who's been to St. Michael's and Cambridge, had all the advantages in the world, and now he wants to throw them all away, after all that you and his father did for him. It's colour bar, colour bar, colour bar, sinful and all that, but what about ingratitude? The judge quoted Shakespeare to my uncle, Blow, blow, thou winter wind, thou art not so unkind as man's ingratitude. It was a bit wasted, because the only thing my uncle knows about Shakespeare is his name. You know all the blue blood of Pietermaritzburg belongs to the Club, and my uncle is almost embarrassed to go there. But the great Henry Mainwaring is even more embarrassed, and he has threatened to disinherit Hugh if he doesn't resign from the party. Now about the anonymous letters. The woman is obviously sick, and you needn't worry about her. But the other two are disturbing. The man sounds as if he could be dangerous. Have you shown them to Naomi?

– Most certainly.

– How does she react?

– As you might expect. But I can see that they worry her. And then the Security Police. You know my aunts and uncles are very respectable, and they didn't like the police attending my cousin's funeral. When I say they attended it I mean they parked a little way off, and got out of the car and leaned against it, watching. You know how they are taught to look at people with that merciless stare that frightens the wits out of the more timid ones. Some people just can't stand being stared at. My relatives didn't like it a bit, and whether I was right or wrong, I felt that they thought my attendance at the funeral had introduced an unpleasant note into what was their private ceremony. I tell you frankly, I didn't like it.

– No one likes it, Robert. It's meant to be an intrusion into privacy. It's meant to show you that you can't have anything private once you oppose the Government. They taped Kathie Vermeulen making love to someone she shouldn't have been making love to, and they played it to her, and she left on the next plane.

– Philip, you force me to tell you that I am timid by nature. Because I was good at cricket, no one guessed it. If you've played for South Africa, it's not difficult to run a school. But I thought you ought to know. After all, when you asked me to be the Natal chairman, you didn't know me at all.

– You mustn't think you're unique. Now that Emmanuel has become the organiser of NALA, they follow him everywhere. They visit his wife in his absence and urge her to get him to give it all up and go back to being messenger of the court. One of them declares he is Emmanuel's dear friend, and Lydia Nene told me she had seen tears in his eyes as he pleaded with her to save her dear husband and his dear friend from following his dangerous course. He in fact hinted to her, and there was no one else there to hear him but herself, that it might be physically dangerous to Emmanuel. She asked him to say straight out what he meant. Did he mean that Emmanuel might be killed? And who would kill him? Would it be the police themselves? Oh no, he didn't mean that, he didn't mean that at all. But there were enemies who had a great hatred for NALA, and indeed who had a great hatred for any black man who stood up for himself and his rights, and others who had a great hatred for any black man who joined white people in politics. These enemies could kill such a man, run him down when he was walking on the road, or hire black thieves to break into his house and to shoot him if he resisted. Emmanuel doesn't like this any more than you do. Lydia doesn't like it either, but she reacts to it in the same way as Naomi. You must not think, Robert, that you are unique in your feelings. We all get fits of timidity.

– One last thing, Philip. In Durban we have a romance on our hands and I'm timid about that too.

– You mean Prem and Hugh?

– Yes. Shall I speak to Hugh or shall I not?

– I would say not. It's not your job to get your members to obey the laws of the country, especially one that the party has roundly condemned. But I don't suppose you have that in mind. You're afraid they might get hurt.

– Yes, I am.

– That's understandable, but I would leave them alone. They are two of the sanest youngsters in the country. It's their problem, and they must solve it for themselves. Are you worried about the party too? Well, you shouldn't be. You may be sure that they'll think about that too.

The most famous of all the blackspots is to come to an end on 10 February 1955. Its name is Sophiatown, called after Sophia the loved wife of Mr. Tobiansky, who bought the site at the beginning of the century, and laid out a white township, naming some of its streets after his children, Edith, Gerty, Bertha, Toby and Sol. It was only four and a half miles from the centre of the city of Johannesburg, and its plots would have sold like hot cakes if the City Council had not decided to establish a sewage farm next door. Mr. Tobiansky then decided to sell his plots to African, coloured and Asian people, which the law allowed him to do. In 1955 more than sixty thousand people were living there.

Sophiatown is a wild, exciting, tumultuous place. Apart from Tobiansky's plan, it has grown up without design. Plots have been split up again and again, resulting in a kaleidoscopic conglomeration of shops, houses, lodging-rooms, brothels, shebeens, churches. A child might grow up good in Sophiatown but never innocent. It was of this vital, raw, violent, ugly place, that Father Trevor Huddleston of the Community of the Resurrection wrote when he had to leave it, using the words of Walter de la Mare, Look thy last on all things lovely, every hour. Sophiatown had become to him the home of all things lovely. It was the place where old men and women came into the great church of Christ the King on their hands and knees. The humility and faith of it smote him in the inward parts. It was the place where small black children ran out from the houses to hold the hand of the father. It was the place where he and Sister Dorothy Maud could walk safe at any hour of the day or night.

– Father.

– Yes.

– I have killed a man.

– When?

– Now now. In Sithole's yard.

– You were gambling.

– Yes.

– You promised me.

– I promised you, Father, but I broke it.

– What happened?

– This man played a card that was not in his hand. I said, That card was not in your hand. So he pulled out his knife.

– And you pulled out yours?

– Yes, Father.

– Which you promised not to carry.

– I repent, Father.

– Go on.

– He would have killed me, but I struck first. In a minute he was dead.

– And everyone saw it?

– Yes, Father.

– Let us pray, Michael, then we shall go to the police.

– Let us pray then.

Of all the places in the world, Huddleston will never find one like this again. He has given his heart to it. The beauty of Switzerland, of Italy, of the moors of his own West Country, cannot compete for his love with the beauty of Sophiatown. He is known to all, his lean and handsome face, his dark hair greying, his expressive hands, and a kind of purity and vitality that shines out of his eyes.

This purity and vitality is more marked than ever in this year 1955. He has the appearance of one who is burning to serve the world. This burning quality does not show in any fierceness in the eyes, or hollowness in the cheeks, or fever in the skin. The ruddiness of his cheeks is that of spiritual health, not of fanaticism. He is a dog of the Lord, not fierce but faithful. And now he burns to save Sophiatown. He is seen everywhere. He is seen with leading members of the African Congress, and the Security Police watch every move that he makes, listen to every speech and to every telephone call, read every letter that is written to him. He is pitting himself against the might and power and glory of the State.

On 9 February the Minister of Justice banned all public meetings in the magisterial districts of Johannesburg and Roodepoort for twenty days. The Minister said the position was serious, not because of the resistance from the people to be moved, but because of the agitators. He was sorry to say that there were certain clergymen amongst the agitators, among them Father Huddleston. What right had an Englishman who could speak no language but his own, who had been in the country for a mere eleven years, what right had he to say that the laws were unjust?

At dawn on 10 February a whole fleet of army lorries arrived in Sophiatown. A couple of thousand armed police, white and black, were there in case of trouble. The Commissioner of Police patrolled up and down in a radio van, in hourly communication with the Minister in Cape Town. Wherever Huddleston went he was surrounded by black people. His progress was a series of banned meetings, and no sooner had he obeyed the order to move on from one than he was in the middle of another. At this very moment his name was going round the world.

Not everyone who condemns the destruction of Sophiatown approves of Huddleston's actions. Not even all the members of his own Community of the Resurrection approve. Some of them think that his actions make all their works more vulnerable, and that the authorities will make the Community suffer for his defiance. Some think he courts publicity in a way not fitting for a monk. The Community has already lost all its schools, but there were many other projects that could be harmed. No white priest could enter a black township without a permit from the Government, and if it was decided to withdraw permits, all mission work would come to an end.

Two powerful Ministers, Dr. Hendrik of Bantu Affairs, and the Minister of Justice, have said in Parliament that Father Huddleston was encouraging the use of violence in the Sophiatown campaign. Huddleston has challenged them to say so outside Parliament, when he could sue them, but they have not done so. He is prepared for this kind of attack, but it has hurt him that none of his ecclesiastical superiors have come to his defence. He takes very seriously those words of the prophet:

The Spirit of the Lord is upon me, because He has anointed me to preach the Gospel to the poor; He has sent me to heal the broken-hearted, to preach deliverance to the captives and recovery of sight to the blind, to preach the acceptable year of the Lord.

That was what Huddleston really believed, that he had been sent to heal the broken-hearted. But his Archbishop, the Most Reverend Geoffrey Clayton, even if he believed it, didn't think that Huddleston was doing it in a sensible way. Clayton was also known as a champion of the oppressed, but he was deliberate and judicial, whereas Huddleston burned with zeal. Clayton wrote to the Father Superior of the Community, saying that he did not wish to be Visitor to the order so long as Huddleston was the South African Provincial.

It was in fact impossible to be lukewarm about Huddleston. You either approved of him or you didn't. In Sophiatown, although he was white, he was the best known, the best loved, of all its people.

– Father, I am too old to be moved.

– I know you are too old, mother, but if you do not go they will lift you up in their arms and put you into the truck.

– Father, I do not want to go.

– I do not want you to go either. But tomorrow maybe they will come with the big machine and smash your house to pieces. Then what will you do?

– I do not want them to touch me, Father. But if you help me into the truck I shall go.

– I will help you, mother, and as soon as I can I shall come to your new house in Meadowlands.

– Give me a minute, Father. I must say goodbye to my house. My husband built that house many years ago when we were both young. I am glad he is not here today.

The old woman stands for a minute at the gate of her house. She shuts her eyes, she is praying. What is she praying for? That some angel with a sword will come down to defend it? Or does she give thanks for the life that she lived there? Or does she ask forgiveness for those who have taken her house from her?

– I am ready, Father.

Meadowlands. The name is beautiful. The huge machines come, and day after day they raze Sophiatown to the ground, the shops, houses, lodging-rooms, brothels, shebeens, churches. For some reason the huge church of Christ the King is left, standing guard over the desolation. Other huge machines come and take away the rubble. The new streets are laid out and paved, and thousands of houses are built for the white workers of Johannesburg. The name of Sophia, loved wife of Mr. Tobiansky, which in some other dispensation might have lived for ever, goes into oblivion.

The new town gets a new name, Triomf, meaning Triumph. One assumes it means the triumph of the Great Plan, of the philosophy and practice of separate coexistence. One must not be surprised if one day the name is changed, back to Sophiatown perhaps, or to Huddleston, or to Kwa-Lutuli.

. . . You must not have any doubts, my dear aunt, about the demolition of Sophiatown. It was a giant slum, dirty and overcrowded, full of thieves and murderers and prostitutes. The new place Meadowlands is a place of order and spaciousness. The houses are small but well built, and when the trees grow up it will be a place to be proud of. It is another great step forward in the Great Plan. It will certainly not be a place for South Africa to be ashamed of, which Sophiatown certainly was.

Another notorious slum that will be demolished is District Six in Cape Town. It too is full of thieves and murderers and prostitutes. The Government is determined to put an end to mixed residential areas. There is no need to feel guilty about these demolitions. Ethembeni about which I last wrote to you, Sophiatown, District Six, and all the other blackspots are not Afrikaner creations. Ethembeni was allowed to come into being by the Natal Government, Sophiatown by the British rulers of our defeated Transvaal Republic, and District Six by the Cape Government. Mixed residential areas were never permitted in our two republics.

The man Father Huddleston is an agitator. The title 'Father' is Romish, and is alien to our Reformed churches. He would much rather be with black people than white, and he takes every opportunity to be photographed with laughing black children. He is laughing himself and has his hands on their heads in the act of what is known as 'blessing', another Romish custom.

His attempts to stir up violence in Sophiatown ended in total failure. But he did great harm to our country by inviting foreign newspapers to come to Johannesburg and to publicise the removals. This time he took every opportunity to be photographed with old men and women, who naturally take such a resettlement much harder than the younger ones. The newspapermen get the old people to weep or, if they cannot weep, to hold handkerchiefs to their eyes and, if they can get Huddleston there too, looking full of sorrow, they feel they have done their work well. Then they send their pictures overseas so that all the world can see how cruel are the white South Africans, especially the Afrikaners.

A friend in London sent my Minister a picture from an English newspaper showing Huddleston helping an old woman into the army truck that is to take her to Meadowlands. A couple of young policemen are shown laughing, and unfortunately it looks as if they are laughing at the old woman. I happened to be in my Minister's office when he received the paper, with this photograph on the front page, and the caption 'Seeing the Funny Side'. He sat and looked at it without speaking, but his face was black with anger. At last he threw it over to me. 'Look at it, look at it, Van Onselen,' he said. 'What do you think of it?' I said, 'Minister, it's a scandal.' He said, 'Of course it's a scandal, but if I were to touch this Huddleston, there would be still more pictures.'

He then told me to find out the names of the two young policemen, why they laughed, why they laughed when there was a photographer there, and why they allowed Huddleston to help the woman into the truck.

In fact the removal was a great triumph for the Minister. It was carried out with a minimum of disturbance, and many of the people laughed and joked with the police. The Minister kept in touch throughout the day with the Commissioner of Police in Johannesburg, and had the messages typed out and put on his desk. Each time I went to his office he showed them to me, and he was full of pride in the police and the officials. His cup overflowed when he received congratulatory messages from the Prime Minister and from Dr. Hendrik. His happy mood lasted exactly ten days, and then he received the picture from London. My Minister has the reputation of being a hard man, but in fact he is not, and he was deeply upset by the false impression given by the photograph.

I have taken very seriously your advice as to how I should deal with my intense dislike of my immediate superior Dr. Fischer. It is too early to say if my efforts have borne fruit. While we are in Cape Town he spends a great deal of time at the Houses of Parliament, and I do not see much of him. I will see much more of him when we all return to Pretoria.

I must finally report to you that the congresses, the African, the Indian, the white and the coloured, are planning to hold a great Congress of the People in Johannesburg in June. One good thing is that Lutuli will not be able to be there, as my Minister has confined him for two years to the area around Groutville, where you may remember he was once the chief. At times it makes me anxious to see how the work of the congresses persists. I had hoped that when the Defiance Campaign came to an end, there would be a lull in their activities, but it does not seem to be so. I can tell you in confidence that I and many others will rejoice on the day that Dr. Hendrik takes over the reins of the government of the country. I do not like to appear disloyal to the P.M., but he does not have the vision or the intellect of Dr. Hendrik, and when he speaks he does not evoke the Afrikaner pride that Dr. Hendrik can call forth and which our revered Dr. Malan could certainly evoke in me (and which I am afraid Dr. Fischer does not; his Afrikaans is generally recognised to be superb, but I find it too cold and logical).

The Congress of the People is going to last for two days, and it is going to present a new Charter for the People of South Africa. That means of course that it will reject totally Dr. Hendrik's Great Plan for peaceful and harmonious separate coexistence. My Minister is facing the grave decision as to whether he should ban the gathering altogether as a danger to the peace of the country.

Father Huddleston
Church of Christ the King
Sophiatown

I am getting sick and tired of seeing your photograph in the papers, patting the heads of black children. Do you ever pat the head of a white child? Have you no love for the children of your own kind?

The latest photograph is of you with your arms round a black woman. It makes me ashamed to be a member of the Anglican Church. Why cannot we stick to our own kind? In God's creation dogs do not mate with cats, and lions do not mate with antelopes. Why is it a crime to want to stick to your own kind? God created us different, yet according to you He will bring down judgement on the Government for moving blacks out of white Johannesburg, and sending them to live with their own kind.

As a priest you make me sick. Why must you always paw the black women? I know all about your vows. But why are there thousands of infants' graves in every nunnery in the world? They are monks' children and you know it, and as soon as they are born they are put to death so that your holy name can be preserved.

Now that Sophiatown has gone, what will the white men do who used to go there to visit the black dollies, and kiss the black tits and the black — ugh! I cannot bring myself to write down such filth. And you, are you so holy? You know as well as I do that if you start pawing black women you won't stop there. And you a priest! It makes me want to get out of the Anglican Church.

I have never touched a black skin in my life and I never shall. The thought fills me with disgust. My mother would never let a black woman touch any of her children. She taught us not to hate anybody but she would not let us be touched by the black nation.

I look in the paper every day to see if the Government has sent you back to England.

Proud White Christian Woman

. . . I can understand your puzzlement, my dear Max, and I do not take offence at your question. It was a pleasure to hear from you after all these years. You were nineteen and full of reforming zeal, and it was exciting to you to be taught by a man who was proud to be a Marxist and a member of the

toughest party in the world. You are by no means the only one
who asks how I, an aging professor of Biology, thought by
many to be a world authority on certain obscure matters, and
having such a fiery past, can join a political party which is
made up of cranks, utopians, and impractical idealists; des-
perate black people who think their threatened rights can be
saved by white liberals just because they are white; scheming
black people who think there might be pickings in it; and
other black people who for some extraordinary reason join
white people to fight for things they both believe in.

It's a good question and, if it puzzles you, it puzzles me
too. It has made me take time off from my work and turn my
instruments on myself. What's going on there in that queer,
supposedly autonomous entity Edward Roos which I call my
self? In my idealistic days I was a card-carrying member of
the Communist Party, but I left in 1936, partly because I
could no longer endure the hostility of the 'real believers'.
My belief in dialectical materialism was shaky and I could
never really accept the idea that the right and only way to
bring about social and political change was to provoke
hostility between class and class, which in South Africa
meant hostility between white and black. I suppose I was in
truth a socialist who wanted to be a democrat also. However,
my resignation in 1936 did not prevent the Nationalist
Government from 'naming' me in 1950. That meant that
nothing I said or wrote could be published, but it did not
prevent me from joining the Liberal Party.

I had several reasons for doing this, but I shall mention
only one. It was the conduct of the white members of the
party during the campaign to resist the destruction of
Sophiatown. Here were men and women who had not taken
part in any resistance before, who were sent for at all hours
by black members of the party in Sophiatown, to trace
people, sometimes members and sometimes friends of members, who had been taken away by the police, for a whole
host of offences that only black people can commit, such as
being caught in the street without their passes, but really
because they opposed the destruction of Sophiatown and of
their freehold. Some were taken away for no other reason

than that they objected to being questioned in the street as to what they were doing and where they were going. Some no doubt objected in stronger terms than others, and there is no easier way for black persons to get arrested than to object strongly to being interfered with when they are strolling or gossiping or shopping in the streets of the township which they regard as their home, and where they expect to be able to walk about in freedom.

There is nothing more difficult for most white South Africans than to go to a police station and make inquiries about some black person whom they believe to have been detained unjustly. I know this well because when I was young I did it myself, and I had to force myself to go into the police station. One is conscious — and this is a terrible thing to say — that one is being disloyal to something, and that something is nothing less than the cause of white supremacy. One feels that one is poking one's officious nose into affairs which every decent white South African should leave in the hands of the police with perfect trust in their probity and humanity.

It almost made me weep to see little Laura de Kock in the Newlands police station. She is only a slip of a girl, very shy, very conventional, and absolutely terrified of the police. She went to inquire what had happened to Elizabeth Mofokeng, who went out to the shop and didn't come back again, but people reported to her husband that the police had taken her away. 'Yes,' said the young policeman, 'there is a Bantu female Elizabeth Mofokeng in the cells.' Laura asked if she could see her and the young policeman referred the question to his sergeant, who said no. He wanted to know what authority Laura had to inquire on behalf of Bantu female Mofokeng and she replied that she was a friend of the family, and had been asked to make inquiries by Mr. Mofokeng. It was easy for Laura to see that the sergeant disapproved of white people who had black friends, and of white people who called black men 'Mister'. He wanted to know why Bantu male Mofokeng had not come to inquire about his wife, and Laura explained that he had had to stay with his distraught children, who had heard a neighbour say that the police had taken their mother away. The sergeant informed her that she had no status in the matter, but that he would supply information to Bantu male Mofokeng.

Laura de Kock left the police station with a sense of her complete powerlessness in the face of the State. Some value that she regarded as fundamental, call it what you like, the sanctity of the Mofokeng family, the security of the Mofokeng children, the security of Elizabeth Mofokeng who could not even go in safety to the shop, seemed to count for nothing in the Newlands police station. A decent woman had been arrested on her way to or from a shop, for some offence unknown, yet no friend of hers had any right to know what offence she had committed. On the one side of the counter complete powerlessness, on the other side a power terrifying in its omnipotence, totally indifferent to the anxiety or distress of the husband and children, and, what was more, a power totally unaware that it was destroying the future of its own society.

Laura went to look for a telephone, and public telephones in Newlands are notorious. At last she found one that worked, and she rang Ruth, the doyenne of us all, Ruth with the eager face, not beautiful, but burning with an inner fire and a consuming passion for justice, and as far as I know without fear of any policeman or magistrate or judge. She is a lawyer, and of course that made it easier for her than for Laura.

It was now getting near midnight, and Ruth had gone to bed, but she told Laura she would be there in thirty minutes. She came to the house and got me out of bed too so that I could keep her company. She swept into the police station and asked to see the sergeant. She told him she was an attorney, and she had been asked by Mr. Mofokeng to represent his wife. She wanted to know why Elizabeth Mofokeng had been arrested.

It was easy to observe a change in the attitude of sergeant and constable. They could ride roughshod over liberal house-wives but they had to be careful of attorneys. When the sergeant was preparing to hum and ha, Ruth said to him forthrightly, in that eager way that was uncompromising but not offensive, 'Sergeant, I am Mrs. Mofokeng's legal representative, and I demand to know why she has been arrested.'

'Lady, she was arrested for loitering.'

'Loitering!'

'Yes, lady.'

'Let me tell you, sergeant, I know this lady well, and she does not go in for loitering.'

'The court will decide that, madam.'

'And I'll be there, sergeant, and I am warning you that the police evidence will have to be good. Now I would like to put up bail for Mrs. Mofokeng.'

'Madam it is not in my jurisdiction to set and receive bail.'

'Then I shall ask you to release her into my custody, on the understanding that I shall deliver her to the court at the time set down for trial. Here is my card. You will see that I am an attorney-at-law, 1605 New Court Chambers, in Ferreirastown.'

'Madam, I would have to release her on her own recognisances, but I would do it on the understanding that you will deliver her to the court at nine a.m. tomorrow. Court number 24.'

'Well, thank you, sergeant, that will be an arrangement satisfactory to all parties.'

We delivered Elizabeth Mofokeng to her overjoyed husband and children, and drove behind Laura's car to her home in Parkwood. As soon as we approached the house, her architect husband Hendrik came out to meet her, and enfolded her in a long and silent embrace. It was two o'clock in the morning, but there were no reproaches. I must say that the sight affected me. I said to Ruth, 'All right, I'll join your damned party.'

– I didn't phone you, Mr. Mansfield, because I didn't want anyone listening in to have the satisfaction of knowing what had happened to your engine. Mind you, they'll probably find out anyway.

– And the engine is ruined?

– I'm almost certain it is, but I won't know for sure until I've stripped it down.

– How did they do it, Jeff?

– It's easy. You park your car outside a hall or a cinema or whatever, at night preferably. The chap lifts the bonnet, takes the cap off the oil filler pipe, pours one tin of grinding-paste into the sump, puts the cap back, and closes the bonnet. I should say he would take less than a minute. The filthy oil gets into the oil pump, but before the pump packs up pumps the oil into the engine, where it begins to erode the bearings and to eat away the cylinders. If you go on using the car, then finally the whole thing seizes up. The red light gave you three warnings, and if you had left the car and got us to fetch it the damage would have been less. But you did what most people would have done, you decided to get to your service station as soon as possible. You had to travel twenty miles to get there, and the damage done in those twenty miles would have been considerable.

– If you can repair it, Jeff, what will it cost?

– I'd say four to five hundred pounds.

– And a new engine?

– Double that. I'm sorry, Mr. Mansfield.

– I'm sorry too.

– Will you go to the police?

– I'll have to think it over. I'd say not. Since I went into politics — unpopular politics, Jeff — I have no confidence in the police. I imagine them saying to each other, Here's this fellow Mansfield who wants to give votes to blacks, and who wants to do away with the Immorality Act, and now he comes running to us when people muck up his car. And does he think we are going to work night and day to find out who did it? So you see, Jeff, I wouldn't have any confidence. I'm ashamed to say that. I feel almost like a criminal too, because they see me as a traitor to white South Africa. They can't get me under any law, but if anyone ruins my car they'll never find out who did it.

– I'm sorry, Mr. Mansfield.

– Jeff, you'll let me know the final verdict.

– Yes, I will. If you have to buy a new engine, perhaps you ought to buy a new car instead. It must have a bonnet that can open only from the inside, and we'll have to put a padlock on the oil filler cap. You'll also have to have a petrol tank cap that can be opened only with a key. I don't know why they didn't try that on you, it's even quicker. Put some sugar in the tank, and you'll have the same trouble, only not so quick or so deadly. Goodbye, Mr. Mansfield, I'll let you know.

Mansfield went to his study and sat there doing nothing. He could find the five hundred pounds, the one thousand if he had to, but the discovery of his vulnerability was a shock to him. Was there something special about a car, or did this desolate feeling follow the loss of any possession? Perhaps a car was special. Archie Berrigan of Johannesburg, stout member of the white Congress, defending lawyer in a dozen 'political' cases that no other lawyer would touch, had been undeterred by abusive letters, threats of death, even by shots fired through the windows of the sitting-room. But when his enemies poured paint remover over the hood and bonnet of his new Pontiac, he and his wife gave up and went to live in Australia.

– Robert, what are you doing?

– Nothing. Absolutely nothing.

Naomi Mansfield went to her husband quickly, and lifted up his head so that she could look at his face.

– Robert, don't frighten me. What's wrong with you?

– The time is out of joint. O cursed spite, that ever I was born to set it right!

– Is it the car?

– Yes, it's the car. The engine's gone. Someone put grinding-paste in the sump. So the whole car ground to pieces.

– Have you been to the police?

– Of course, of course. Have you any suspicions who might have done it, sir? No, sergeant. When did it happen, sir? I don't know, sergeant, some time in the last two weeks. Where did it happen, sir? I don't know, sergeant. Thank you, sir, your information is invaluable, and will greatly assist us in our resolute search to find the villains. No, I have not been to the police, and I do not intend going. I don't like going to them anyway, but even if I did, I wouldn't see any point in it.

Now listen, Naomi, I don't want the children to know about this. I must confess to you, dear, that I feel almost ashamed of it.

. . . Why did I leave the Communist Party? I have already told you, Max, that I could not endure the hostility of the true believers. I had begun to realise that the State was not going to wither away. The stories about Stalin's liquidation of millions of peasants who resisted collectivisation troubled me deeply. The true believers realised that I was beginning to have doubts, and if I had not resigned they would have forced me out.

You ask why I did not finally identify with the white Congress? It would have been like returning to the Communist Party. All the members of the Congress are not communists, but their real inheritance is from the C.P. They regard the sanctity of home and family, the rule of law, the freedom of the press, the speaking of the truth, as bourgeois values that liberals have exalted to the rank of absolutes, whereas the only true absolute is the party. I don't want to pontificate, but my work is a search for the truth. The case of Lysenko, who was prepared to adapt his theories of heredity to suit the party, shocked me deeply. If the white Congress ever came to power it would not hesitate to abrogate the rule of law, and to make the press an instrument of the party.

Most of the members of the Liberal Party have no conception of the toughness and relentlessness of the white Congress. The two bodies are temperamentally, politically, and philosophically incompatible. A girl like Laura de Kock is brave, she has a passion for justice, but she is gentle of nature. A girl like Eve Briscoe is also brave, she also has a passion for justice, but if she came to power she would have me shot because I deserted the C.P. A dear simpleton like Peter Ross actually belongs to both the Liberal Party and the white Congress. He has an ecumenical and holistic credo, and believes that somehow the two will become one. Eve would have him shot too.

A rare creature is Helen Joseph. She is a member of the

Congress but she has said herself that she was not promising material for the ranks of communism. Yet she was more at home in the Congress than she would ever have been in the Liberal Party. She was certainly not relentless but she had a quality of militancy that is more evident in communists than in liberals. The Black Sash kept their distance from her, and in any event she disapproved of their decision to keep the Black Sash white and their declaration that it was a white women's fight, just as the Torch Commando had fought for coloured rights but would not admit coloured members. How does one explain these riddles of human nature? But the most difficult of all are the riddles of white South African nature.

At present our delegates are at Tongaat discussing the proposed Congress of the People with the members of all the congresses. Why the white Congress agrees to meet with us, I cannot quite fathom, even with my communist past. No doubt Lutuli and Z. K. Matthews wanted us to be there. However, I guarantee that our delegates will come back with the feeling that they have been manipulated. I'll go further and say that the Liberal Party will never go to the Congress of the People at all. That will be a great pity, and it won't do us any good, but that is what the white Congress wants, for us to agree to attend this great gathering of the people, and then for us to chicken out.

I am afraid of our ecumenical members. They will find a 'formula' to embody all the points of agreement and to leave out all the points of disagreement, and it is the points of disagreement that are the most fundamental. They are in fact the way that liberals look at the world.

I joined the C.P. so that I could help to build Utopia. Now I don't believe in Utopia any more. I didn't join the Liberal Party because I thought it would achieve Utopia. I joined it because I had a lump in my throat.

The Congress of the People has come and gone, and it was a cheerful affair. Huddleston said it was like a bank holiday on Hampstead Heath, thousands of people milling about, laughing, joking, giving salutes, buying tea and scones and cold drinks and pies, listening to brave speeches, applauding the resounding clauses of the Freedom Charter that gave every conceivable freedom and happiness to mortal man, who is born of a woman and has but a short time to live, and is full of trouble.

Well, not quite like Hampstead Heath or a bank holiday. This is Kliptown, Johannesburg, and the police are here in their hundreds. Still, if you fight for freedom you must learn to live with the police. There is a kind of truce between police and people, an armed truce for the police, an unarmed truce for the people. You can see the revolver holsters of the police, but you cannot see the guns that would be brought out if there were trouble. However, there is no trouble. You are searched when you come in and you are searched when you go out. You do not look at the police, and they do not look at you. It is an impersonal affair, and you shout and talk to your friends while they are searching you. Everyone is shouting and laughing, as though they had come to a bank holiday fair, and not to a gathering where the freedom and happiness of men and women were to be set out in moving words.

A new heaven and a new earth, that's what it is. And the police are here in force to maintain the other new heaven and the other new earth of Dr. Hendrik and the National Party, the new heaven and earth of separate and peaceful coexistence. It looks peaceful enough here, in this gathering that has come to frame the charter of another kind of coexistence, earnestness and resolution mixed with the shouting and the laughing. But neither the shouting nor the laughter is directed at the police, it is meant for your friends. Huddleston is laughing too, enjoying himself like a boy, but of course he knows that his every movement is closely watched. And he knows that his Archbishop, the formidable Geoffrey Clayton of Cape Town, does not approve of his being here, and he knows too that his own order, the Community of the Resurrection, are more and more troubled by his doings.

Huddleston receives the title of *Isitwalandwe*, the Courageous Warrior, amidst deafening applause. So does

Dr. Yusuf Dadoo, the national president of the South African Indian Congress. There is special applause for Chief Lutuli, who also receives the title, but he cannot be here, because he is banned to the magisterial district of Stanger for two years. He could not have come in any case because he has suffered a stroke.

This is 25 June, and it is winter in Johannesburg. The air is cold and crisp, but the sun is warm and pleasant. You would hardly know that you were attending a gathering of people who are fighting to be free, to be free of every law that prevents them from enjoying life and liberty, and pursuing happiness. But when you hear the Freedom Charter you will know.

The Security Police are confiscating every dangerous document. One of them will be used at a famous trial that is still to come. It reads: 'Comrades. Tea 3d. Tea and Sandwich 6d.'

∞∞∞∞∞∞∞∞∞∞∞∞∞

Adopted at the Congress of the People at Kliptown, Johannesburg, on 25 and 26 June 1955.

We, the People of South Africa, declare for all our country and the world to know:

that South Africa belongs to all who live in it, black and white, and that no government can justly claim authority unless it is based on the will of all the people;

that our people have been robbed of their birthright to land, liberty, and peace by a form of government founded on injustice and inequality;

that our country will never be prosperous or free until all our people live in brotherhood, enjoying equal rights and opportunities;

that only a democratic state, based on the will of the people, can secure to all their birthright without distinction of colour, sex, or belief.

And therefore we, the people of South Africa, black and white together — equals, countrymen, and brothers — adopt this Freedom Charter. And we pledge ourselves to strive together sparing neither strength nor courage, until the democratic changes here set out have been won.

All apartheid laws and practices shall be set aside.

The national wealth of our country, the heritage of all South Africans, shall be restored to the people;
The mineral wealth beneath the soil, the banks and monopoly industry shall be transferred to the ownership of the people as a whole;
All other industry and trade shall be controlled to assist the well-being of the people;
All people shall have equal rights to trade where they choose, to manufacture and to enter all trades, crafts and professions.

No one shall be imprisoned, deported or restricted without a fair trial; no one shall be condemned by the order of any government official.

The law shall guarantee to all their right to speak, to organise, to meet together, to publish, to preach, to worship, and to educate their children;
The privacy of the home from police raids shall be protected by law;
All shall be free to travel without restriction from country-side to town, from province to province, and from South Africa abroad;
Pass laws, permits and all other laws restricting these freedoms shall be abolished.

Education shall be free, compulsory, universal and equal for all children.

Let all who love their people and their country now say, as we say here:

These freedoms we will fight for, side by side, throughout our lives, until we have won our liberty.

∞∞∞∞∞∞∞∞∞∞∞∞∞∞∞∞

And I saw a new heaven and a new earth, for the first heaven and the first earth were passed away, and there was no more sea.

And I John saw the holy city, new Jerusalem, coming down from God out of heaven, prepared as a bride adorned for her husband.

And I heard a great voice out of heaven, saying, Behold the Tabernacle of God is with men, and he will dwell with them and be their God.

And God shall wipe away all tears from their eyes, and there shall be no more death, neither sorrow, nor crying, neither shall there be any more pain; for the former things are passed away.

– Well, Robert, it is good of you to come to see me.

– They wouldn't let me come before, Chief. I tried many times. How are you, Chief?

– I'm much better, but I'm sluggish. This is not a time to be sluggish. We Puritans don't like it when we're not working. What made it worse for me was that while we were holding the Congress of the People, I was so helpless. Why weren't you there, Robert?

– Chief, the national committee decided that the party would not be there.

– They made a mistake. They didn't want to be there because the white Congress was going to be there. They think the white Congress plays the tune and we all have to dance. Is that a compliment to me? Or to the African Congress?

– No, it isn't.

– You ought to know, Robert, we also have members who don't like the white Congress. They say there's only one thing worse than being ruled by Pretoria and that's being ruled by Moscow. We also have black Nationalists who dislike the whole Congress alliance. They don't want to have anything to do with whites or Indians. You liberals are too afraid of the white Congress. If a communist or a member of the white Congress wants to work with me for an end to apartheid and for work and food for everybody, I'll work with him. Look, Robert, when my house is burning down, and we are all running to the fire, I don't say to the man next to me, Tell me first, where did you get your bucket, where did you draw your water?

– Chief, some of our members take fright at all this talk of nationalisation of mines and banks and factories. They are afraid not only of the end of private property, but of the very incentive to work. They are afraid of a dead level of mediocrity, with millions of powerless workers ruled by powerful party bosses, and they see the hand of the white Congress in it.

– Robert, black people don't feel the same about mines and banks and factories as you do. They've never had any. All they had to do was to work in them, and to live in mean houses while the bosses lived in mansions. Just take the sugar country where I live. We work on the plantations for next to nothing, and do they think we can't see the houses where the sugar barons live? I don't want to see the end of private property but I want to see the end of private property that has been built on the labour of people who have no private property. Why is the gold industry so rich? It's not because gold is so rich, but because the people who dig it are so poor.

– Chief, it's not just the loss of private property. What we fear most of all is that you can't nationalise everything without destroying all freedom, the freedom to speak and teach and protest as you have been doing. We *are* afraid of some of your colleagues. They put fine words in the Freedom Charter, but do you believe that if they come to power, no one would be imprisoned or restricted without charge or trial? We don't believe it.

The Chief wiped his brow and his face, down which the sweat was pouring as it always did when he was putting his heart and soul into something, which he did often. Then he gave his tremendous laugh.

– Robert, you know the Freedom Charter well, although you weren't there to help us make it. And don't you know I mustn't get excited? Look at me now. The sister won't let you come again.

– Sorry, Chief, but you make me excited too. If I think

freedom is in danger, I must defend it, even to you.

– Well, let's change the subject. I still think it's a pity you didn't come to Kliptown. You could've saved us from putting in all the Marxist doctrines. You know Patrick Duncan came to see me?

– Yes, I knew.

– We invited him to Kliptown but he said he wasn't well enough. That was an even greater pity. If a white man goes into Germiston location on crutches, then we make a hero of him. Then when he doesn't go to Kliptown we don't know what to make of him. It seemed like a snub to the African Congress, and especially to Z. K. Matthews whose idea it was. Patrick gave his reasons for not going, besides his illness I mean. It was like listening to you, except that his anti-communism is much worse than yours. Don't let him make you into an anti-communist party.

– We know the danger, Chief.

– Robert, I can't let you go away looking so gloomy. I must tell you . . .

– I'm not gloomy, I'm sober. It makes me sober talking to you. But I must go on talking to you for the sake of us all.

– Of course. Listen to me. I've a story to cheer you up. A couple of nights ago I dreamt I was elected the Prime Minister of South Africa. And I sent for you, Robert, to ask you to be my Minister of Education.

Mansfield felt his heart suddenly warm to this big man, whose big voice could electrify a gathering as no other voice in the country could, the voice that had been silenced by the Minister of Justice at the very time when the Minister should have listened.

– Well, Robert, nothing to say?

– Lots to say, but at the moment I don't seem able to say it. I can't speak, Chief, because you've touched me.

– So I ought to touch you. God help us when we can't touch each other any more, because then, Robert, we're going to kill each other. All right, sister, I'm sending him off. Come again, Robert.

. . . You see, the Congress of the People passed off quietly. Your fears were unjustified. Not a stone was thrown, not a shot was fired. The police behaved impeccably as you would expect our police to behave, firm and controlled. Huddleston was there of course, having taken a day off from his religious duties. It surprises me that he performs any duties. He and his picture are always in the English papers, I mean our English papers, but he also gets a lot of space in the papers of England. He is always smiling. He simply has no conception of the danger of the forces he is playing with. If they came to power, that would be the end of him and his church, indeed the end of all churches, the end of freedom of worship. These enemies of ours pick on anything they can find wrong in our country, but they do not say that there is complete freedom of worship, and the Government does not interfere in any way with the churches, or the synagogues and the mosques and the temples. Our President Kruger was held in great respect by the Jews of the Transvaal. You will remember the story of how he was invited to open the synagogue in Pretoria. He made a little speech and then he declared the synagogue open 'in the name of our Lord Jesus Christ, Amen'. But they didn't hold it against him.

The Congress of the People adopted a Freedom Charter, full of high-sounding clauses about freedom and equality, attacking apartheid and the doctrines of separate coexistence, and of course strongly anti-Government and anti-Afrikaner. The Charter has been thoroughly investigated, not only by our legal people, but by our greatest experts on Marxism and communism. One section of it, the one on the country's wealth, is pure communism, and would make South Africa a kind of Soviet republic. Another section of it, the one on the law and restriction of liberty, advocates freedoms that don't exist in any Soviet republic. Mines, banks, and industry are going to be nationalised in one section, but in another section people are going to be allowed to trade and work where they choose. The whole Charter was obviously written by white hands, and was designed to meet the demands of the communist left wings of all the congresses as well as the demands of what could be called the democratic right. In any event, the Congress of the People swallowed it whole.

I can tell you in confidence that our experts, Dr. Andrew Munnik of the University of Cape Town, Dr. Willem van Amstel of the University of Pretoria, and Dr. Koot Wollheim of the Nederduits Gereformeerde Kerk, are unanimous in their belief that the Freedom Charter has a deeper and more sinister meaning than that which appears on the surface. These three men are probably three of the greatest experts in the world on communism, and indeed it makes one proud to be an Afrikaner. It seems to me as if it requires a true Afrikaner son to understand the deepest meanings of Marxism–Leninism–Communism, to strip away the façade of the liberation of the masses, and to expose the hidden menace to true freedom and true religion.

The view of these three men — and don't forget I am telling you this in confidence because their opinion may have momentous consequences and lead to momentous steps that must be prepared in absolute secrecy — is that the Freedom Charter is in fact a treasonable document. Their argument is that the changes proposed are so far-reaching that they would be realised only by revolution and that therefore those who took part in the Congress of the People are co-conspirators in a gigantic plan to overthrow the State.

My Minister is giving their opinion the very deepest consideration, for if their views are accepted by the Government then all those who took part in the Congress have exposed themselves to the gravest penalties, even that of death, for the offence of high treason. The mechanics of the matter are not easy. One cannot arrest and charge three thousand people. It will require time and thorough investigation to determine what persons were actually behind the whole business, and what persons actually prepared the Charter, for it is ridiculous to suppose that such a document was composed on the spot from the alleged thousands of proposals received from branches of the different congresses in various parts of the country. I doubt for example whether Huddleston would be a candidate for arrest. He is a vain and silly man, with a liking for the limelight, but he has no conception of the evil forces that are using him.

One notes that the Liberal Party, and particularly your Newcastle friend Mr. Robert Mansfield, had the sense to stay away from the Congress. I know you had a high opinion of him until he started to challenge the laws and customs of the country. It was a stupid thing to do in Newcastle. But it was even more stupid for him to resign his headmastership when he was likely to have been the next Director of Education. It is tragic to realise that he represented South Africa in cricket, and can wear the Springbok blazer.

Talking of cricket and football — did you read that our enemies have launched a new organisation, ESAWS, which means Expel South Africa from World Sport? I don't think it will do much damage to us, but one can never be sure. ESAWS was launched in London, and soon after that in Stockholm, Oslo, Copenhagen, Amsterdam, Toronto and New York. So the whole thing was planned. It is a pity to see Britain and Canada mixed up in it, and it only confirms my view that the sooner we get out of the Commonwealth the better. ESAWS is largely run by exiles from South Africa, who have left to escape the 'unjust laws', but the Security Police are keeping a close eye on a certain Mr. John Parker of Johannesburg, who is said to be their South African agent. It is difficult to understand how a born South African can so turn against his own country, but the difficulty is lessened when one learns that he is a member of your friend Mr. Mansfield's dangerous Liberal Party. Sorry if I appear to be a little acrimonious, but I get decidedly edgy when I smell the whiff of treason.

I have heard some good news, Well, it is not really news, it is only a rumour. I have heard that Dr. Hendrik is trying to get my Minister to agree to the transfer of Dr. Fischer to his department. I sincerely hope he succeeds. Dr. Hendrik has told my Minister that Fischer is much more than a lawyer. He is a prophet and an apostle and should be used as such. I must confess to you that working under him is a burden to me. My only consolation is to observe signs — not big signs, but I know my Minister well — that he and Dr. Fischer are not as friendly as they used to be. This does not surprise me, for my Minister is a warm man. I am sending you a cutting

that may interest you. It comes from the *Ohrigstad Dagblad*.
Don't forget to look out for the momentous steps at which I
hinted. If they are taken it will be a deathblow to Moscow.

OHRIGSTAD'S MOST FAMOUS SON

Respected Editor
   I visited Pretoria last week and I thought your readers
would like to know that I went to the Groot Gedenksaal to
hear Ohrigstad's most famous son, Dr. Jan Woltemade
Fischer, B.A., B.Ed., LL.B., Ph.D. The occasion was the
celebration of Oom Paul's birthday, and the hall was full to
overflowing. It was one of the most wonderful speeches that
I have ever heard. I have listened to General Hertzog, Dr.
Malan, Mr. Strijdom and Dr. Hendrik, probably the four
greatest speakers in the history of Afrikanerdom, and Dr.
Fischer will in due course join their ranks.
   There is nothing in Ohrigstad to show that Jan Woltemade
Fischer is one of our sons. Why do we not name a street after
him? I suggest that Jan Smuts Street should be renamed Jan
Fischer Street. What do your readers think?
      Yours faithfully
      Barend Hertzog van Rensburg

Mr. Robert Mansfield
Natal Chairman
The Liberal Party

Have you thought of getting Chinks and Japs to join your
party? I can see them from my window, these dago sailors
from the East, with their white and black dollies. The dollies
go down every night to the ships. The black ones take my
breath away. Everyone knows what they are and where they
are going and what they are going to do. You know too, eh,
with your knowledge of the poker game?
   The black dollies are not supposed to get into the ships, but
they do it all right. They go down to the crew's quarters,

they open up their . . . ugh, it's disgusting, it makes me ashamed to be a woman.

Why don't you get these Chinks and these Japs and their white and black dollies to join your filthy International Club? Everyone knows what goes on at your club. Isn't it wonderful to get all the men and women of the world together, so that they can paw one another in your private rooms, and spawn their mongrel babies all over the place, except they're too clever, eh? The police found a Portugoose and a black dolly in your reading-room, they weren't reading, ha! ha!, because the lights were off, and all their clothes too. One day God will strike you down, that's for sure.

I read in the paper about your meeting at Port Shepstone. So you've got a teenage daughter, eh? Is she safe from you? If I were your wife I'd keep my eye on you, but I bet she's too busy with black lover boys.

Do you wonder sometimes who I am? I'll bet you do, and I can read your filthy thoughts. Well, you'll never know. My mother warned us against all men, especially those of the black nation. But don't be disappointed, you'll hear from me again. I'll keep in touch.

I sign myself like I did before
Proud White Christian Woman

Mr. Robert Mansfield
Natal Regional Office
The Liberal Party

You will no doubt have observed that you have not so far been eliminated. Your observation is correct. We have decided that this would be too easy for you, and that you should pay materially for the treachery of yourself and your party. In fact you have already paid the first instalment.

You must look after your new engine very carefully. A few locks here and there are not much protection. But of course we will not necessarily confine our attention to your car. You have a son and a daughter, have you not, not to mention a wife who no doubt values the good looks which she has at the moment? Are you going to lock them all up too?

We sign ourselves

The Preservation of White South Africa League

. . . Yes, my dearest aunt, the Government has at last been able to change the Cape coloured franchise. I wrote to you, last year I think, to say that the Prime Minister was going to enlarge the Appellate Court so that the Government would be able to expect a more enlightened attitude towards its constitutional legislation. Well, he did this, but he still was unable to get a two-thirds majority of both Houses sitting together, which he required to alter the Cape franchise.

He has now made sure of his two-thirds majority, by enlarging the Senate in such a way that it will be overwhelmingly pro-Government. The achievement is magnificent, and was the work of the finest legal brains in the Public Service.

The Prime Minister was not able to increase his majority in the Lower House by any honourable method. The number of seats he holds is decided at every general election and, if he had called a general election, he might have gained more seats, but not enough to secure the two-thirds majority.

Therefore it was decided to reform the Senate. Up till now the four provinces have each elected one-quarter of the elected senators, but now they each elect a number of senators proportionate to their number of members in Parliament. That in itself increases the number of pro-Government senators.

The next step was to increase the Senate from forty-eight members to eighty-nine. That again increased the majority.

The third step was the most brilliant of all. Up till now, if a province had twenty National Party M.P.s and ten United Party M.P.s, the National Party would get two-thirds of the senators and the United Party one-third. But now the candidates are put up individually and voted upon, and therefore in this case every National Party candidate would be elected by twenty votes to ten.

This meant that there would be seventy-seven National Party senators for the Cape, Transvaal, and the Orange Free State, out of a total of eighty-nine. The Prime Minister thus secured his two-thirds majority, and Parliament, on 27 February 1956, by one hundred and seventy-four votes to sixty-eight removed the coloured voters to a separate roll and gave them four separate constituencies, which must return white members of Parliament to the Lower House.

As the Prime Minister explained, there was no diminution of rights, quite the contrary, for, whereas coloured voters previously constituted a fraction of each constituency, now they have four constituencies of their own and are therefore directly represented in Parliament. They were previously used as pawns in the game between the two big parties, but now the Government has saved them from any further humiliation of this nature. White South Africa also derives benefit from the amendment, which goes part of the way to make reparation to the two defeated republics of the Transvaal and the Orange Free State, who were forced to enter a Union in which their sacred principle of 'no equality in Church or State' was allowed to be flouted over a large part of the country.

Of course the liberals and the leftists are howling. The biggest squealers are the women of the Black Sash. They wear a black sash over their white dresses to show that they are mourning the death of the constitution. They stand on street corners to protest against this and that, and hold vigils in churches and at monuments. Whenever a Minister opens a bridge or a roadway, or visits an institution, they parade near the site of the occasion. They do not speak, but carry signs and placards. It is interesting to note the reactions of the Ministers. The Prime Minister tries to take no notice of them, but you can see that he is trying. Minister Louw takes off his hat and bows to them. My own Minister, while trying to avoid them at Westville near Durban, took another route and got into deep mud and had to be rescued. Minister Hendrik does not like them at all; he thinks they are impertinent to picket a Minister of State on a public occasion, and his irritation shows plainly. I do not blame him. It is irritating to see these women standing in the amphitheatre of the Union Buildings. These majestic buildings have become almost sacred to me. I started my career there, and was there till I went to the Palace of Justice.

In any case it is not in the Afrikaner tradition for women to demonstrate in public places. My dear mother — your dear sister — would never have done such a thing. She was a power in our home, but we always regarded my father as the head of the house. It pains me to see the wife of the leading surgeon in Pretoria standing holding a placard outside the Union Buildings. Even though she is English-speaking, I am ashamed to see her standing there, with apparently no conception of the way in which she and her friends are lowering the status of womanhood. The real beauty and dignity of womanhood has been captured for ever in the Vrouemonument at Bloemfontein, where Anton von Wouw immortalised in stone the story of the death of the twenty-eight thousand women and children in the concentration camps of the War of Freedom. Those British sins may be forgiven, but they must never be forgotten.

Dr. Hendrik goes from strength to strength. He gives to me not only a feeling of pride that I am an Afrikaner but a feeling of total security for the future. He predicts that in twenty years, that is in 1976, the black tide to the cities will turn and will flow back with ever-increasing volume to the homelands, which will by that time have become increasingly attractive to black people, not only because the eroded lands will have been restored, but because white industrialists will have established more and more factories on the borders of these countries.

This idea of border industry must be one of the most creative that has ever been thought of in the history of our country. Black workers will leave their homes in the early morning, cross the border to the factories, earn good wages, and return to their homes in the evening to rejoin their families. The whole idea has a kind of beauty about it because of its very simplicity. It must surely come from Dr. Hendrik, who is undoubtedly the greatest intelligence that South Africa has ever produced. Of course one can quibble and say that he was produced in Holland, but it was South Africa that nurtured him. Dr. Hendrik towers over the Cabinet, and I do not want to be disloyal to the Prime Minister, but my feelings of pride and security will be even further strengthened when Dr. Hendrik rules our country.

I believe that under Dr. Hendrik we shall enter a new age. In fact I believe we have already entered it, an age in which all of our nations — and do not forget that we have at least ten of them — will have their own identity, cherish their own customs and culture, preserve their own languages, and enjoy the freedoms which white South Africa enjoys.

In addition to the economic forces which Dr. Hendrik is setting in operation, I believe also that there is a powerful desire on the part of black people who have been drawn willy-nilly into our cities, to return to their homelands. We must not think that black people do not resent the eternal surveillance of the police, the humiliating pass laws, the crowded trains, the crime in the townships. They resent them bitterly and endure them because at the moment it is only in the cities that they can find work.

I must admit that the coloured people pose a problem because they have no land of their own, but I am confident that Dr. Hendrik will solve that also. The Indian people also pose a problem for the same reason, but I do not see why they should not be given the north and south coasts of Natal. The white Natalians will squeal of course, but what have they done for South Africa except to grow a bit of sugar?

The year 1976! I cannot wait for it, my dearest aunt, and I shall probably be alive to see it. For I believe that in that year the world will admit that we were right.

I must confess to you that this letter has been written in a mood of euphoria. This is not entirely because I have such trust in Dr. Hendrik. It is because my own Minister said to me yesterday, 'Van Onselen, I want to tell you that you are my ideal of a public servant. I know that if I ask you to do something, and if I tell you how I want it done, it will be carried out in every detail. I can't say that for everybody.'

I could not help thinking, of course, that perhaps he found Dr. Fischer lacking.

Black man, we are going to shut you off
We are going to set you apart, now and forever.
We mean nothing evil towards you
You shall have your own place, your own institutions.
Your tribal customs shall flourish unhindered
You shall lie all day long in the sun if you wish it
All the things that civilisation has stolen
Shall be restored. You shall take wives
Unhindered by our alien prohibitions
Fat-bellied children shall play innocently
Under the wide-branching trees of the lush country
Where you yourselves were born.
Boys shall go playing in the reed lagoons
Of far Ingwavuma, the old names
Shall recover old magic, milk and honey
Shall flow in the long-forsaken places
We mean nothing evil towards you.

On this morning of this ninth day of August 1956, ten thousand women, most of them African, gathered near the statue of General Louis Botha in the grounds of the Union Buildings, the most majestic building in the whole continent of Africa, if one excepts the monuments of antiquity.

These women gathered to protest against the issuing of passes to African women and against the pass laws themselves. Most of them were members of the Federation of South African Women and the African Congress Women's League. Two of the most prominent were Miss Lilian Ngoyi, chairwoman of the Federation, and Mrs. Helen Joseph, its secretary. Both of these women were also prominent delegates to the recent Congress of the People.

Mrs. Joseph said that today's demonstration was the result of a three-thousand-five-hundred-mile journey through the length and breadth of the country. Asked to what organisation the white women belonged, Mrs. Joseph said they belonged to the white Congress, the Federation, and other organisations.

At least ten thousand women, some claim twenty

thousand, gathered at the Botha monument. It was one of the largest crowds ever to assemble at the Union Buildings, and probably the largest gathering of women in the country's history. Just after noon the women, in ranks of ten, moved in a solid phalanx through the grounds of the Union Buildings, to the great amphitheatre. There they sat down, a vast chattering throng that fell silent immediately their leaders stood to address them. Miss Ngoyi announced that the Prime Minister had refused to meet the deputation, and the crowd gave a great shout of *Mayibuye Afrika!* Miss Ngoyi then announced that a delegation of nine women, including Helen Joseph, would take seven thousand petitions to the Prime Minister's office, asking for the repeal of the pass laws. This announcement was also greeted with shouts of *Mayibuye!* and thousands gave the thumbs-up signal.

Led by Mrs. Helen Joseph, the delegation threaded its way through the densely crowded amphitheatre. They were attended by photographers and movie cameramen. At the entrance door the delegation was told that only white persons might enter. Mrs. Joseph questioned this decision and was told that it had been made by the Head of Police. However, later Mrs. Joseph and four others were allowed to enter and to proceed to the office of the Prime Minister. They knocked repeatedly on the door and were at last admitted, but the Prime Minister was not there, and they had to leave their seven thousand petitions on the floor of his office.

On their return to the amphitheatre the five women were received with shouts of jubilation. The women then stood for thirty minutes in absolute silence. The demonstration ended with the singing of *Nkosi Sikelel' iAfrika.* During the singing the women stood with upraised thumbs, the sign of the militant African Congress, and at the end of the anthem gave three rousing hallelujahs.

A strong force of members of the Security Police, both white and black, mingled with the crowd. There were no incidents, and the women dispersed peacefully.

Helen Joseph? She was born in 1905 in England, and came to

South Africa in 1931 to recuperate after an accident. Although concerned with social questions, she was first moved to political action in 1952 by the Defiance Campaign. She helped to found the white Congress in 1952 and the Federation of South African Women in 1954. She has great gifts of organisation, and has won the deep respect of black women. She is in fact an extraordinary woman, and appears to be fearless. She herself records that she began her political career by taking part in a march to the Johannesburg City Hall and 'was absolutely terrified'.

Helen Joseph? She is not a South African but she presumes to teach us about justice. She is playing with fire, and is going to get burnt. She is regarded by the Security Police as one of the most dangerous agitators in South Africa. If she does not change her course, she will get into big trouble.

Dear Philip

The Chief was delighted to receive the message of goodwill from the party on the occasion of the expiry of his ban. He was behaving just like a schoolboy who has been given an extra holiday. He was laughing most of the time, a great laugh that you could hear all over the house and the garden. People were coming and going, and his wife Nokukhanya was giving them tea. Her name, as you know, means 'a person of light', and that is what she is.

It is a solemn thought that this joy and exuberance and downright gaiety is the gift of the Government. It is also a solemn thought that the effect of a ban is so powerful. The Chief has found the isolation, the absence of communication, the ban on all gatherings, very painful to bear. Now that the ban has expired, he has opened out like a great flower, a giant sunflower I would say. He radiates light and joy to all around him. I have never seen anything like it. Of course in another way the ban is powerless. Its influence on the Chief's beliefs and aspirations and courage is exactly zero.

He and Z. K. Matthews are in striking contrast to each

other, the one exuberant and spell-binding, the other massively self-contained. Lutuli is the fire, and Z.K. the brains. The comparison is not perfect, but they remind me of Botha and Smuts. Botha was a true man of the people, and commanded the affection and respect of his soldiers, whereas Smuts after a day's march withdrew from them with Kant and the Greek Testament. After Botha's death Smuts called him the 'cleanest, sweetest, soul of all my days'. Matthews could well say that of Lutuli.

Lutuli is waiting for Conco and Yengwa to emerge from their bans and then they and Nokukhanya and Mrs. Conco plan to take a holiday trip to Swaziland. His eagerness has a kind of innocence about it, and his joy is infectious. I did not know he was a poet, but he told me that he could not wait to have 'a shake in the air of freedom'. I have never heard that phrase before. At first I thought it described the shake given by a horse setting off on a journey after a long spell in the stables, but the Chief says he is no horseman. He gave his great laugh and said to me, 'Robert, I am too heavy for a horse.' I think he has forgiven us about the Congress.

Yes, I am worried about the car. How can one stop an ill-wisher from forcing open the bonnet? He did just that, and poured oil into the brake fluid. That is fatal, or rather it could be fatal, for if after the oil had done its work I had been faced with an emergency and jammed on the brakes I would have got no response at all. Luckily for me I put on the brakes on a level piece of road to give a chap a lift, and the results were not fatal, though it was an unnerving experience. I was much more worried about Naomi and the children. I have had to tell them of course, and have had to ask them to be on the alert for any unusual situation. They took it well.

I had a good meeting in Underberg, and they all sent their good wishes to you. How you with your offhand bantering manner win the confidence of people is a mystery to me, but you do. Their situation is distressing. Most, if not all of them, were given their land by the British government after the battle of Isandlwana, because they remained 'loyal'. That is more than seventy years ago. The land was good, and they were able to keep some cattle and to grow mealies and pumpkins and a few fruit trees. But the Government is determined to wipe out every such place. The people are likely to be resettled in the Impendle district, parts of which consist of rocks and shale and kranses. Emmanuel was there of course, and manages to radiate confidence and courage in what seems a hopeless situation. He is an incredible fellow.

See you Tuesday.

    Yours
      Robert

In June 1940, when the Allied fortunes were low, a peace procession of white women, most of them wearing Voortrekker dress, marched from Church Square to the Union Buildings to present a petition bearing signatures to the Prime Minister, urging the withdrawal of South Africa from participation in the war. Smuts passed the job of receiving them on to Hofmeyr, who performed the task gallantly, offered them refreshments, and was thanked by them for the excellent police arrangements. With the Prime Minister's permission the women held a religious service in the grounds of the buildings.

. . . You are quite right to correct me, my dearest aunt. I should certainly have remembered the procession because I saw it myself. I told you how my own present Minister got stuck in the mud at Westville trying to avoid the Black Sash, but Smuts was no less anxious to avoid the Voortrekker women, and he passed the job over to Hofmeyr, who, though he never got married, because of his mother of course, could handle women with the greatest charm and courtesy. There was one difference between Hofmeyr and myself. If it hadn't been for his mother, he would certainly have got married, whereas I would have not. There was one difference between our mothers too. They both possessed their sons, but Mrs. Hofmeyr ruled hers and mine did not. People used to tell the story of how Hofmeyr, when he was Administrator of the Transvaal, hurt himself on the tennis court, and was rushed off by his mother to a nearby chemist's shop; and when he jumped at the iodine, she called out, 'Jantjie, don't jump like that. How can the lady help you if you jump like that?' And Jantjie replied, 'But it hurts, ma, it hurts.' My mother would certainly never have said that to me, and I would certainly never have said that to her.

In any event the women's demonstration at the Union Buildings passed off in the most dignified way. I still would not compare them with the Black Sash. They did not carry placards, and they did not attempt to picket the Prime Minister. They behaved indeed as you might expect Afrikaner women to behave.

My Minister is in a very bad mood. He is now quite satisfied with the Appellate Court as it has been reconstituted, and reckons it can now be relied upon to give reliable and impartial judgments. But Mr. Justice Olivier is to him like a red rag to a bull. A representative of the Opposition appealed against the Senate Act, and asked the court to declare it invalid, but only one judge supported the appeal and that was of course Judge Olivier. He said that although Parliament had acted within its powers by enlarging and reconstructing the Senate, the motive was not to have a better Senate but to amend the Cape franchise and to remove coloured voters to a separate roll. He therefore presented a minority opinion, but the court voted ten to one to reject the appeal.

I remember writing to you that I would sometimes play a little game with the Minister and mention the judge's name quite innocently, just to watch the Minister's reaction. Well, I don't play it any more. His hatred of the judge has become almost pathological, and he would be extremely angry with me.

My own legal knowledge is now getting a bit rusty, but I was taught by the late Professor Streicher that of course Parliament had motives and the question was not whether you liked the motive but whether Parliament acted constitutionally in passing the legislation. It is the Appellate Court that has kept on telling Parliament that it cannot amend the Cape franchise without a two-thirds majority, and now that

the Government has obtained the two-thirds majority, Judge
Olivier wants to tell Parliament that the motive is bad and
therefore the law is invalid.

I once prophesied to you that Judge Olivier would never
become the Chief Justice. It seems now more certain than
ever.

I can tell you in the strictest confidence, my dear aunt, that
you will hear and read of the heroic steps that will shortly be
taken to crush for ever the forces which oppose and try to
obstruct the Great Plan for the creation of a society of
separate and peaceful coexistence.

The trip to Swaziland was a great success. The joy of being
able to move again through the country went to their heads.
They laughed incessantly, the Chief loudest of all. They
called in at Nongoma to pay their respects to the King and
the Royal House.

Not long after that they entered the white farming country
with mile upon mile of mealies, running in their measured
lines across the countryside, and lush orchards of pawpaws,
oranges, bananas, avocados. Here they fell silent, awed by
the richness and beauty of man's achievement, and dumb
with the realisation that there was not one black farm in the
whole expanse of South Africa that looked anything like this.
Into their minds, certainly into the minds of the three men,
came the memory, though it was only the Chief who actually
remembered it, of the Natives Land Act of 1913 that took
away from the African people the right to buy land outside
their own pitiful Reserves, where only by one chance in a
thousand or one in ten thousand could people buy any land at
all, because it was held, by immutable custom, in community. So this richness and this beauty of man's achievement
was the white man's achievement, because no black man had
the land on which to achieve them.

Lutuli and his party would have liked to say, 'Ah, but the
land is beautiful', but the words would not come out of their
mouths because it was the land that was taken from them.
'By right of conquest' — those are the words, but they can be

used only by the conqueror. The Chief's mind went back ten years, to 1946, the year that he was elected to the Natives' Representative Council, the council that was the white man's reparation for the taking away of the common-roll vote in 1936, the council that Mosaka called the toy telephone. The Acting Prime Minister, the Right Honourable J. H. Hofmeyr, came to open the seventh session of the Council and made them a speech which was meant to be friendly and conciliatory. Dr. James Moroka, seconding the vote of thanks, said to Hofmeyr, 'In your speech you say that we must love our land . . . We love it and we shall always do so. We only hope it will be made possible by the rulers of this country that we may have some land to love.'

And when they did find some land to love, as Emmanuel Nene's father did at Ethembeni, and in all the other black-spots, then laws were passed to take it away. These sombre thoughts intruded on the shake in the air of freedom, and in a way they were glad to enter the country of Swaziland, where everything was less rich and less alien, and where the Swazis spoke a language that is as close to Zulu as any language could be. Here in Swaziland a great honour was shown to the Chief, when the King paid the party a courtesy call.

Then they returned to their own country, and as they crossed the border they experienced what all such travellers feel, a sudden tension within themselves, a premonition, no, rather a certitude, of trials ahead, which would call for a stiffening of the will, and a strengthening of the determination to die for the cause of freedom if that should be asked of them. They still had their legal freedom, not quite the same as the freedom of Swaziland. But even that did not last, for on the morning of the fifth of December, the police came to the Chief's home in Groutville and arrested him on a charge of high treason.

One of the policemen greeted him with the words, 'Yes, the day has come.'

. . . The great step of which I hinted to you has been taken. No fewer than 156 people have been arrested on charges of high treason. They include ex-Chief Lutuli, Professor Z. K. Matthews and Dr. Naicker of the Indian Congress, all of whom have repeatedly flaunted their disloyalty to the lawfully constituted authority. It is indeed lamentable that there are white people among them, including Mrs. Helen Joseph who led the impertinent march to the Union Buildings last August.

This step has been taken only after my Minister was satisfied that the chances of a successful prosecution were good. It is possible that the Department will build a new security prison to house those found guilty. It is expected that there will be at least a hundred, and it would be undesirable to place them with other prisoners. It is unlikely that the death penalty will be imposed; it is more likely that the guilty will receive life sentences. In any case it is fairly well known in responsible circles that neither the Prime Minister nor my Minister wants the death penalty. The hostility of the United Nations, and of the outside world in general, is bad enough already, but it would be immeasurably increased if the death penalty were imposed.

The real test that faces the State is that of proving that the 156 accused were co-conspirators in a plot to overthrow the State by violence. The evidence that will be led will be unique, for it will be the evidence of philosophers, political scientists, and scholars rather than that of policemen. As I wrote to you before, Dr. Andrew Munnik, Dr. Willem van Amstel, and Dr. Koot Wollheim are probably the greatest experts in the world on communism. Dr. Munnik's works in particular are said to be so profound that the number of people who understand them is small.

Now I am a lawyer, not a philosopher, but I am going to try to explain the argument to you. You know that the science of identifying handwriting is highly advanced. You can say that the chances are ninety-nine out of a hundred that this particular piece of writing was done by this particular person, even if that person has changed from right hand to left or has tied a handkerchief round his writing hand, or is not looking at the paper at all but into a mirror. The characteristics of a particular piece of handwriting are like fingerprints; they belong to this person and to no one else.

Now this is also true of thinking, and particularly of ideological thinking. You can try to disguise your ideology, as indeed people tried to do in the Freedom Charter, but the profound expert will identify the Marxist elements and will prove that they come from Marx or are inspired by Marx. You can be a Marxist and you can try to speak or write as a Christian, but you will not be able to disguise the ideology. And this is the task of the prosecution, to examine the writings and speeches of all these 156 people, and to identify the ideology common to them all, and to prove that it is communist and could be nothing else.

Take for example these clauses from the Freedom Charter:

Every man and woman shall have the right to vote for and to stand as a candidate for all bodies which make laws;
All people shall be entitled to take part in the administration of the country;
The rights of the people shall be the same, regardless of race, colour or sex.

Now these demands are in direct contradiction to the policies of separate coexistence. We do not have *one* country, we have many countries. We do not believe, to use the jargon of the day, in a common society. There is no way in which a common society could be realised, except by the violent overthrow of the lawfully constituted authority, and this could be done only by revolution, and such a revolution could succeed only with the help of hostile forces from outside.

This is the task which confronts the State, to prove that this is true, to prove that these 156 people, or most of them, *knew* that they could achieve the common society only by revolution, and that therefore, when they continued to demand a common society, they accepted the necessity of revolution.

My dearest aunt, I must admit that these ideas trouble me. As I said, I do not pretend to be a philosopher. I do not really like living with ideas, I much prefer facts. I am writing to you in the strictest confidence, and in the confidence also that what I write to you is for you, and you alone, as indeed I would once have written to my mother. There are times when the problems of our country seem insoluble. I felt this strongly on the day that Mrs. Helen Joseph and her ten thousand women came to the Union Buildings. On that day I happened to be at the Union Buildings on the Minister's business. These women had no power whatsoever, they had no guns, they had no votes, they had no members of Parliament, nothing. Yet they had a strange kind of other power. They marched in that solid column from the Louis Botha statue up to the very amphitheatre. There they sat down and were addressed by one of their number, a Mrs. Ngoyi, I believe. Well, I have never heard a woman speak like that, although I could not understand everything. I have heard Mrs. Smuts and Mrs. Malan, and Mrs. Leila Reitz when she was in Parliament, and Mrs. Ballinger too of course, but not one of them could speak with her fire. There she was, standing up in the amphitheatre of the Union Buildings, and you would have thought that the buildings belonged to her. She told the crowd that the Prime Minister had refused to meet their deputation, and they gave what sounded like a shout of jubilation. They called out their slogan, *Mayibuye Afrika!* which means something like 'Give us back Africa'. Why the Prime Minister's refusal should make people jubilant is beyond my understanding, but worse than that, it gives me this feeling of unease. Then this Mrs. Ngoyi said that Mrs. Joseph and others would now present the petitions, and again they shouted *Mayibuye!* Eventually they had to leave the petitions on the floor of the P.M.'s office, and you may be sure that by evening they would be in the incinerator, yet when the women returned to the amphitheatre they were greeted by triumphant shouts as though they had achieved something great. Then all the women sang the Bantu anthem, *Nkosi Sikelel' iAfrika*, which I must admit is very beautiful. And to crown it all, they shouted, *Hallelujah! Hallelujah! Hallelujah!* As you know, this means 'Praise the Lord!' but what they were praising the Lord for, it would be hard to know.

Then they all dispersed in a very peaceable fashion,

obviously pleased with the day's work. Yet what had they done? Whatever it was, they were pleased with it.

I observed my fellow public servants while they watched the demonstration. Some of them were openly contemptuous, some thought the whole thing was very funny. I didn't see anyone looking angry, but it is in fact characteristic of public servants that, if the Prime Minister and the Head of the Police allow a demonstration to proceed, then it is not their place to get angry about it. There were some who watched it all without smiles or contempt, quite soberly in fact, as though they wondered how real it was, and what kind of strength lay behind it all. I found myself remembering Roy Campbell's 'Zulu Girl', where the girl is feeding her child by the pool.

> Yet in that drowsy stream his flesh imbibes
> An old unquenched unsmotherable heat —
> The curbed ferocity of beaten tribes,
> The sullen dignity of their defeat.

We learned it at school, and the words came back to me while we were watching the demonstration. There was dignity all right, but it wasn't sullen. In fact it was determined and confident. One had the feeling that it would show itself again, that in fact it would go on showing itself, until, well — yes, well — until it triumphed. That's a gloomy thought, isn't it? You see my feeling of euphoria has gone. Dr. Fischer is back in the Minister's good books, perhaps because the university has announced that he will receive an honorary doctorate of Laws at the next graduation, for services to the cause of justice, or words like that.

I shall feel neither happy nor safe, my dear aunt, until Dr. Hendrik is the head of the Government. I expect him to lead us, and especially Afrikanerdom, into a new world.

PART FOUR

Death of a Traitor

– Hugh.

– Yes, Mrs. M. K.

– I don't want to pry into your private affairs, but this particular affair is ours too. You know what I'm talking about, don't you?

– Yes.

– Well, what is the relationship between you and Prem? Are you in love with each other?

– We are, Mrs. M. K., and we are not. What I mean is, I love Prem and she loves me. But if we'd wanted to get married, we'd have had to go to some other country, and what is more, we'd have had to stay there. We thought it over very seriously. Then decided we ought to stay here, and that meant we couldn't be in love.

– So you just decided not to be in love?

– Yes.

– Well, it's extraordinary. It seems almost supernatural. But then I sometimes think my daughter is supernatural.

– There's another side to it, Mrs. M. K. Supposing we went to England, would we do anything? Wouldn't we always be thinking that we had gone there for our own private reasons?

– You and Prem are far too serious for your ages. I was never so serious. But I was one of a large family, and you can't be so serious in a large family. Prem is an only child, and she has grown up very serious. You mustn't think I worry about you and Prem. I brought her up to know what is right, and I trust her to lead her own life. That's why we never interfered with her when she took part in the Defiance Campaign. Her father used to get up in the night and walk about the house, but he didn't try to stop her. Tell me, do your parents know?

– If my father knew, Mrs. M. K., I just don't know what he would do. He was ashamed to walk around in Pietermaritzburg when I went off to join Patrick Duncan. But if he had heard that I was in love with an Indian girl, I just don't know what would have happened.

– Hugh, you're a Christian, aren't you? I mean you take it seriously?

— That's a hard question, Mrs. M. K., but, yes, I do.

— And you might become a priest?

— Yes.

— Then what about Prem's religion?

— It's difficult, Mrs. M. K. . . .

— You mean it's difficult to tell me that if you could have married, she would have become a Christian. Well, it wouldn't shock me. I don't think her father would have liked it, and of course some Hindu parents would be horrified. Some Indians would have thought Prem was a traitor, and they would have said, Look what the Christians have done to us, look at the Group Areas Act. You know, if Prem had a saint, it was Francis of Assisi, not Mahavira or one of our other saints. You know the great Mr. Ahmed Bhoola, he is the director of FOSA, that's the Friends of the Sick Association, he has given his life to the service of the sick and thinks he is a kind of Mahatma. He's an educated man but he had never heard of Francis of Assisi till Prem mentioned his name. He said to her, 'Prem, let me give you some good Hindu advice: if you ever become a Christian, you must keep your eyes on Christ so that you will not get a chance to look at Christians.' Well, what are you going to do? Are you going to stop seeing each other? If you go on seeing each other, you will be preventing Prem from ever getting married and she will be preventing you.

— Mrs. M. K., I shall never marry anyone but Prem.

— How do you know that?

— I just know it.

— And Prem?

— You must ask her, Mrs. M. K.

— I suppose she just knows it too.

— That is what she says.

— Well, it's supernatural. And if it's not supernatural, it's unnatural. It's not the way young people should be. And I can tell you, Hugh, lots of older people couldn't be that way either. And when do you think they will let you marry? When your party comes to power, I suppose, and that means never. Or are you going to convert the Afrikaners? If you converted them ten a day for the next ten years, you

wouldn't be any nearer to marrying Prem. It's no use looking
so gloomy, Hugh. You and Prem have made up your minds
and I don't think you'll change them. The Afrikaners think
the Group Areas Act is sacred, but the Mixed Marriages Act
is as holy as God. You know the Padayachee boy. He went to
study in Canada and married a Canadian girl, and when he
brought her home to meet his parents, they had to sleep in
separate rooms. And I'm telling you, the parents were
terrified when they even touched each other. Mrs.
Padayachee couldn't sleep at nights because she was afraid the
police would burst in at any moment, and go through the
bedrooms feeling the sheets and looking for Canadian hairs
on young Padayachee's pillow. That's the kind of madness it
is.

  – I'm sorry I brought all this trouble on you, Mrs. M. K.

  – You needn't be sorry. Just suppose that Prem had fallen
in love with one of these young men whose lives are ruled by
hate. I won't stop praying for happiness for you both.

. . . My Minister is very angry about the Treason Trial
Defence Fund, and rightly so. No sooner has he taken the
grave step of arresting 156 people for high treason than all the
liberals and do-gooders in the country rush to their defence.
The Minister is determined to root out the communists once
and for all, but meantime the liberals, whom the communists
would kill tomorrow, rush round collecting money to
defend them. To me it is incomprehensible, but to the
Minister it is infuriating. He regards the setting up of a
defence fund as treasonable in itself. He would have liked to
ban the fund and some of its sponsors on the very day after its
launching, and he had the support of Dr. Fischer, but the
Prime Minister was against it. However, he has given
instructions to the Security Police to watch closely the
comings and goings of anyone connected with the fund.

  And what a bunch they are! Bishop Reeves of Johannesburg of course, but one would expect it of him. The
Reverend J. B. Webb, the great Methodist teacher of morality to us poor Afrikaners. It was a shock, however, when the

Most Reverend Geoffrey Clayton, the Anglican Archbishop, accepted the presidency of the fund in Cape Town. You may remember that he opposed the Bantu Education Act, but we did not expect him to go as far as this. One must add another big churchman to the list, and that is the notorious Canon Collins of St. Paul's Cathedral in London, who is one of the most poisonous Afrikaner-haters in the world. He raises tremendous amounts of money to defend political prisoners and wastes the precious time of our higher courts.

And then of course the members of the Liberal Party, Robert Mansfield the Springbok cricketer, Mrs. Carmichael, the wife of our leading surgeon in Pretoria (she is one of the Black Sash women who come to the Union Buildings to picket the Ministers), Donald Molteno, who ought to know a good deal better, Philip Drummond of the Natal aristocracy. In fact they are all what they call in England upper middle-class, and they do the impossible, and the ridiculous too; they hobnob with black labourers and have them to tea. It is now not the proper thing to give them tea in special cups, but to use the same for all. The famous Springbok cricketer has just condemned the South African Railways for using separate crockery and cutlery, and he is not an Englishman, he was born and bred in Natal, though I suppose that is much the same thing. The Liberal Party is edging towards the left. It started off with a suffrage for all who had passed Standard Six, but now advocates a universal adult suffrage. Our reports say that it is people like Patrick Duncan, the new national organiser of the party, who are pushing it to the left, and this is quite incomprehensible because he is violently anti-communist, just as extreme as some of our own people who find, as the English say, a Red under every bed. We know that he and Molteno have an antipathy for each other, and that sooner or later one of them will push the other out. We are watching the party very closely. It seemed to be coming to its senses when it refused to attend the Congress of the People, but now it has thrown all its gains away by being so active in the treason fund. Its members use the stupid parrot cry that a man is innocent until he's proved guilty.

I must tell you that I am coming round to Dr. Hendrik's

point of view about mixed worship. When I look at people
like the Bishop of Johannesburg, the Archbishop of Cape
Town, the Reverend J. B. Webb, and Father Huddleston, I
think it is desirable to keep them away from our Bantu
people. Our Bantu have a great respect for law and authority,
but when they hear people like Bishop Reeves and Huddleston condemning the Government and the separation laws,
they are bound to lose it. Neither Reeves nor Huddleston can
speak a word of Afrikaans, but they think they can teach
Afrikaners to run their country. When you think they have
been here only a few years, and that we have been here for
three centuries, their actions cannot be regarded as anything
less than impudent.

The Archbishop also cannot speak a word of Afrikaans. He
was educated at Rugby and Cambridge and, however
famous these may be in England, they cannot possibly
provide an education which would fit a person to make lofty
pronouncements on South African affairs. He holds the
erroneous idea that if you are a Christian you can pass moral
judgements anywhere and everywhere in the world. He has
no conception of the meaning of Christian–Nationalism, a
philosophy which helps one to set one's Christianity firmly
in the context where one was born and where one lives. *Die
Kerkbode* put it well. It wrote: 'Educated in England, unac-
quainted with the history, language and ideals of our nation,
and totally lacking in feeling for the circumstances of our
country, these men give themselves the right to say precisely
who and *what* we are. How can they criticise us without even
knowing us?' *Die Transvaler* put it even better: 'As long as
liberalistic bishops and canons, professors, students and
politicians can freely attend church and hold meetings and
socials together with non-whites, apartheid will be infringed
in its marrow. It is high time for this to end.'

Now Dr. Hendrik is absolutely determined to stop the
abuses of mixed worship. He has submitted a Native Laws
Amendment Bill to Parliament, and one of the clauses, 29(c),
provides that no church in a white area will be able to admit
Africans to worship without the permission of the Minister
of Native Affairs, given with the concurrence of the local

authority. This will apply not only to worship but to any meeting held on church premises. It will apply also to schools, hospitals, and clubs in all areas zoned for white occupation under the Group Areas Act.

There is a block of flats next to mine, and one at least of the flats is occupied by liberalists, probably members of the Liberal Party, or perhaps even leftists belonging to the white Congress. They have black guests, and almost certainly break the law by supplying them with liquor. There would be much less resentment in the neighbourhood if the parties were quiet, but they are not. The worst noise is when the party breaks up, and they congregate on the pavement, laughing and shouting and slapping each other on the back, and calling one another Fred and Lucy and Thembi and Lancelot. The white men kiss the black women quite brazenly, and vice versa. You can understand how a white citizen of our city reacts to this provocation, because that is what it is. And no one reacts to it more strongly than Dr. Hendrik. It is lucky for him that he does not have to live in flatland.

It is of course a tricky thing to control visitors to private dwellings, and these dwellings are not affected by the clause, but you may be sure that Dr. Hendrik will not rest until some control is achieved. He has already taken steps in flatland to control 'locations in the sky', which is what we call the concrete roofs of the flats where the servants are quartered, and where the noise and the immorality are unbelievable. That is why there is a move to have our cities 'white by night', as they say in English. You can imagine how intolerable it is for a dweller in one of these very tall flat buildings to have to look down on to the roof of a lower block of flats.

So you will see why I have decided, after much struggle, my dear aunt, to back Dr. Hendrik's move to stop mixed worship. This is another of those cases where neither alternative is perfect, and one has to choose the one that seems less imperfect.

PS. I must learn not to use the term 'political prisoner'. I used it the other day to the Minister, and it made him very angry, which I can assure you is not pleasant. He says such people may be political persons, but they are being charged with criminal offences. Treason is not a political offence, it is a criminal offence of the gravest kind.

Mr. Robert Mansfield
Natal Chairman
Liberal Party

So you don't like separate cups and saucers on the railways, eh? You want us all to drink from the same cups, eh? The day that happens I want to be dead.

I suppose you all use the same cups at the International Club, don't you? It's to be expected from you. Anyone who can suck — ugh, you disgust me with your thoughts.

I suppose you've been wondering who I can be. I can guess your filthy thoughts. Wouldn't you like my phone number? I suppose you think it'd be a change from the black dollies and their — ugh, I wouldn't be touched by a shit like you.

How is your reading-room at the club, ha! ha! Have they caught any more Portugooses in the act of reading with the lights off, ha! ha!

I'm watching your career of corrupting our kids. You'll hear again.

I sign myself
        Proud White Christian Woman

His Grace The Archbishop
Bishopscourt
Cape Town

Your Grace

My mother brought up her children to have great respect for bishops and of course greatest of all for an archbishop. So don't think it is easy for me to write to you.

I am a white Anglican woman but I am thinking of leaving the Anglican Church and joining one which has more Christian views about mixing with blacks.

This mixing is not natural. Have you forgotten the story of Zimri who brought a Midianitish woman into his tent? When Phinehas, the grandson of Aaron, saw this, he took a javelin and went into the tent and thrust the man through his back and the woman through her belly. There was only one thrust, not two. You understand what was going on, don't you?

I support Dr. Hendrik in his plan to stop blacks going to white churches. Don't they have churches of their own? But you like it, don't you? I know you have condemned the Mixed Marriages Act. I suppose you condemn the Immorality Act too. Then you can't blame people if they think certain things.

You will lose lots of members of the Anglican Church, especially those who won't drink the wine from a chalice that's touched the lips of the black nation.

I have just found another passage and I think you ought to read it before you deliver any more of those charges that are widely reported in the English press, and only incite racial hatred in our law-abiding country. I'll quote only two verses of this chapter.

'And when the Lord thy God shall deliver them before thee, thou shalt smite them, and utterly destroy them; thou shall make no covenant with them, nor show mercy unto them. Neither shalt thou make marriages with them: thy daughter shalt thou not give unto his son, nor his daughter shalt thou take unto thy son.'

I am sick and tired of the Anglican Church. I am sick and tired of seeing pictures of Father Huddleston patting black children. He also puts his arms round black women. You know what people say, don't you?

You are always using the name of God. Well, God used Phinehas to stab those two in the act. I would not stab anybody but I would not hesitate to defrock you with my own bare hands.

I sign myself
                    Proud White Christian Woman

– Good morning.

She looked at him suspiciously. For one thing he did not look at her when he said it. One might have thought he did not wish to be seen saying it. She moved from *Cereals* to *Jams* and he followed her, not with any obvious intention, but as though he wished to move to *Jams* also.

– What is your name?

– My name is my own.

– Yes, I know that, but I would like to know what it is.

– Why do you like to know?

– When you see people and you like them, you like to know their names.

– I do not tell my name to any stranger.

– I have seen you before, more than once.

– Anyone can see me. If I go to a shop anyone can see me, but my name is my own.

– Do you always come on Monday?

– Yes, I buy for the week, for me and the madam. She is too old to buy.

A white woman was drawing nearer to them with her basket.

He said to her in a low voice,

– I shall come again on Monday at this time.

– You can come. The shop is open and any person can come.

. . . Yes, the lump is still in my throat. This Ruth woman, to use a slang expression, absolutely slays me. I have never seen such eager, questing, and apparently inexhaustible energy. If someone is being unjustly treated, or hurt, or cheated by the powers-that-be, she's there. She has just come back from Newcastle, having been called there by Emmanuel Nene, who is another one of these very rare human beings on whom has been bestowed a genetic fortune. Neither of them seems able to tire. Emmanuel seems able to smile on the most calamitous occasions. He is very religious and believes that his power is the power of the Holy Spirit. Quite a lot of people think that religion gives you this vitality. It is nonsense of course, Emmanuel has vitality and religion. Ruth has vitality and no religion, well, certainly not any formal religion. It is a matter of the genes, and it is quite unnecessary to invoke any supernatural agency. I am afraid that Emmanuel has got me on my rationalist high horse, and I try to keep my rationalism quite separate from my liberalism, or should I rather say, I try to avoid any discussion of rationalism in party circles. So many members of the party are there because of their religious faith, like Laura de Kock and her husband Hendrik, and I love them both and would not like to hurt them. I love Emmanuel too, with his big hat and his riding-breeches. I would guess that he has never had a nasty thought in his life.

The party conference in Pietermaritzburg also gave me a lump in my throat. I am getting more sentimental as I get older. There we were, white aristocrats from Natal, black landowners correctly dressed in ancient clothes, brilliant Jews from Johannesburg, foolhardy Afrikaners from Pretoria, those beautiful young Indian girls from Durban, old-fashioned coloured liberals from the Cape; and of course Patrick bursting with grand ideas, and Molteno eying us all with a kind of benign malignity, and this aging professor of Biology, who would watch the whole thing with scientific impartiality, if it weren't for the trouble he has with his throat.

The sight of Molteno addressing this motley mob is not easily to be forgotten. Out of his mouth came forth those exact, controlled, faultless sentences, warning us against Utopia and against alienating the wise, steady, devoted liberals of the Cape. Ruth can hardly keep still and Philip Drummond has to tell her to sit down and await her turn, and when her turn comes she tears Molteno to pieces for his equivocal espousal of justice. Molteno looks at her as though he were some Olympian Judge of Appeal, astonished and mystified that a lawyer could exhibit such passion.

We closed the conference with a braaivleis at Philip Drummond's house. The braaivleis proved again that the Liberal Party is a gigantic *tour de force*. Drummond's house is three times the size of mine, and probably six to eight times the size of the house of the average black landowner. The dining-room alone is as big as many a black house. Yet no consciousness of it is to be detected anywhere. All the members call him Philip. He himself is a mixture of earth and sky. His philosophy, his creed if you like, is a blend of utopianism, pragmatism, and scepticism. His political morals are impeccable, but he hides what Molteno would call his evangelistic zeal behind a mask of banter, and it is very noticeable that his banter towards African members is decidedly milder than his banter towards the white ones, which at times can be quite cutting. He moves among his guests, teasing them in English and in Zulu, and I watch him. I am sitting next to an African woman from Underberg, and she watches me watching Drummond, and she says to me, 'We love that man.' And that is true, I think. The African membership of the party is increasing rapidly, and they will soon outnumber the wise, steady, devoted liberals of the Cape or anywhere else.

Because of my past I am very conscious that the party is not yet aware of its *tour de force* nature. The question as to why Drummond's dining-room is as big as many a black house has never been raised, nor the question as to why ninety-five per cent of the cars at the conference belonged to white members. The party has committed itself to the fight against all unjust laws, to the elimination of discrimination, and to the destruction of the colour bar. Within the party itself there appears to be a total absence of racial prejudice and racial thinking. I would not say, of racial fear, because it has so long been a factor in our history. Prem Bodasingh, the beautiful young woman from Durban with two of the most beautiful hands that have ever been seen, told me that her fear of the African people had much abated since she had met Emmanuel of the big hat and the riding-breeches. Well, that is something, but there is so far no discussion as to why there are all these laws, nor any discussion as to their economic causes. I have long since ceased to believe that the causes of all social ills are economic, but so far the party seems almost unaware that many of the causes *are* economic.

We shall all miss Manilal Gandhi very much. Patrick

Duncan will miss him especially, because Manilal was always a reminder to him of the power of *satyagraha*, and Patrick with his very militant and at times aggressive nature needed such a reminder. Manilal was if anything too gentle. He lacked the steel-like quality of his father. He was brave enough, and went and sat in all the public places where Indians are not allowed, but the police must have had special instructions because they simply took no notice of him. That was of course before the Defiance Campaign.

It can't be much fun to be the son of one of the most famous men in the history of the world. Although the Mahatma proved a very indifferent kind of father, Manilal was intensely proud of him, and did his best to continue his father's work. I shall also miss him especially, not because he reminded me of the power of *satyagraha* but because I could see in him all those virtues and defects of gentleness that are in myself.

I must stop now because in a few minutes I must go to earn my bread and butter.

PS. On re-reading I see that I wrote that on people like Ruth and Emmanuel had been 'bestowed' a genetic fortune. My rationalist self disapproves of this expression. Nor would it approve of saying that they had been 'given' a genetic fortune. I should have written that they had 'inherited' it.

Early in 1957 the Most Reverend Geoffrey Clayton, Archbishop of Cape Town, decided that the Church of the Province of South Africa, that is the Anglican Church, should inform the Prime Minister that it would not be able to obey Clause 29(c) of the Native Laws Amendment Bill if the Bill passed into law.

Clause 29(c) was the clause which would forbid any church in an area designated as 'white' under the Group Areas Act from admitting any African to worship without the permission of the Minister of Native Affairs after he had consulted the local authority.

The Archbishop was not empowered to make a decision which would bind the Church, and he therefore summoned to Cape Town the committee appointed by episcopal synod in 1956, to deal with any crisis of this nature. The committee was composed of the bishops of Grahamstown, Johannesburg, Pretoria, and Natal, and they arrived at Bishopscourt on the fifth day of March 1957, the day called Ash Wednesday.

The Archbishop did not take this step eagerly. On the contrary he took it with great heaviness of heart. There were two reasons for this. He was in his seventy-third year and had never during his long life thought that he might one day defy the State. He had preached many times on the text, We ought to obey God rather than man, but had not looked with a very favourable eye on people like Huddleston and Scott who thought that was what they were doing. Now he was about to do it himself.

His second reason was personal and very human. The idea of going to prison filled him with a revulsion that was almost fear. On the Sunday before the bishops' meeting he preached for Ted Langton, a man very dear to him. He said to Langton, 'Ted, next Sunday I may be in prison.' Langton exclaimed, 'Your Grace!' The Archbishop said, 'It's true. I have written a letter and it will not be liked by the Government, who might send me to prison.' Langton said, 'If you go to prison, I think the majority of us would follow.' The Archbishop said, 'I don't want to go to prison. I am much too old. But if I have to go I'll go.' Langton was near to weeping.

The bishops immediately agreed that the law must be disobeyed, and after a few changes had been made, agreed to the Archbishop's letter, which contained these sentences:

'We recognise the great gravity of disobedience to the law of the land. We believe that obedience to secular authority, even in matters about which we differ in opinion, is a command laid upon us by God. But we are commanded to render unto Caesar the things which be Caesar's, and to God the things which are God's. There are therefore some matters which are God's and not Caesar's, and we believe that the matters dealt with in Clause 29(c) are among them.

'It is because we believe this that we feel bound to state that if the Bill were to become law in its present form we should ourselves be unable to obey it or to counsel our clergy and people to do so.'

The bishops left Cape Town on the Thursday morning, and the Archbishop worked in his study. One of his tasks was to sign the letter to the Prime Minister. After lunch he dictated letters to his chaplain. About three o'clock the chaplain heard him singing and moving about his study, which he always did very noisily. Down in the garden below the head gardener saw the Archbishop at the window. His head was out of the window and he was looking down at the ground. This was not unusual. The head gardener would say to himself, 'The Archbishop has a lot of work to do and he is thinking.' The Archbishop left the window and soon after the head gardener heard what seemed to be books falling, followed by a cry, but he thought nothing of it. At twenty-past three the chaplain found the Archbishop lying on the floor of his study. He thought it was some kind of a game, and said, 'Get up, your Grace.' But his Grace was dead. The chaplain and a brother priest said together the office for the Commendation of the Soul, which begins, 'Go forth, O Christian Soul, on your journey from this World.'

By the wish of the Archbishop the funeral service was not to be one of thanksgiving, but of penitence for one who had been a sinner. It was attended by many notables and dignitaries, but neither the Government nor the Governor-General was represented.

COLOURED MOURNERS ASKED TO LEAVE FAMILY POSTPONES SERVICE

Loeriestad — This quiet village in the forests of the Outeniqua mountains has been torn in two by the action of Dominie Krog, who yesterday ordered coloured mourners to leave the funeral service of the late Mr. Cornelius Bezuidenhout. Mr. Bezuidenhout was one of the most respected farmers in the district, and some twenty of his workers came to the service, taking their seats unobtrusively at the back of the church.

Dominee Krog refused to take the service until the coloured mourners had left the church. An elder of the congregation ordered them to leave. As soon as the sons of the deceased became aware of this, they went to the vestry to remonstrate with the dominee, who told them that he had acted in terms of a synodal ruling, and had no power to do otherwise.

After consulting with their mother, the sons postponed the funeral, which will take place today in the Loeriestad Methodist Church.

'It was a great shock to me,' said Mrs. Bezuidenhout. 'I could scarcely believe it. My husband was a most considerate employer, and his workers wished to pay their last respects. I did not believe that such a thing could happen in a Christian church.'

White opinion in Loeriestad is sharply divided over the dominee's action.

. . . I understand your feelings about the Loeriestad affair. Of course the English press has made great ado about it, and has blown it up out of all proportion. I am told that the coloured people left the church very quietly, and even willingly when the facts had been explained to them. I do not like interfering with the freedom of the press, but I quite understand the Prime Minister's anger. A small affair in a small village in the Outeniqua forests becomes news throughout the world, and the press must carry the sole responsibility. This kind of reporting makes our work at United Nations almost impossible.

Nevertheless you are right in thinking that the whole thing is very sad, and that it does not do any good to our nation. But you may comfort yourself that when Clause 29(c) becomes law, this kind of thing will not happen. People will know beforehand who is allowed to enter the church and who is not, and if it is a funeral the family can if they wish make other arrangements.

The Archbishop's death has also strengthened opposition to Clause 29(c). I do not for a moment share the view of those who believe that he was struck down by the Almighty because he intended to defy those whom the Almighty has put in charge of our affairs. I think this is an extreme view to take. I am fully prepared to believe that at his age he found the task which he thought he ought to perform too onerous for him.

Yet I disapprove totally of the way these English churches perform what they think to be their tasks. They issue statements to the English press, they talk of defiance, they are in fact threatening Dr. Hendrik that he will be facing a most serious problem if all the bishops go to jail, and perhaps a great number of their people. The one truth is that the jails could not cope with an influx of churchmen and perhaps churchwomen. The other truth is much more unpalatable. The news will go round the world and will do us irreparable harm.

That is why I so admire the methods adopted by our own churches. They have issued no public statements but have been to see Dr. Hendrik privately. The Federal Council presented a statement to him, and one of the clauses stated the right of the Church to determine when, where, and to whom the Gospel should be proclaimed. After listening to the Minister's point of view, the Council agreed to omit the word *where*. Another clause stated that it was the duty of the State, as the servant of God, to allow full freedom to the Church to execute its divine calling, but after discussion the word *full* was omitted. Dr. Hendrik persuaded the Council to drop certain clauses altogether, and you may be sure that the delegation found his arguments acceptable. They parted from the Minister with expressions of mutual regard. There was no acrimony, and no talk of defiance. It was a perfect example of harmony between State and Church, and it is a great pity that the English churches seem totally incapable of following it. I must tell you, my dear aunt, that I ponder with something like anguish over the fact that the English and the Afrikaner churches both claim to be Christian, and that they all declare that Christ is the Lord of the Church, yet disagree so completely on vital principles.

By the way, Dr. Fischer is going to add another degree to

his impressive total. The university is going to confer on him an honorary LL.D. for his services to the church, the law, and the nation. This will put me in a strange position. I am the president of the Convocation, and it will be my duty to hood him and to shake his hand in congratulation. After that he will deliver the oration. The only way I could get out of it would be to go sick, and I really cannot do that.

I fear, my dear aunt, that I like him no better than ever I did. That he is upright, I have no doubt, but he is a hard, humourless man. My father was upright, and he was stern, but he was neither hard nor humourless. I suppose that Dr. Fischer will have to get a new piece of wood for his desk, because his degrees reach to the end already. He is endlessly ambitious, and I am sure that his goal is Parliament and finally the Cabinet. He is moving upwards in the Broederbond, and that makes his success a certainty. I tell you, and I would not tell anyone else, that I worry a good deal over the way I feel about him. I know it is not right.

I should add one thing. Some people say he is not humourless, but that on the contrary he has a great wit. I think that is possible. Wit can be very cold, humour never. For my part, I have heard neither humour nor wit from him.

They are walking again in Alexandra. They walked there twelve years ago, and for the same reason. They have been asked by PUTCO, the Public Utility Corporation, to pay five pence for the daily journey to Johannesburg. That means tenpence a day, two extra pence every day. They say they cannot afford it.

– You cannot afford two pence a day?

– No, I cannot afford it. It's a loaf of bread less every day. That's what we eat, mister. Yes, take my photograph. My name is Samuel Bukosini.

– Where do you come from?

– I come from Ingwavuma. It's a far place, there in Zululand. But there's no work there. So I came to Johannesburg.

– What are your wages?

– I get eight pound and sixteen shillings a month. Now I shall have to pay one pound and two shillings for a bus. So I rather walk.

– What do you eat?

– We eat bread, mister, and we drink tea. We have sugar with our tea, and milk when I have overtime. And the big luck is meat. And jam. You should see my children when I bring meat.

– Are your children here?

– Will you put that in your paper, mister?

– If you say no, no.

– I must say no. Because if you put it in your paper, the police will come, and they will send my wife and children back to Ingwavuma, and what will they do there?

– I see you carry your shoes.

– Yes, I cannot buy new shoes, so I carry my shoes.

– What time do you leave home, Mr. Bukosini?

– I leave home at four o'clock. My wife wakes me at half-past three and gives me tea and bread and mealie-meal with milk. I am the only one who always has milk. My wife says it must be so because I have to do the walking. I get to work at seven o'clock and I leave Johannesburg at four o'clock and I get home at seven o'clock. Then I talk to my children. A man must talk to his children, otherwise he will lose them.

– Mr. Bukosini, can I ask you a private question? Not for the paper.

– Yes, ask it.

– Do you get time to make love to your wife?

– Well, sometimes I do. But sometimes I am too tired. You can't always make love when you have walked for six hours and worked for eight hours. At lunch time we all sleep.

– Well, thank you, Mr. Bukosini. It has been an honour to me to talk to you.

– Listen, mister. You can put my name and my picture in the paper, but you must not put my wife and children, and you must not put my street in Alexandra. But you can put this. I am strong. I can walk every day. Now you see that woman there? How can she walk twenty miles a day? She was last year in hospital for her chest. Do you see how she breathes? But she has four children, and her husband has left her for another woman.

– Why don't they let her take a bus?

– They do not let anyone take a bus, mister. If she took a bus they would hurt her.

– Do they let her take a lift?

– Yes, they let her take a lift. But she has had no luck today.

– Who are these white people who are giving lifts?

– I don't know. They come every day. They have *ubuntu*. Do you know what that is?

– No. What is it?

– It is . . . well . . . they see a woman, and she is breathing badly, but they do not see a black woman, they see a woman breathing badly so they take her to Johannesburg. That is *ubuntu*.

– Yes, I see. Thank you again, Mr. Bukosini.

– Thank you, mister. Don't forget. No wife, no children, no street.

The leaders of this boycott do not want disturbances. The people are asked to walk in twos and threes. Otherwise the police will catch you for attending riotous assemblies. The people were also asked not to assault those who used the buses. Some of those who work in Johannesburg are old, and some are crippled, and some are ill. It would not be right to assault them. This injunction is by no means always obeyed.

Members of the white Congress and white members of the Liberal Party and other white people have taken their cars to Alexandra, and there they choose their passengers from the old and the sick and the crippled. Their actions are approved. Often a black man or woman who is preparing for the ten-mile walk to Johannesburg will, according to an ancient custom, thank the giver for the gift that is being given to others. Laura de Kock is there every day, and her husband Hendrik comes when he is able.

The Minister of Transport has announced that the boycott is a political movement, and that the Government will not be intimidated. Representatives of industry have asked for legislation to require employers to meet the increase in fares. But the Minister will not intervene. The boycott must be broken. Employers could help by refusing to pay for time taken up by walking. If they wanted to increase wages, that was their own concern. In the meantime he would give instructions to take action against any person who contravened the Transportation Act.

The Minister said that the boycott was the work of the African Congress. It was testing its strength. He appealed to 'all the thousands of law-abiding Natives' to repudiate these leaders. But the 'thousands of law-abiding Natives' did not listen to the Minister. On 20 January 1957 twenty thousand Africans from Moroka, Jabavu, and Dube joined the boycott of the PUTCO buses. This brought the number of boycotters to forty-five thousand. The people are talking of boycott in Randfontein, Brakpan, Port Elizabeth, East London, Bloemfontein, even in faraway Worcester in the Cape. The Minister has asked what further proof is needed that agitators are the real cause of the boycott. He would countenance no concessions whatsoever. Law and order must be maintained. Agitators must be rooted out. Peaceful natives who appreciated that the apartheid laws were made for their advancement must be protected. Communists masquerading as liberals and defenders of freedom must be rooted out. Liberals would be closely watched. They were the ones who led you into ambush so that the communists could kill you. There was no difference between liberals and communists except in the names they gave themselves. Last year the Government had closed the Russian consulate, but let no one deceive himself — the aim of the Russians is to gain control of South Africa, of its gold and its platinum and its coal and its chromium. And if they do so, black boycotters will not be able to march daily up and down Louis Botha Avenue because they will be dead. The Minister received a standing ovation.

— Kindly draw over here, lady.
— What do you want with me, officer?
— It's a safety check, lady.

– Will it take long?

– It will take as long as it needs to take, lady. Not a minute more, not a minute less. If everything is O.K. it won't take long. But if everything is not O.K., it may take a very long time.

– But I was checked last week.

– Last week is last week, lady. And this week is this week. This week is not the same as last week, lady. Can I see your licence? Laura de Kock, housewife. Are you Afrikaans-speaking, lady?

– That has nothing to do with you.

– That's in order, lady. I see you have passengers. Where are you taking them?

– Are you entitled to ask me that question?

– If I suspect a crime has been committed, yes, lady. There was a big robbery in Johannesburg this morning and we are checking all traffic.

– But my passengers are women.

– I don't suspect they did the robbing. But we are looking for the stolen goods. Will you please open your boot, lady?

So the boot is opened. The three women passengers are used to such treatment, but they have never seen a white woman treated like this. The officer finds nothing in the boot and turns his attention to the passengers. He asks for their passbooks. His manner to the white woman has been covertly insulting, but towards the black women he shows an open contempt.

– What are you paying this lady?

– We are paying nothing.

– Why don't you use the buses?

– Because of the money.

– Because of one penny?

– Yes.

– Who is paying you to do this?

– Nobody.

– That's what you say. But we know it is the Congress.

A woman of spirit says to him,

– Then you know more than we do.

– You cannot speak to a policeman like that.

– I can say to a policeman that he knows something I do not know. There is no law about that.

– Your lawyer is clever, eh?

– I have no lawyer.

– When are you going to use the buses?

– When they bring back the fare to four pennies.

– But they are not going to bring it back.

– Then we are not going to use the buses.

– Are you going to walk for ever?

– If we have to, yes.

– You kaffirs are getting too cheeky. But one day we'll get you. Then many of you will die. And I warn you, be careful when you speak to white policemen. We like to be called baas.

– I do not call anyone baas. My employer will not let me call him baas.

– What's he? A Jew?

– He is an Afrikaner.

The policeman spat on the ground to show what he thought of such Afrikaners.

– Well, you can go. But don't let me catch you again in a white car. Lady, you can go.

– Before I go, officer, will you give me the name of your commanding officer?

– Why do you want it, lady?

– I want to report you for the way you speak to my passengers. What do you mean when you say that one day you'll get them? What do you mean that many of them will die?

– So you do understand Afrikaans?

– I understand it well.

– Well, my commanding officer is Captain Smith of the Hillbrow station. And I wish you luck, lady. You'll need it when you talk to Captain Smith. No, don't go yet, lady. I want to have another look at your tyres.

This time the officer spent a long time examining the tyres. Then he came back to Laura de Kock.

– I suspect that the tread of your right front tyre does not conform to the requirements of the regulations drawn up under the Transportation Act. But your tyres must be examined by an expert.

He wrote an address on a leaf of paper from his book and handed it to her.

– Tomorrow morning at ten o'clock, lady, at the inspection centre.

– But I'm teaching, officer.

– I'm sorry for that, lady, but most of the people who have to report there are in employment of one kind or another. The inspection centre doesn't work at nights, lady. They also have homes to go to.

– Can't you make it Saturday, officer?

– I'll do you a favour, lady, I'll make it Saturday. Let me give you a warning, lady. Every white car that carries boycotters is going to be stopped in future. It is going to be checked for defects. Its passengers are going to be checked too. Our orders are that the check must be very thorough.

He looked at his watch.

– You have been here an hour, lady. And if you are stopped tomorrow, that'll be another hour.

– But I've been checked today.

– Tomorrow's officer won't know that, lady.

– Can't you give me a piece of paper, anything, to show that I've been checked?

– We don't do that, lady. Lady, you must move on. There are hundreds of cars on this road.

– But you're stopping only the ones with white drivers and black passengers, isn't that so?

– It might be so and it might not be so. Drive on, lady.

– Good morning.

For a moment he thought she would not reply. Then she replied.

– Good morning.

A wave of excitement went through him. The chase was on. At least she had answered him.

– I am glad to see you.

– You can be glad. I cannot stop you.

– Are you glad to see me?

– I see you. I am not glad. I am not sad. But I see you.

– I want to tell you something.

– Tell me then.

– I think you are beautiful.

He could see a slight sign of pleasure. But she was frowning also. She looked this way and that. She spoke in a low voice.

– Don't you understand? Are you so foolish? Don't you know I am dangerous to you?

– Yes, I know. But if I think you are beautiful, how can I help that?

– You are not supposed to think me beautiful. Don't you know the laws?

– Yes, I know them. Will I ever see you?

– You can see me now.

– I mean some private place.

– Don't you understand? I am dangerous to you, and you are dangerous to me.

– Will I ever see you?

– Don't talk to me. I am going.

– Will I not see you here?

– Anyone can see me here. The shop is open and anyone can see me.

And she was gone. He found that he was breathing hard, as though the chase had been physical. He was trembling too, with excitement and with fear. Of course it was dangerous, but she was one of the most beautiful of women. When he came out of the shop, she was already far up the street. He stopped and thought that she might perhaps look back. But she did not.

The people have been walking now for nine weeks, and they are still walking. The Minister has said that they must first stop the boycott, and then he will consider what steps can be taken. The boycotters say that the Minister must announce what steps will be taken, and then they will consider whether to stop the boycott. Meetings are held day and night, employers whose output is declining, PUTCO which is losing thousands of pounds a day, boycotters who are prepared to go on walking, church leaders who believe that the boycotters' cause is just, police whose patience with these do-gooding white motorists is almost at an end, city council-lors who feel that the whole thing is a disgrace to one of the richest cities in the world. And of course Government officials, who maintain that the boycott is political, that it is not the twopence a day that is the cause of the trouble but the agitators, that the Government will not yield to intimidation. The officials smell a rat, a red rat from Moscow.

The Minister has introduced a Bill which provides that if any transportation service is discontinued, he may prohibit the Transportation Board from licensing any substitute ser-vice. When the bus boycott started in Lady Selborne, outside Pretoria, workers began to use the trains, and the South African Railways augmented its service. But the Minister of Transport protested to the Minister of Railways, these two Ministers being one and the same person, whose right hand obviously did not know what his left hand was doing, and the augmented service was withdrawn.

Nine weeks is a long time, and the sick and the weak and the cripples have dropped out, and a fund has been started by white women of Johannesburg and Pretoria to provide them and their families with food. This has enraged the National Party member for Pretoria South-West, Mr. Louis Smith, who has urged the Minister of Justice to introduce immediate legislation to make such assistance illegal, punishable by fines not exceeding five hundred pounds or imprisonment not exceeding five years. His fellow members have asked him to withdraw his proposals; they do not tell him that they think they are extreme, because that would only enrage him further, but that they will be publicised abroad and will harm the country and, as is well known, no true Nationalist wants to harm the country; Mr. Louis Smith certainly doesn't want to harm the country, but the trouble is he does not know what will harm the country and what will not. However, he withdraws his proposals, but it doesn't really help because they have already been publicised abroad, thanks of course to the press, which believes in some mythical value known as the freedom of information.

The Institute of Race Relations has of course been interfering in the boycott. They have urged the Commissioner of Police to stop acting against white motorists. They have challenged the view that the boycott is political. Two pennies a day was a lot of money to people who could not balance their budgets anyway. It simply meant they had to eat less bread. Or do without a cup of milk. Or eat less mealie-meal. The Institute urged the restoration of the old fares. The director of the Institute reports that he senses a new factor in the racial situation, and that is a determination on the part of African people to act for themselves, a new awareness of a common interest and a common passive strength.

What does he mean, a passive strength? Does a passive strength ever become an active strength? He could have added that white South Africa could go down on its knees and thank God for this passive strength, for this unbelievable patience, and this unbelievable courage that enables not only the strong, but also the weak, the lame, the old, to walk fifteen miles, eighteen miles, twenty miles, twenty-two miles a day, week after week, and when they reach work, to work as hard as they are able. Ah, but your land is beautiful, and what in it is more beautiful than those who walk to their work, along the hard pavements of Louis Botha Avenue, day after day, week after week, in sickness and in health, because they think their cause is just?

– There's nothing wrong with your tyre, lady.

– I didn't think there was.

– People like you come here every day. They're clogging up the whole works. There's most often nothing wrong with their cars. Their trouble is like yours, lady, they've been giving lifts to black people. I see them every day in Louis Botha Avenue. Lady, it breaks my heart.

The Minister of Transport has increased the levy that employers must pay for every worker, and this will be used to increase the subsidy to companies like PUTCO. The fare

from Alexandra to Johannesburg has gone back to fourpence.
The long battle is over, for this time at least.

. . . I agree with you that we took too long to increase the
subsidy. I visited Johannesburg three times during the
boycott, and found travelling along Louis Botha Avenue
very painful. I tell you in confidence, my dear aunt, that
governments often react foolishly and childishly to anything
they construe as a threat or as an attempt to intimidate them.
This is what has happened in this case. My own Minister is
inclined to take the whole boycott as a personal affront.

I did not play sick on the occasion of the graduation
ceremony. I hooded Dr. Fischer LL.D. and shook his hand.
He then delivered the graduation address. You will be
interested to know that he had quite a lot to say about the
Loeriestad affair. He used the argument that one was here
dealing with two apparently absolute goods and that one
could not have them both. That was the complexity of life,
and life was the work of the Creator and we could not
criticise it or try to oversimplify it. The one good was that
the employees of a good employer should be allowed to
attend his funeral and pay their last respects to him. The
other good was the separation of the races, and their separate
development in every sphere, in the home, the school, the
university, the church. All true Afrikaners believed that this
was the will, and one might say, the wish of God.

He quoted Professor Geoffrey Cronje, whom he regarded
as one of the great prophets of Afrikanerdom:

'The racial policy which we as Afrikaners should promote
must be directed to the preservation of racial and cultural
variety. This is because it is according to the Will of God, and
also because with the knowledge at our disposal it can be
justified on practical grounds.'

He also quoted Dr. P. J. Meyer, whom he also regarded as
one of our prophets:

'The Gospel is not directed to the human being as an
absolutely autonomous and isolated entity, but to the human
being as creature and therefore as a member of a specific

nation . . . Not only the individual, but also the nation, as part of the Creation, has been called by God . . . The Afrikaner accepts his national task as a divine task, in which his individual life-task, and his personal service to God has been absorbed in a wider, organic context.'

I must admit that Dr. Fischer developed his theme with that professional skill for which he is famous. I do not know if something is wrong with me, for although I accept his view of the divine calling of Afrikanerdom, and his conviction that the Afrikaner was planted in South Africa for a divine purpose, he does not inspire me. He dealt with these great themes in a way that to me was intellectual and cold. Therefore when he argued that, seen in the light of these eternal verities, the incident at Loeriestad was not a matter of tremendous consequence, and certainly not fitted to become an item of news to be flashed across the world, he did not convince me. Perhaps that is because my mother, and you my dearest aunt, could never bear to see a fellow being, of whatever race or colour, humiliated as these coloured folk were humiliated at Loeriestad.

I should not omit to say that Dr. Fischer received a very laudatory citation. The orator said that it was the university that was honouring itself by honouring him. He was one of the most distinguished lay sons of the Church. His career in the law had been one of outstanding achievement, and he was regarded as one of the most brilliant sons of the university. But it was as a son of Afrikanerdom that he was most cherished, and one of the most revered of Afrikaner theologians had called him 'God's gift to the nation'. 'Mr. Chancellor, sir, I present to you for the honorary degree of Doctor of Laws, Dr. Louis Woltemade Fischer, churchman, lawyer and patriot.'

You must admit that it went a bit far. I give you my opinion confidentially that the Minister doesn't like all this. There is a joke going round and I don't know if he has heard it, but if he did hear it he wouldn't like it. It goes: 'Oh, the Palace of Justice? Isn't that the place where Dr. Fischer works?'

The Prime Minister did not answer the letter from the bishops of the Church of the Province. He sent it to the Minister of Native Affairs, who didn't answer it either. He gave the job to his private secretary, who wrote that the Minister regretted that the bishops should threaten disobedience to the laws of the land without waiting for the second-reading debate to see 'how the clause is to be redrafted to eliminate all possibility of suspicion and misunderstanding'.

In Parliament Dr. Hendrik announced amendments that would eliminate all suspicion. The most important of all was that if the law were disobeyed, it would be the African worshipper, not the church, who would be guilty of an offence. He condemned those people in Pietermaritzburg and Durban who founded international clubs. He condemned the Liberal Party, and said that its activities compelled Parliament to take steps.

The Minister made no attempt to conceal his loathing of interracial association. He said:

'We find that there are whites who take pleasure in arranging special social gatherings where whites and non-whites mix freely, not because they feel the need for contact but because they like to demonstrate . . . They even throw open the doors and windows so that everyone can see what is going on. They allow whites and non-whites to lean out of the windows to annoy the neighbours. That is what has been happening . . . There are, for instance, areas where nobody in the whole neighbourhood would think of doing such things, except for one liberalist who does them deliberately.'

On 24 April 1957 the Bill became law. On 14 July letters were read in all Anglican churches in South Africa. These letters contained these words:

'Before God and with you as my witnesses, I solemnly state that not only shall I not obey any direction of the Minister of Native Affairs in this regard, but I solemnly counsel you, both clergy and people, to do likewise.'

This was followed by similar declarations from most of the English-speaking churches. The Pietermaritzburg and Durban international clubs closed down rather than seek ministerial permission to continue, a permission that would not

have been granted. The Institute of Race Relations, the
Liberal Party, the National Union of Students, decided to
continue as usual.

A fascinating interlude was provided when the white NGK
congregation at Pinelands invited an African minister to
occupy their pulpit. *Die Kerkbode*, the national periodical of
the NGK, assured its readers that this was not a demonstration against Clause 29(c). It explained the whole situation,
making telling use of italicisation.

'It is an *exception* that will occur very *seldom* in our Church,
but which however is also again completely *natural* in the
light of the spiritual bonds that exist between us and Bantu
Christians. Our church policy is not *undermined* by this, nor
renounced, not even *changed*, but rather *refined* to stand out in
its spiritual light and clarity.'

Dr. Hendrik made it abundantly clear that he had not
reworded the clause because of the Archbishop's letter, but
because of the decorous and Christian representations made
to him by those who would never stoop to deliver attacks
which were 'distorted and unreasonable'. This was the only
time in Dr. Hendrik's career that he had been known to bow
to the wind. The church clause was seldom if ever invoked. It
was a retreat disguised as a victory.

Mr. Robert Mansfield
Natal Chairman
Liberal Party

So you decided to close down your International Club, eh?
You didn't have the guts to stand up for your principles. I'm
disappointed in you, Robert.

Where are your Portugooses going to read in the dark with
their black dollies now, eh? You know what they read in the
dark, don't you, those books with the fuzzy hair, eh? You
disgust me, with your Christian talk, playing poker with the
black dollies.

I would never belong to any international club, but if I did,
I'd stand up for it, I wouldn't come running like a dog just

because a Minister blows his whistle.

Wouldn't you like to know my name, Robert? Wouldn't you like to know what I look like? but you won't. I wouldn't have your hands on me, not the hand of a man who paws his own daughter.

I sign myself
Proud White Christian Woman

Mr. Robert Mansfield
Natal Regional Office
The Liberal Party

You were fortunate to discover the defect in your brakes on a reasonably safe stretch of road. We warned you that a few locks here and there would not be enough protection. You clearly do not take our warnings seriously.

We read, however, that you have decided to close down your International Club. Does that mean that you are becoming amenable to reason? It may interest you to know that our committee takes some credit for the closing down of the club. We supplied the Minister with full details of your activities, all of which are contrary to the doctrines and policies of racial separation.

Our committee is, however, dissatisfied with your performance. We have come to the conclusion that you do not intend to dissociate yourself from the Liberal Party. We therefore wish to warn you again that we are planning to take more serious action against you. This would be taken some time in the next few weeks. This would give you an opportunity to take action yourself, of the kind that we suggested to you in our first letter.

We sign ourselves
The Preservation of White South Africa League

– Good morning.
 – Good morning.
 – I am glad to see you.

– You can be glad. I cannot stop you.

– You are still beautiful.

He could see again that slight sign of pleasure. But it was not unalloyed. He could see conflicting emotions, fear perhaps, pride too perhaps, that would not yield easily to a stranger.

– When shall I see you?

– Why should I see you?

– Because I love you.

– That's a big thing.

She said to him with sudden vigour,

– I have told you before, I am dangerous to you, you are dangerous to me.

– Yes, I know that, but I want to see you.

– Where?

– In the park.

– That's a big thing. I must think about it.

– Not too long. Will you tell me next Monday?

– Perhaps next Monday. Please leave me now. Now, now.

She spoke so urgently that he left her. For a moment he felt that he ought to draw back, that the whole thing was indeed dangerous. But the feeling lasted only for a moment. She was too beautiful for him to draw back. He made a click of annoyance with his tongue and teeth. He had forgotten to ask for her name.

NALA is going from strength to strength. That is due to the determination of the black landowners to keep their rightful land, and the organising skill and vigour of Emmanuel Nene of the big hat and the riding-breeches. Though he is still a young man, he enjoys the confidence of the landowners, some of whom are white-haired and venerable. He also enjoys the close attention of the Security Police, who turn up at every branch meeting of NALA. They sit at the back of the humble halls where the meetings are held, usually school-rooms in those few schools that are not yet controlled by Dr. Hendrik and his Department of Bantu Education, or church buildings. They make notes of all the speeches, which are of the very essence of law-abidingness, but which one and all condemn the law which empowers the Minister to take away their land. They photograph all the speakers and a good many of the listeners too, moving about noisily and arrogantly while the meeting is in progress. One of their favourite ploys is to station themselves and their apparatus in front of the speaker so that he cannot see his audience and they cannot see him. If he moves, then they move too. And what can he do? This is the power of the State, and the State is white and he is black. But if Philip Drummond is there he will give them five minutes to take all their photographs, after which they must resume their seats at the back. Otherwise he will have to report to their commanding officer in Pietermaritzburg.

After the meeting is over, the police visit the authorities who have lent the schoolroom or the church. Does the reverend gentleman want a visit from the government building inspectors, who will condemn his church building or his schoolroom as dangerous for human occupation?

– It will cost a lot of money to build a new church, reverend. We advise you, reverend, not to lend your church to subversive organisations like the Natal African Landowners Association.

And now for Bantu female Dorcas Hlophe.

– Do we understand, Dorcas, that this man Nene slept in your house on the occasion of his last visit? We advise you, Dorcas, not to do this again. You have a motor car, do you not? Bought in 1937? It could be stopped on the road by the transport police, and taken to Estcourt for examination. It might cost a lot of money, Dorcas, to have your certificate of roadworthiness renewed. Sometimes they don't renew the certificate at all. They just order you to take the car off the road.

– Philip, my car is looked after by Gasa. Everyone knows he is a first-class mechanic. He says the car is in good condition. What shall I do if they take it to Estcourt?

– You must go with it. You must not let it out of your sight. When you get to Estcourt you ask to see Mr. Wainwright. You tell Mr. Wainwright that Philip Drummond asks him to keep a special eye on your car. He will do it.

However, not every official has been to school with Philip Drummond. Up here at Drayton Moor, old Mrs. Mbele has been visited by the Security Police. Her son Lucas is a member of the Liberal Party in Pietermaritzburg. His mother has been told to warn him to get out of the party, otherwise he may be banned under the Suppression of Communism Act and ordered to be confined to the area of Drayton Moor. In Pietermaritzburg he has a good job at good wages, and he is a good son to his mother. But at Drayton Moor there is no work at all. If the Security Police so decided, he could live the rest of his life here in this desolate place, one of the least favoured of all the blackspots. For it was too heavily subdivided, and carries the largest population of them all. Through its once-fertile fields run ugly dongas which in places are ten feet deep. Rain is not a blessing here, but something to be feared. The dongas become red rushing rivers, carrying the precious soil to the sea.

Emmanuel Nene had a good meeting at Drayton Moor. It was held in the Holy Church of Zion, minister the Reverend Zachariah Nyembe. There were two hundred people at the meeting, and six policemen, three white and three black, who took many photographs. It is a sight to see, men and women coming over the veld from every point of the compass, and waiting for them, leaning against their cars, the six policemen, who have been trained to frighten people by the intensity of their stares, eyes which will remember every face, ears which will remember every word, till that day of reckoning when every subversive person will have been utterly destroyed, when every enemy of the Great Plan will have been converted or silenced for ever. If these men and women of Drayton Moor are frightened, they do not show it. They do not laugh or joke, for the might and power and glory of the State is not to be laughed away. They go quietly into the church, some of them kneel for a moment as they enter, for this is the building of the Lord. Some of the young people are now saying that he is a white Lord, and that no black man or woman with any pride should worship him, and that the white man gave the black man the Bible with one hand and took his land away with the other. Some of the young people are saying that all white men are the same, even people like Philip Drummond and Robert Mansfield and Patrick Duncan, and this grieves their elders, coming here in their black suits and their best dresses, to protest against the rape of their land.

Dr. Edward Roos, professor of Biology, the aging professor as he calls himself, has come from Johannesburg to encourage the landowners to persist in their fight for their land. When he sees an old woman go down on her knees to pray, no doubt for the blessing of God on their cause, he gets that lump in the throat that troubles him from time to time, hardened rationalist though he is. Emmanuel also encourages the landowners. It is very hard not to be encouraged by him.

Emmanuel tells the people about the great meeting of affirmation and prayer that is to be held by NALA at Roosboom, the blackspot near Ladysmith. The rumour is that Roosboom will be the next to go; also it is in a central position, and that is why the meeting will be held there. It is hoped that all the blackspots of Natal will send as many people to the meeting as possible, so that the voice of black landowners will be heard by the Government. His speech is punctuated by cries of approval and clapping. A black man jumps to his feet and cries out, shaking his fist in the air,

– Yes, we will make them listen to us.

The police photograph him immediately, for that day when Nemesis will overtake him, and he cries out at them,

– Yes, take my picture, take the picture of the man who got his land honourably from his father, and now the Government wants to take it away.

They take more pictures of him.

Their actions, and the enormity of the deed that the Government proposes to commit, and the thought of losing his house and land, bring on a kind of hysterical sobbing, and he cries out at the police.

– The British gave it to me, and now the Boers are trying to take it away. I tell you, I tell you . . .

Now such things are not said. They may be thought, but they may not be said. Mr. Robert Maguza, chairman of the

Drayton Moor branch of NALA, goes to the sobbing man, and leads him to the door. He gestures angrily to the police who are taking photographs of the dramatic subversive scene. At the door he gently advises the wife of the sobbing man to take him home. When he returns the church is silent. He turns to the white policemen and says to them,

– You do not know what you are doing, you are sowing the seeds of your own destruction, and the destruction of many of us also.

He turns to the black policemen and says to them,

– A prostitute sold her body and Christ forgave her, but you sell your souls, and whether you will ever be forgiven, I do not know.

Mr. Maguza returns to the chair, and says to the police,

– You have done your harm now, I ask you to go.

The policeman in charge says angrily,

– We have our duty to do, and we shall not go.

– Then, said Mr. Maguza, I apologise to the professor that we cannot hear him speak. The meeting is now closed.

But the professor held up his hand, and said a few words to the chairman. Mr. Maguza smiled and said to the meeting,

– The professor is sorry he cannot speak, but he wants you to know that there is one Boer here who will do all he can to save your homes and your land.

The closing words were received with the clapping of hands and other expressions of approval.

Quite a number of the people of Drayton Moor have come to the station to see Emmanuel Nene take the train home. Among those who come to see him off is Mrs. Dorcas Nyembe, at whose home he had slept the night before. The Security Police have also come to see him off, but they stand apart from the others. As the train passes through the settlement of Drayton Moor itself, which is about two miles away, many people will come to wave and shout their farewells to him.

But it does not happen that way. When the train is passing through the settlement, the police stand on the track and order the train to halt. When the train has stopped, the police ask in loud voices,

– Is there a passenger called Emmanuel Nene on the train?
Emmanuel says,
– Yes, I am on the train.
Then he is ordered to pick up his bag and to descend from the train. The train is then ordered to proceed. Then passenger Nene is ordered to get into the police vehicle.

This of course has been seen by hundreds of people. They have seen with their own eyes what can happen to a man who defies the Government, and who advises people to fight for their land. The police drive off with Emmanuel Nene. There is no smile on his face, nor on the faces of those hundreds who have witnessed this event. They came here smiling, but now they smile no more. They have been insulted by six foolish men, who, as Mr. Maguza has said, are sowing the seeds of their own destruction, the seeds that are known as dragons' teeth.

– Will you come?
– Yes, I will come.
– To the park?
– Yes.
– When?
– Tonight. At eight. Where in the park?
– Do you know the pond?
– Yes.
– You know the trees there?
– Yes.
– Wait for me in the trees. Or if I get there first I shall wait for you.
– You know that it is dangerous?
– Yes.
– I must go now.
– Tell me quickly. What is your name?
– Elizabeth.

It was a dark night, and warm. With a beating heart he went

to the park. Then as quietly as he could he went to the trees by the pond. A low call told him she was there. He went quietly into the trees and took her into his arms. She was tense and trembling and showed no passion.

– Don't be afraid, Elizabeth.

– Are you not afraid?

– No. There is no one here.

– You know that it is dangerous?

– Yes, I know, but I love you. You are beautiful, Elizabeth. Kiss me, Elizabeth. No, not like that. Can't you open your lips?

She opened her lips but she was still both tense and trembling. She kissed him, still without passion.

– Elizabeth.

– Yes.

– I want to kiss your breasts.

With shaking hands she opened her dress. She was still trembling, with fear no doubt. He was trembling with passion. Her breasts were soft beyond all imagination, warm and beautiful.

– Let us lie down, Elizabeth.

And then the white blinding light, the white pitiless light, the light that strips away all the pretensions of a man, and destroys him for ever. Men come running, with lights and cameras.

– Dr. Fischer, I arrest you under the Immorality Act of 1927.

The captain added with a kind of grim joy . . .

– Amended as you know, I am sure, in 1950.

But Dr. Fischer does not hear the jest. He is full of terror. His life, his honours, his fame, all come to an end. A black policeman says to the girl,

– Daughter, you may go now, go quickly home.

She turns to go. She does not look at the man she has destroyed. She makes haste to get out of the park with the pond and the trees. She wants never to see it again.

White Pretoria is struck dumb by the Fischer arrest. There are of course those who enjoy the story, who indeed enjoy the story of any of the mighty who have fallen. But they are not laughing up there at the university, and they are not laughing at the big Kerk in Plein Street. They are not laughing at Ohrigstad, where they have just changed the name of Jan Smuts Street to Jan Fischer Street. And they are certainly not laughing at the Palace of Justice. There is an air of apprehensive expectation, for they are waiting for the Minister to arrive, and when he arrives he looks like some angel of vengeance. He sends for Van Onselen, who expects to bear the burden of the Minister's wrath. But the Minister confines himself to departmental business, and does not mention the man who has brought such shame on the Palace of Justice and on the Afrikaner nation.

. . . The Fischer affair has cast gloom over the Palace of Justice, and indeed over the Union Buildings also. My Minister is grim and controlled, but his anger is immeasurable. At ten o'clock he telephoned me and told me that he wanted me in his office. Fischer's mother was coming to see him, and he did not want to interview her alone.

So I was waiting there with the Minister when she arrived, a small frail woman. I must admit, my dear aunt, that my heart went out to her, but the Minister did not look at her except for the briefest of moments. If he had looked at her, perhaps he would not have loosed upon her the torrent of his anger that such a scandal to the nation had come from the Palace of Justice. He is a hard and severe man, but his pride in the Palace of Justice is immense. He motioned Mrs. Fischer to a seat and introduced me to her.

'Minister . . .'

The small woman's opening word seemed to open the floodgates of the Minister's wrath. His grim self-control had gone.

'Mevrou Fischer, you must understand that justice must take its course. There is no way that anything could be done to change that course. Nothing can be done to soften the blow that must fall on you and your house . . .'

'Minister . . .'

'Let me finish, mevrou. Remember that you are the
mother of a man who has disgraced the university, the
church, and most unforgivable of all, the nation. We are
sorry for you, but your personal happiness can never be the
first concern of this department . . .'

'Minister . . .'

'I said, Let me finish, mevrou. This disgrace will be felt
deeply by the university, the church and the nation. But
nowhere will it be felt more deeply than in the Palace of
Justice. Your son has damaged beyond computation the
cause of justice. He has brought bitter shame to all those who
honoured him. Look at this cutting, mevrou. Only a few
days ago the Town Council of Ohrigstad changed the name
of Jan Smuts Street to Jan Fischer Street. Now Jan Smuts is
not a hero to true Afrikaners, but at least he was the Prime
Minister. He was also Minister of Justice and in his own way
upheld the honour of the Palace of Justice. But now the
Town Council has removed his name, and has given the
street the name of a man who has brought disgrace to the
nation.'

I must say, my dear aunt, that I was overwhelmed by the
Minister's treatment of this small, frail woman. But what
could I do? One does not say to the Minister, Minister, I
think you have said enough. He sat there, obviously exhausted by passion, and she sat there, with her burden of
grief. I watched the Minister struggling with himself. He
knew he had lost his self-control and he did not like to think
of it. He is the tallest man in the House, and she must be one
of the smallest women in Pretoria.

'Minister.'

'Yes.'

'I did not come here to ask for mercy. I did not come here
to ask you to change the course of justice. I came to express
my sorrow to you, and to the Department of Justice, that my
son should have brought this disgrace upon you. That is why
I came, Minister.'

A tear gathered in one of her eyes, and rolled down her
cheek. She took out her handkerchief to wipe it away. The
Minister could hardly not see it. He sat exhausted and bitterly

ashamed. His remorse struggled with his pride and his anger, and his pride and anger triumphed.

'It is fitting that you should have done so, mevrou. It was your duty and you did it. If there is any essential matter that must be dealt with, any matter connected with your son and the department, I must ask you to deal directly with Mr. van Onselen. I do not wish to deal with it. And now, mevrou, I must bid you good day.'

The Minister did at least stand up, but he did not look at her or offer his hand to her. She stood up also, and seeing that he would not offer his hand to her she bowed to him and turned to go. She stumbled and nearly fell, like a drunken woman. She put one hand on a chair to steady herself and the other she put on her breast. She started to walk again, and again looked as though she would fall, so that I went quickly to her and took her arm.

'Come, mevrou.'

She gave me a little smile, and I could see that she was full of grief and pain. I guided her to the door and, aunt, I was glad to get her and myself out of that office.

– Where do you live, mevrou?

– In Sunnyside, meneer. In Hofman Street. I can get a bus from here.

– You cannot go on a bus. I shall take you home.

So he took her home.

– Meneer, will you have a cup of coffee? It will not take long.

– Yes, mevrou, I'll have a cup of coffee.

– What is your Christian name?

– Gabriel, mevrou.

– Gabriel. The archangel. It is a good name for you. You have been as an angel to me. May I call you by your name?

– Of course, mevrou.

She left him to make the coffee, and to think strange thoughts. He was drawn to her by strange and inexplicable forces. Pity, of course, because of her smallness and her frailty, and because of her grief also. Well, perhaps the forces were not strange and inexplicable. She looked like his mother. She brought him his coffee, and said to him,

– Gabriel.

– Yes, mevrou.

– I have something big to ask of you.

– What is it, mevrou?

– I have no one to help me, and I need a man's help. Read this letter. It is from my late husband's sister.

He took the letter and read it. It had been delivered by hand, by one Johannes.

Dear Alida,

I have just seen the news. I have no words to describe my feelings. I am afraid we must rather wait for your next visit, till things settle a bit. You must not take this too badly. We are all in a state of turmoil.

  Hannah

– She lost no time, mevrou.

– The others will do the same, Gabriel. All my husband's family. And I have no family of my own. That's why I am asking your help. Can you find out when the case is to be?

– I'll do that, mevrou. The case will no doubt be adjourned, and they will let your son come home.

– That's why I need your help, Gabriel. How can he come home through the streets? I know him. He will be filled with terror. The higher you go, the harder you fall. All the bones of his soul must be broken. Will you go quickly and find out, and bring him home?

– I'll do that, mevrou.

– I do not know how to thank you.

– It will not be necessary.

– This day has been a day of grief for me. But sometimes God sends an angel in the hour of one's need. That's what He has done for me. May I tell you something?

– Tell me, mevrou.

– My son said of you that you were the perfect public servant.

He flinched, but he bowed to her. She did not know how

he had come to hate those words.

 – Will you need money, Gabriel? For the court?

 – It is possible.

 – How much?

 – A hundred. Two hundred maybe. Don't worry now. I'll stand good for it. They know me well. I think the sooner I go the better. Goodbye, mevrou.

 – Goodbye, Gabriel. I shall not thank you again. But my heart is full.

She stood at the door and watched him go down the path to the gate. At the gate he turned to salute her, a small, frail figure who would now face the contempt and the ostracism of the righteous world.

 – I will read to you a passage from the *Pretoria Times*. These are the words: Any white man who offends against the Immorality Act offends against the law. But any Afrikaner who offends against it offends against the nation. It is in fact the greatest of all offences. No punishment can be too great for the offender. Do you know who said those words?

 – . . .

 – I cannot hear you, Dr. Fischer.

 – I said them.

 – Do you remember where you said them?

 – . . .

 – I cannot hear you, Dr. Fischer.

 – In the church. The church in Plein Street.

 – That is right. I shall read another passage to you. These are the words: He is one of the most distinguished sons of the Church. His career in the law has been one of outstanding achievement, and we esteem him as one of the most brilliant sons of the university. But it is as a son of Afrikanerdom that he is most cherished, and one of our most revered Afrikaner theologians has called him, God's gift to the nation. Did you ever hear those words?

 – . . .

 – I cannot hear you, Dr. Fischer.

 – Yes, I heard them.

– On what occasion did you hear them?

– . . .

– Dr. Fischer, you must answer me.

– At the university.

– Yes, go on.

– My honorary graduation.

– Did you not think to yourself, I do not deserve these words? Did you not think of crying out, Stop the graduation, I am not a gift to the nation, I am a traitor?

– . . .

– Please lift up your head. I cannot hear what you are saying.

– I did not think of saying that.

– Why did you not?

– Because I am two men. The one who received the degree. The other . . .

– Yes, continue.

– The other . . .

– Shall I continue for you? The other is the man who went to the park. The man who went at night to the park, to break the most sacred law of the nation. Is that right?

– Yes.

– But there are not two men in this court. There is only one. The one who received the honorary degree is the same as the man who went to the park. I must ask you one last question. I shall read you another passage. These are the words: To offend against the Immorality Act is not to commit a sin of the flesh. It is to commit treason against the nation. It is to break the law that was made to preserve the purity of the nation. There is no offence greater than to sin against the purity of the nation. Do you remember these words?

– Yes.

– Who spoke them?

– I spoke them.

– My lord, I have finished my examination.

– Prisoner in the dock, have you anything to say?

– No, my lord.

– Then I must do my awful duty. Jan Woltemade Fischer,

B.A., B.Ed., LL.B., Ph.D., and of course honorary LL.D., I find you guilty and I pass on you sentence of death.

The man cried out,

– You cannot do that.

– Why not?

– There is no death penalty under the Act of 1927, nor the amended Act of 1950.

– I do not sentence you under either of those Acts. I sentence you to death for the crime of treason.

– Treason?

– Did you not say yourself that to offend against the Immorality Act was to commit treason against the nation?

– . . .

– You must answer me, Dr. Fischer.

–Yes, I said it.

– Therefore I sentence you to death. Gentlemen of the police, lift up the prisoner. I cannot speak to a man scrabbling on the floor. Dr. Jan Woltemade Fischer, it is an act of mercy that I am doing. Where could you live now? Could you live in Pretoria, where you are known to many? Or in Cape Town, where you are known also? Or would you perhaps seek refuge in Ohrigstad, the town that named a street after you, the town you plunged into shame? Whom will you ever look in the face again? When will you ever smile or laugh again? Or tell a witty joke perhaps, as you sometimes did to your friends? Therefore mercy is shown to you, and you are sentenced to death. And may God have mercy on your soul.

And a small, frail woman stands up at the back of the court, and cries out, God have mercy, Christ have mercy. But the messengers rush to her and take her away. One may not cry out for mercy in this court.

Dr. Jan Woltemade Fischer
17 Hofman Street
Sunnyside
Pretoria

So they caught you with your trousers down, eh? The great speaker, the great leader, caught in a park with his trousers down. You're a clever man, Dr. Fischer, but you never thought you would be caught. You never thought that the black dolly might be a policeman's daughter. How stupid can a clever man be, ha! ha!

What were you doing in the park, doctor? Looking for flowers, the kind that open up at night, ha! ha!

I suppose you'll get six months, suspended perhaps. But a man like you should be shot to death. You are a disgrace to the white nation.

I sign myself
Proud White Christian Woman

Dr. Fischer will not get your letter, Proud White Christian Woman. For, as you wished, he has been shot to death. He took his father's revolver and went to the bathroom and shot himself in the temple. His mother came running, and took a small wet cloth and wiped away the blood from the wound. Then she knelt and took his head to her breast, and said to him, *My kind, my arme kind*. That means in English, My child, my poor child. But the deep meaning of it cannot be written in any language, for its grief is unutterable.

Ah, but your land is beautiful. Cruel and beautiful. A man is destroyed for a small sin of the flesh. For it is not a small sin of the flesh but a great sin against the nation. When you know that you will never look any man or woman in the eyes again, when you know that you will never smile or laugh again, when you know that you will never jest again, then it is better to die than to live.

May God have mercy on your soul.

The council and the senate of the university have met together. Their problem is very difficult. Has the university the power to take away a degree that it has given? And if it does take it away, then would that do more harm to the university than to do nothing at all? The difficulty is that there is a magnificent board of honour that confronts you as you come into the entrance hall of the university. This board commemorates the names of all those who have received honorary degrees, and the name of Jan Woltemade Fischer has already been added. The council and senate were unanimous that it would be unthinkable for the name to stay there. It was finally decided to consult eminent counsel, to determine whether the university had the right to revoke the award of an honorary degree.

The big Kerk in Plein Street has had no problems. The portrait of Dr. Jan Woltemade Fischer has been quietly removed from the church refectory, and has been privately burned at the back of the building.

The Ohrigstad Town Council met privately to consider the renaming of Jan Fischer Street. It was decided unanimously that it should be renamed. It was also decided unanimously that it should not be renamed Jan Smuts Street. After discussion it was decided unanimously to rename it Hospital Street.

According to the *Pretoria Times*, the Mayor was not available for comment, having been called out of town on private business. The Town Clerk said it was not the practice of the Council to talk to the English press. When asked for a personal opinion he said that it was also not his practice to talk to the English press. What had happened was a painful matter and had caused the people of the town great distress, but to the English press it was only a titbit to titillate their readers' palates. He would welcome any move on the part of the Prime Minister to curb the English press, which would do well to emulate the example of the Afrikaans press, and to show restraint when dealing with delicate matters. He considered that the *Pretoria Times* was a thorn in the side of the nation.

The City Council has decided that in future Louis Botha Park will be opened at sunrise and closed at sunset. A motion to limit entrance to the park to whites only, was defeated by one vote.

. . . The shock of Dr. Fischer's death, coming as it did on the same day as his arrest, has been tremendous. My Minister sent for me and spoke to me briefly.

'Van Onselen, listen to me carefully. The name of the man is never to be mentioned in my hearing. Anyone who mentions it in my hearing can expect no further advance in the Department of Justice. Now I can hardly issue instructions to that effect. I am therefore instructing you to go to the head of every sub-department, and to any person who has others under him, to instruct them to instruct all those under them that the name of the man is never to be mentioned in my hearing. Is that clear to you?'

'It shall be done, Minister, and immediately.'

'Further, Van Onselen, no telegram or letter or minute that concerns the man must be referred to me, no matter how important it seems to be. I authorise you to deal with all such matters without any reference to me. I said *all* such matters, Van Onselen. Is that clear to you?'

'Yes, Minister.'

'And there is one thing more I wish to say to you, Van Onselen. I want you to know that in this terrible time, the like of which I hope never to experience again, you have been a tower of strength to me.'

'Thank you, Minister.'

The Minister gave a shadow of a smile.

'I am leaving in a few minutes for the airport. I am going to Heunisstad to open the new police station. Therefore for the first time, Van Onselen, you will be the head of the Department of Justice.'

There was not much to say to that, so I bowed modestly, wished the Minister a good journey, and went to carry out the instructions he had given me. And when that was done I went to the house in Hofman Street.

– Gabriel!

– Mevrou.

– Ah, I knew you would come. I was sure you would come.

– Mevrou, there are arrangements to be made.

– And you have come to help me?

– Yes, mevrou.

– That is my fortune, Gabriel, for I cannot make them any more. My courage is failing. Dominee Vos will not bury my son, and he will not allow any minister from the big Kerk to bury him. What shall I do?

– Do you know the Reverend Andrew McAllister, mevrou? Or do you know of him? He is the minister of the Presbyterian Church here in Sunnyside?

– I have heard of him.

– I shall go to see him now. If he is able to do it, he will.

– Gabriel, I have not been to the undertakers. I am afraid to go there. I am afraid they will say no. And I am afraid to go to the cemetery too.

– Mevrou, I shall see them all.

– She looked at him with such trust that he felt his heart was breaking, and he hurried away from her.

. . . The funeral service was held in the smallest chapel at the undertakers. I had thought that Mrs. Fischer and I would be the only persons there, but there were three young men there also. I knew by some kind of instinct who they were. They were the three Berg brothers, the boys who had been sent to school and university by my Minister, and had repaid his generosity by joining the Liberal Party. They had all gone to the same university as Jan Woltemade Fischer.

We could not have had a better man than the Reverend Andrew McAllister. He took the service in English, but gave a little address in Afrikaans. He told Mrs. Fischer that the hearts of many Christians had gone out to her in these last days. He said that God would give her courage to face the times that lay ahead. He referred to her son as 'our brother now departed'. He closed by asking that God's blessing would rest on her all her days. He said to her:

'Though you walk through the valley of the shadow of death, you need fear no evil. For God is with you, and His rod and staff will comfort you.'

I must say it was very moving.

– Who are you three young men?

– Mevrou, I am Jan Berg. And these are my brothers, Frederik and Izak.

– The sons of Cornelius Berg?

– Yes, mevrou.

– So you are my junior cousins. Is that why you came?

– That is one reason. But we also came to pay you our respects.

He saw her lip trembling, that these three young men should come to pay their respects to the mother of a man who had offended against the Immorality Act and had then taken his own life, and whose funeral service had been taken by a stranger from another church.

The three young men had another reason too, but they did not tell her that. They had come to make their protest against the Immorality Act of 1927, amended in 1950.

He went back with Mrs. Fischer to the house in Hofman Street, and she asked him to have a cup of coffee with her.

– I want you to see the library, Gabriel.

The library astonished him. It must have been one of the best private libraries in the whole country. There was no doubt the man was very learned.

– What am I to do with them, Gabriel? I am sure the university would not take them.

– There is more than one university. I shall see what can be done.

On the way back to the sitting-room, she opened a door and said to him,

– This was his room, Gabriel.

He could see that she meant him to go in, so he did so. It was a quite ordinary room. There was a Bible on the table by the bed, and a photograph of herself on the dressing-table.

He picked it up and looked at the tender and innocent face.

– Did you know all about this, mevrou?

– Yes, I knew. I knew that one day it would destroy him. But I could not speak to him. He was an arrogant man, Gabriel, like his father before him. One could not speak to them. You must understand, Gabriel. I loved them both, but they were arrogant men. My son was two men, and one was clever and good, and considerate of his mother. But the other was a doomed man. He never looked at a white woman, Gabriel. Do you understand these things?

– I do not say I understand them, but I know that is the way we are made.

– You are humble. You are not made that way.

– You know the English saying, mevrou? There but for the grace of God, go I. I say that also.

– Are you arrogant, Gabriel?

– I do not believe so. Mevrou, I think you should go away for a time. You should get away from Pretoria. I have an aunt in Natal. She lives on a farm under the Drakensberg. She is a woman of your own kind, and if you allow me, I shall write to her, and ask her to write to you and invite you to stay with her.

– Yes, I would do that, when things are settled here, Gabriel.

– Of course. I shall help you to settle them.

. . . Something has changed in my life, my dear aunt. You know, don't you, that since my mother died I have become the perfect public servant? Strange that her death should change me into a dry old stick and that Fischer's death should change me back again. At least I think that is what it is going to do. I remember writing to you to tell you that I was ashamed of the way I felt about him. It was jealousy, I suppose, and resentment that he got the job that should have been mine. And now it has gone. My dear aunt, I want you to invite Mrs. Fischer to the farm. You will like her. Her courage puts me to shame.

So I have been a tower of strength to the Minister. I was a

bit surprised because I have done nothing out of the ordinary. But he would not be pleased to know that I have become an archangel as well, and to a woman whom he treated so cruelly. I have to face the possibility that his displeasure could rob me again of my promotion. And somehow I don't seem to care. Do you remember Shakespeare's 'Full fathom five'? Well, I seem to be suffering a sea-change, into something rich and strange. It is an extraordinary thing to be happening at my age.

PART FIVE

The Holy Church of Zion

Three shots were fired last night into Robert Mansfield's house in Ridge Road, Durban. The first bullet went harmlessly into the wall. The second went into the face of Rembrandt's 'Man in Armour'. The third went into the face of Prem Bodasingh. She lies, close to death, in the special ward at St. Bartholomew's. Dr. Monty, down from Johannesburg during an adjournment of the Treason Trial, visits her night and day. The Archbishop has been to pray at her bedside. Prayers are being said in temples, mosques, churches, and synagogues. This coming Sunday there will be a special service of intercession at Chief Lutuli's church in Groutville, and he is going to preach a sermon on steadfastness.

Miss Dorothea Mainwaring, sister of the Chairman of the Natal Provincial Executive, head of the reference section of the Durban City Public Library, has won the support of the Chief Librarian, who has recommended to the City Council, that a plaque be placed in the reference section commemorating the fact that Miss Prem Bodasingh sat there during the Defiance Campaign of 1952. But the City Council has turned down the recommendation. Members of the Council are hostile to defiance campaigners, and to the commemoration of criminal acts. One might as well face the truth that most of them are hostile to Indians also. In the end a very practical view prevailed. How could you put a plaque to a young woman in a room which she is not allowed by law to enter? Her feelings must also be considered, for if she is against the colour bar, would she want a plaque in a colour bar library? This argument was put forward most persuasively by Councillor Barrington, who has a reputation for unbreachable urbanity.

Mr. and Mrs. Bodasingh are silent and withdrawn. For twenty-four years this girl has been the apple of their eyes. She has frightened them more than once, with that will of steel. Her father has always been helpless to turn her from her course; her mother has always been confident that, if her daughter has chosen a course, it must be right. They have both poured out their love upon her.

Mr. Jay Perumal comes to see them, but they do not make

their jokes. Mr. Perumal does not make jokes about his wife who is a saint, and Mr. Bodasingh does not make jokes about his wife who is not. Mrs. Bodasingh's tongue has lost its edge. They will not joke again until they know whether Prem will live or die. And at the backs of their minds is always the fearful thought that, even if she lives, she will be disfigured for life.

Robert Mansfield is looking very old, and Naomi Mansfield's face is full of care. Mansfield feels that he is responsible for it all. He feels this even after the Bodasinghs have told him that he is not. The son and daughter have gone back to school, but they have gone silent too.

And the Liberal Party has also gone a bit silent. Philip Drummond has made a public statement, but what can he say? That the party will go on? That the members will not swerve from their course of opposition to the policies of racial separation? He is a wise man and he does not say anything of the kind. This is not a time for boasting. He expresses the sympathy of the party for Prem and her parents, and says that the party will try to be faithful to the principles for which she has paid so high a price.

. . . I can tell you in confidence, my dear aunt, *and I really mean in confidence,* that my Minister is not at all pleased with the progress of the Treason Trial. 156 people were arrested on 5 December 1956, and the preparatory trial lasted twelve months, and came to an end in January of this year. The Minister has been told that in no circumstances whatsoever could the charge of treason succeed in the overwhelming majority of cases. It would appear that the police acted in haste, that the evidence against the accused was not only ill-prepared but in many cases was valueless, that their reportage of speeches made in English was at times so ridiculous that the presiding magistrate was not able to prevent the accused from breaking into laughter. On one occasion the magistrate summarily fined one of the accused for contempt of court, and a great number of his fellow accused left their prescribed seats and surged forward towards the Bench. The police were powerless to control them, and it was Lutuli who mounted a chair and ordered them all to return to their seats, which, I may say, they did immediately. The irony did not pass unnoticed that one of the most notable of those accused of treason should come to the aid of the court in preserving law and order.

My Minister is truly unhappy. Advised by the police and supported by the Cabinet, he had given a tremendous display of governmental power, which was intended to cow all subversive elements. He had also been given the assurance of our leading experts on communism and subversion, that the utterances of many of the accused could mean one thing and one only, that they planned the violent overthrow of the State. Now the grave doubt has arisen as to how conspiracy can be proved of 156 people, most of whom knew hardly any of the others.

The question arises as to whether the Freedom Charter is in fact a communist document. It bears a close resemblance in many respects to the United Nations Charter, a document which was not adopted by the Union of Socialist Soviet Republics. I wrote to you some time ago — my, my, it must be two and a half years ago — that Dr. Andrew Munnik of the University of Cape Town, Dr. Willem van Amstel of the University of Pretoria, and Dr. Koot Wollheim of the Nederduitse Gereformeerde Kerk, were unanimous that the Freedom Charter, although it pretended to be a kind of liberal human rights document, had the unmistakable signs of a Marxist-Leninist source. Now the Minister's big lawyers are telling him that the philosophical and theological evidence just cannot stand up in a court of law, and they are telling him — in the most tactful and indirect way they can find — that he made a grave error in paying too much attention to these clever scholars, that in fact they influenced him to do what *he wanted to do*. Dr. Hans Geyer, who says what he wants to whom he wants, said to the Minister, 'Tom, you shouldn't trust these extreme anti-communist advisers. Anti-communism is an irrationality and law is the highest rational pursuit of man.' You may be sure that the Minister didn't like it at all, for he is fiercely anti-communist himself.

There is another thing that I know is troubling the Minister. The defence lawyers quite outshine the State lawyers. The best lawyers never go to work for the State. They either make fortunes at the Bar, or if they put status above money, they become judges. Many of the defence lawyers are Jews, and one has to admit that the Jews have more than their reasonable share of brains. I told you that some of our police don't understand English very well; indeed some of them don't understand high Afrikaans very well either, and they are absolutely terrified of lawyers. They can bluff a lot of people in the police stations, even some of their own officers, but if they try to bluff these lawyers they make fools of themselves. You can imagine what they feel when a judge stops the cross-examination and says, 'Sergeant, you are not answering the question, either because you don't want to answer it or because you don't know what it means. Mr. Maskelson, I must ask you to put your questions in a simpler manner.'

Well, the preparatory examination came to an end, and it put the Minister in what the English call a quandary. Did he want the magistrate to commit the whole 156 for trial, or did he want the magistrate to discharge at least half of them? If the magistrate were to commit the whole 156, then it would show how right the Government had been in arresting them, and then what would it look like when after another year the judge in the Supreme Court ordered the discharge of half of them because the judge would in fact be saying to the country that the police had wrongfully arrested them, and what kind of police action is this when they wrongfully arrest eighty people, especially on a charge of treason? Geyer said to the Minister, 'Tom, you're going to be made a fool of sooner or later, and I advise you to choose sooner rather than later. Send for this magistrate very privately and secretly, and say to him, *Kêrel,* let eighty of them go. Of course if you were in Russia, you could send for him openly, and say to him, *Babushka,* or whatever they say, let eighty of them go or you will end up in Siberia.' Geyer is totally irreverent, and he will argue that an independent judiciary and strong Nationalism are totally incompatible, because you are expecting a

Nationalist judge to put his personal integrity above the nation itself, and he says that really good Nationalists make really terrible judges. Well, in the end the magistrate committed all 156 for trial, and some people are predicting that the whole trial will end up as a farce.

There is still another serious criticism that is being made of the trial. 156 people, many of them virtually unknown to many of the others, have been brought together in a way that they could never have organised themselves, and have been given a sense of common purpose. Their arrest was the direct cause of the establishment of the Treason Trial Defence Fund, and in London of the Defence and Aid Fund. They sing their 'freedom songs' when the court is not sitting, and there is nothing that we can do about that. The moment the orderly calls for silence in the court, they obey him instantly. I must admit to you that it is somewhat frightening. It is a kind of power that hasn't got a gun or a uniform, the same kind of power that Helen Joseph and those women had up at the Union Buildings. I sometimes have the fear that it is invincible, that we are going the wrong way about it all, that we put on a great show of force and we are met by a resistance that is totally immune to any action by us. It is bad enough to try to cow people, but it is even worse to try to cow people and then to have them singing freedom songs at you. Today I am going through one of my bad patches, so I think I shall stop. I feel that the hand at the helm is not strong enough for these dangerous waters. I feel that it is only Dr. Hendrik that can lead us to safety.

Yes, I am sorry about the shootings into Robert Mansfield's house. He has been one of the most active workers for the Treason Trial Defence Fund, and I am afraid that such people inevitably attract the hostility of what is called the Right. You know of course it will be said that the Right can shoot into people's houses with impunity. It will be said — not in public of course — that the police never find out the perpetrators. It will be said too — and again not in public — that the perpetrators are known to the police, and sometimes even that they are policemen themselves, but I do not believe that for a moment.

Aunt, I must stop. I have a rule that I try to keep. If you can only talk gloomily, then keep your mouth shut. You have no right to undermine the hope of others. But I can end on a better note than that. I have been chosen to represent Pretoria in the National Table Tennis Championships.

– Prem.
  – That's Hugh.
  – Yes.
  – What are you doing here?
  – I came to see you.
  – Well, you can't see much.
  – I can see your mouth and the tip of your nose. How are you feeling, Prem?
  – As they say, I'm feeling remarkably well in the circumstances. I'm not going to die. I thought these were your final exams.
  – They are. But they say I can write next week. I had to promise not to try to see the papers.
  – And they believed you?
  – Prem, I haven't come here to make jokes.
  – No. I know why you've come.
  – Why?
  – To ask me to marry you. We'll marry in England, and find a cottage where we can see the daffodils and listen to the nightingales. And we would hate it. You would hate me and I would hate you.
  – Prem!
  – It's true. I'm not going to go through it again. I love you and you love me, but we're not going to marry until we can do so in the open. You've always thought you had a job to do, and you can't do it anywhere else but here. But now because someone has shot me, you think things have changed. Hugh, don't ask me again.
  – I shouldn't have asked you at all. Sorry, Prem. I shan't do it again.

Mr. Robert Mansfield
Natal Regional Office
The Liberal Party

I suppose you are feeling a bit sorry for yourself, but you have no one to blame but yourself. You are still pursuing your dangerous path, but I must warn you that it is becoming very dangerous indeed. That bullet was not meant for the coolie girl but for your daughter. Our man reports that the light was not very good.

Therefore you will see that our plan for you has not yet been completed. It is our intention to complete it when the time is suitable. You can still prevent its completion. You can announce your resignation of the chairmanship of the Liberal Party in Natal. You must announce it in a Durban paper and a Pietermaritzburg paper. You can give any reason you wish, or none if you wish. Most people will now admit that you have a good reason for resigning.

Let me tell you that we are determined to break your party. It is a danger to white Christian civilisation. Let me tell you in plain language that our next target is your daughter. May I advise you not to sit in front of open windows? I am surprised that you were so foolish.

We sign ourselves
The Preservation of White South Africa League

– Prem.
   – That's Professor Eddie.
   – Yes, Prem.
   – What are you doing in Durban, Professor Eddie?
   – I came to see you, Prem.
   – Why did you come all this way?
   – Because I love you, of course.
   – What does Mrs. Eddie say?
   – She says it is understandable. She also says it is a sign of senility. No, don't laugh, Prem. I'm sorry I made you laugh. Dr. Monty will be furious with me.
   – Do you know, it is the first time I've laughed?

– Does it hurt?

– Yes, it hurts.

– I'm sorry, Prem. It's not only *my* love that I'm bringing to you. I bring love from Laura and Hendrik and Mrs. Eddie, and Jan and Frederik and Izak Berg. And from Ruth. She would have come but she had a case. And all the people at Lenasia. And a special message from Helen Joseph.

– That's wonderful.

– Now listen to me, Prem. I have a friend in New York, one of the greatest surgeons in the world. Your father and mother are taking you to see him.

– Why must I go to New York, Professor Eddie? Are they afraid about my face? Will I be ugly?

– You'll never be ugly, my dearest child. But we want to see what can be done.

– You know I never spent much time looking at my face. But now I think a lot about it. What makes one flinch from a girl who has something wrong with her face, even if she is a saint? And why is it more important to a girl than to a man?

– I don't know, child. These questions look very simple, but they are not.

– Do you know the story of the girl with the terrible blemish?

– No.

– She fell in love with a blind man and she married him. He didn't flinch from her. He was the only one who didn't flinch from her. Then along came the great surgeon, from New York too, I suppose. He examined the man and he said, I think I can restore your sight. And the man was filled with joy, and she was filled with fear. She was filled with shame too, because she could not share his joy. Now blind people can see things that we can't, and he knew that she did not share his joy. So he said to her, Why do you not share my joy? But she told him that he was making a mistake, that she did share his joy. He said to her, You have never before lied to me, why do you lie to me now? So in the end she had to tell him about the blemish. And he loved her so greatly that he decided to stay blind, for her happiness meant more to him than his sight. What do you think of that story?

– It is very beautiful, Prem.

– They left my mouth and my nose open, then why did they have to bandage my eyes?

– They wanted you to breathe, Prem, but they don't want you to use your eyes just yet.

– Am I going to be blind, Professor Eddie?

– They don't think so, Prem, but they want to take every care.

– It's a good thing you can't see my eyes.

– Why, Prem?

– Because you'd see that I am weeping. Why do people do things like that, Professor Eddie?

– Because they hate, Prem. Something has died in them. Perhaps something happened to them, in childhood perhaps. The man who shot at you, he hates all black people, but even more he hates white people who treat black people as their equals. They hate and they fear equality more than anything else.

– Like the Lily Maid of Astolat?

– Like whom?

– Elaine, the Lily Maid of Astolat.

– She didn't hate, Prem. She died of love.

– We have our own Lily Maid of Astolat. She comes to our meetings and shouts and chants and curses. She hates all of us. Her name is Elaine, so they call her the Lily Maid of Astolat. She spat in my face once, Professor Eddie. Tell me, how are the Mansfields? Why don't they come to see me?

– Dr. Monty doesn't want them to come yet. He thinks they'd be bad for you. They'd weep and suffer. Your visitors have to be cheerful like me.

– Professor, I must ask you to go now.

– Oh no, sister, not yet, not now.

– Yes, Prem, now. He can come again tomorrow.

– Goodbye then, Prem, till tomorrow.

– Goodbye, Professor Eddie. And take my love to the Mansfields. Tell them I'm getting better. Tell them I'm going to New York. Tell them that's what money can do. If I had been the daughter of a flower-seller, I wouldn't be going.

– That's enough, Prem. This is not the proper time for a

political discussion. And what is more, you've had excitement enough for one day. Professor, off you go.

. . . So off I went, with that cursed lump in my throat, but this time worse than ever, for the land that is beautiful, and for the girl who was beautiful, and may not be beautiful again. If I prayed, I would pray for her, but I say, May she be beautiful again, and I suppose that is a kind of prayer. Ah, well, I am getting old, and my tear ducts are getting old too. The terrible thought comes into my mind, if she's going to be disfigured, wouldn't it be better if she lost her sight as well?

The Minister of Justice is satisfied that Mrs. Helen Joseph is promoting feelings of hostility between whites and blacks. He has therefore issued banning orders under the Suppression of Communism Act, and these prohibit her from attending any gathering, except those of a social, religious or educational nature, and they also prohibit her from leaving the magisterial district of Johannesburg.

Mrs. Joseph has asked the Minister for his reasons for issuing these banning orders, and has received a seven-page reply, claiming that she had actively associated herself with propaganda inciting black people to resist discrimination laws, and had vilified the white people of South Africa, calling them oppressors.

However, Mrs. Joseph is allowed to travel daily to Pretoria, for the Treason Trial has now begun in earnest. She has one comfort. She has bought a house of her own, 35 Fanny Avenue, Norwood, Johannesburg. It is a house that may one day be proclaimed a national monument.

. . . Yes, it is true that when I last wrote I was facing a crisis of confidence. There are days when I feel, as the English say, on top of the world, and there are days when I feel that Afrikanerdom and the Afrikaans language, born in this country of rock and krans and mountain and thorn, fashioned in suffering and fortitude, are doomed to disappear from the face of the earth. The Norman conquerors of England were in their turn conquered by the people they conquered without bloodshed and violence, leaving no legacy of hatred. But the Normans and the English were both Europeans. Their two countries were separated by a mere twenty miles of water. They became one people. Centuries later an Englishman would boast that he had Norman blood in his veins.

I do not see how that can happen here. We are so alien to one another. I fear that the Afrikaner will never be able to undo conquest. His pride of race is too unyielding. Therefore surely the doctrine of peaceful and separate coexistence is the only answer to our problems. I am ashamed that I sometimes doubt it.

The Minister does not know of these doubts, but at times he comes close to discerning them. The closest that he came to it was when he said to me, 'Van Onselen, you have only one fault, and that is that you too often see two sides to a question, and that always leads to indecision and a blurring of policy.' I could not possibly say to him that I shall not feel confident about the future until Dr. Hendrik is our Prime Minister. I could not say to him that it is only Dr. Hendrik who can convince me that there is only one side to a question.

Of course I am writing to thank you for having Mrs. Fischer to stay at Weltevreden. She tells me it is a place of healing, and she needed it. She is a quiet, devout, sensible woman. Her religion rules her life, and it was her tragic lot to bear a son who brought down on her the greatest calamity that can befall an Afrikaner mother. She tells me that she has invited you to come and stay with her, and to see the great city of Pretoria. It would be hard to imagine two places more different than Pretoria and Weltevreden. We have no mountains here, and you cannot wake up in the night and hear the sound of water falling. That is what pleased her most of all, the sound of water falling, and of cows lowing, and the tapping of the bokmakierie on her window. There is still peace in those parts.

I agree that the restrictions on Mrs. Helen Joseph are very severe, but what is the Government to do? It is surely intolerable that a person standing trial for treason should go round making political speeches. No one likes to restrict personal freedom, but we are facing a challenge from world communism, and you cannot fight communism by democratic methods. She absolutely refuses to listen to reason. She is going to go her own way and no one is going to stop her. She tells the Security Police that they are the instruments of a totalitarian society, but she is pretty totalitarian herself. She has been warned that, if she persists, the Minister is fully empowered to cut her off from social gatherings as well. In a way it is farcical to cut a person off from political gatherings and yet allow her to meet freely with anyone she wishes. It is said that she is not a communist, yet she belongs to the white Congress, and that is to all intents and purposes a communist organisation.

I suppose you know that Father Huddleston has gone back to England, and just in time too. He was well on the way to getting a banning order, but his Community recalled him in time. He and Helen Joseph had the same technique. They stand up in front of large black meetings, they give their audience a list of grievances, they condemn the Government, and in particular the National Party, they work up their hearers into a state of frenzy, and then they go home and leave them angry and frustrated. That there are black grievances one has no doubt, but why don't these people work steadily and quietly to remove them, just as our own people do?

I don't think that there can be any doubt that world pressure on us is much greater in 1958 than it was when we came to power in 1948. I can give you a small example of this. It's only a straw in the wind, but the wind is, I fear, going to blow more strongly. Two members of my table tennis club were chosen to go to Amsterdam to represent South Africa in the world championship. But the International Table Tennis Federation has refused to recognise the South African team. Our club belongs to the South African Table Tennis Union, which is white. But the I.T.T.F. has announced that it recognises only the South African Table Tennis Board, which has no colour bar. At first the I.T.T.F. was willing to recognise both the Union and the Board, but the Union barred non-white spectators during the Israeli tour, and that was the end of our recognition.

It is a most humiliating situation. We cannot play any overseas matches without the permission of the Board, and the Board will not give permission so long as we have a colour bar. Our club is adamant against admitting black members or spectators. You will remember the famous church clause. It was part of the Native Laws Amendment Act of 1957, and it empowers the Minister, after consulting the local authorities, to forbid a Bantu to attend *any* function in a white area. Our local authority is the Pretoria City Council, and they would certainly not give us permission, nor would the owners of the hall in which we play, to have Bantu as members or spectators.

Our president swallowed his pride and went to Durban to see a certain Cassim, who is the president of the S.A.T.T. Board, and the man who is certainly behind all this racial agitation. Our president told us that he had never before been spoken to in such a way by a non-white person. This Cassim rejected any kind of federation, and said that any white player was welcome to join any of the clubs controlled by the Board.

The Government has offered generous help to all legitimate non-white organisations, provided there are no inter-racial competitions, no mixed teams, and no mixing of spectators. Non-white teams from abroad would be welcome to play non-white teams in South Africa. Sportsmen from other countries must respect our customs just as we respect theirs. The Government's generous approach has received a surly response from the man Cassim. He says that when the Government orders there to be a separate Afrikaans table tennis union, and a separate English-speaking union, then he might be prepared to negotiate. He says that the Government does not object to racial mixing, it objects only to colour mixing.

The black soccer federation is also stirring up trouble. It

wants FIFA, the Federation of International Football Associa-
tions, to recognise the black federation and not the white
association. It refused to affiliate to the white association,
which offered it affiliation though without voting powers. It
seems that any concession is refused. The Government
announces that it will not grant passports to any person
going abroad to lobby for the exclusion of white South
Africans from world sport.

The South African Olympic Council has decided that no
competition between white and black would be allowed in
any sports association affiliated to the council. But it is said
that prominent South Africans in exile are approaching the
Olympic world body to have white South Africans excluded
from the Olympic Games altogether.

Behind all this is undoubtedly the man John Parker, about
whom I have written to you before. He has one supreme aim
in life, and that is to have white South Africans excluded
from any kind of world competition. How a man can so hate
his own people, I cannot understand. But of course he is a
member of the Liberal Party. So is the man Cassim. So is of
course your friend Robert Mansfield. It is not to be wondered at that they sometimes find themselves the victims of
violence.

In my less confident moods I fear that the next attack will
be on rugby, cricket, tennis, and golf, in all of which white
South Africans have won fame for themselves and their
country. Exclusion from these would be bad enough but I
fear it will not stop there. The final exclusion would be from
any kind of international relations whatsoever, and that, my
dear aunt, would ultimately mean what is known as the
imposition of sanctions. Our extreme politicians say that,
rather than give up our way of life, let us go back to the
ox-wagon. Our extreme theologians say that, if this is God's
will for us, why should we resist it?

I have no time for these fanatics. The history of the
Afrikaner is one of courage but also of resourcefulness and
intelligence. The word *kragdadig* used to be a noble word,
meaning powerful and resolute in deed. But it is gradually
acquiring a second meaning, that the doer of the deed has

more power than sense. This second meaning has been given to it, by our enemies of course, because of the words and actions of these fanatics.

You might say a prayer for me, my dear aunt. I do not like this state of doubt. In fact I am ashamed of it.

Last night the quiet of Ridge Road was shattered by a bomb explosion at the house of Mr. Robert Mansfield, regional chairman of the Liberal Party. The explosion took place at two o'clock in the morning, and completely destroyed two bedrooms. Fortunately the two rooms were unoccupied. Mr. Mansfield's son Lawrence was spending the night with friends, and his daughter Felicity, who had been deeply disturbed by the shooting of Miss Prem Bodasingh, had gone to sleep in her parents' bedroom.

Mr. Mansfield asked his wife and daughter to remain in the bedroom while he investigated the situation. When he was satisfied that there was no other person in the house or grounds, he allowed his wife and daughter to view the damage. It was his daughter Felicity who made the horrifying discovery of a man's body lying by the demolished wall. The body was headless. The girl ran screaming into her mother's arms. By this time friends and neighbours were at the scene, and the family doctor immediately put the girl under sedation. The police also arrived promptly, and after they had thoroughly inspected the damage, they removed the body of the man who had presumably set off the bomb.

He was later identified as Mr. Heinrich Rohrs, nurseryman of New Germany, Natal.

Heinrich Rohrs had been interned by the Smuts Government during the years of the Second World War. He was known as a fanatical admirer of Adolf Hitler, and a sympathiser with the Nazi movement. He was a member of the Greyshirts, a virulent anti-Semitic organisation, and had published a booklet in 1937 producing irrefutable proof that General Smuts was a Jew. Dr. Malan in his campaigns against Smuts never asserted or even insinuated that he was a Jew because he knew perfectly well that Smuts was an Afrikaner, even though not a true one and, what is more, Smuts, though not much older than Malan, had taught him in the Sunday school at Riebeek West, seventy years before. But Malan in his anti-Semitic days certainly thought that Smuts was too pro-Jewish, and he uttered the penetrating witticism that went round the nation, 'General Smuts is on the map of Palestine. Should he be deleted from that map, he would not be on the map of any country.' Another of Malan's jokes went round the nation, namely that when Smuts spoke to the Jews he was General Smutsowitz, and when he spoke to the Scots he was General MacSmuts.

In the internment camp Rohrs met Miss Anna von Maltitz, from the Berlin district near East London. She was an aristocrat, fine-boned and haughty, and Rohrs was a commoner. But she was attracted to him because he shared her hatred of the British, the Jews, and the blacks. They fell in love and decided to marry when the war was over. Acceptance by an aristocrat changed Rohrs from a solitary to an active campaigner for South Africa's secession from the British Commonwealth, the removal of the franchise from Jews, the discontinuation of Jewish immigration, and the unrelenting implementation of the policies of racial separation. During his boyhood he had been secretive and withdrawn. His years at Maritzburg College were a purgatory to him. He was treated as a traitor and an outcast and this made him more anti-British than ever. After the war he devoted his time and his energy, when he was not in the nursery, to proving that Hitler had never ordered the extermination of the Jews, and that places like Dachau, Buchenwald and Auschwitz had never existed except in the imaginations of Jewish–British–American world capitalists. Rohrs strongly approved of Hitler's view that black people were monkeys and were fit only to be slaves and servants. Rohrs claimed to be a Christian, and he wrote that true Christianity was the militant enemy of Judaism, Islam, Hinduism, Liberalism, Freemasonry and Communism. He believed firmly that Jesus was not a Jew but a Persian.

Rohrs was a strong supporter of the racial policies of Dr. Malan and the National Party, but in 1954 he published a bitter attack on the retiring Prime Minister because he had paid a visit to what he called the Holy Land, and had had his name inscribed by South African Jewry in the Golden Book in recognition of his 'contribution to better racial understanding in South Africa'. Rohrs then transferred his loyalty to the new Prime Minister Johannes Gerhardus Strijdom, the Lion of the North, and his powerful Minister of Bantu Affairs, Dr. Hendrik.

Rohrs was a nurseryman of national repute. His rose-gardens at New Germany attracted thousands of visitors. He perfected a new red rose and called it 'Beauty of Berlin'. He was financially highly successful, and the proceeds from his nursery enabled him to publish his pamphlets. He and his wife eschewed luxury so that they could set aside money for his campaigning. Their first child was a boy and they called him Adolf Hitler von Maltitz Rohrs. This meant that the boy grew up as secretive and reserved as his father had done before him. With bitter unwillingness they finally agreed to drop the boy's second name, but the damage had already been done.

The police found an abundance of pamphlets of an anti-Semitic and anti-black nature, and also evidence that Rohrs had directed the Preserve White South Africa League. But they could find no evidence that there had been any other members. In that respect he had continued solitary to the end.

His widow at first continued to run the nursery, but slowly the rose-gardens began to lose their breathtaking beauty. Finally she sold it and returned with her two children to the district of Berlin. The League had come to an end.

It is the kind of news that is very painful for liberal-minded people. They tell it in a low voice, almost as though they hoped that no one would hear it. But it has to come out in the end. The Robert Mansfields are emigrating to Australia. He has got a job there, in a high school in the western city of Perth.

Although the League has come to an end, its consequences have not. The destroyed rooms have been rebuilt, but the girl Felicity Mansfield will not sleep anywhere but in her parents' bedroom. She wakes up screaming in the night. But worse than that, sometimes in the daytime she runs screaming into her mother's arms. When a car passes the house, she stays tense and anxious till she is sure it is past.

The first person to hear the news was Philip Drummond himself. It was not pleasant for him to see the laughing confident giant of a man so stricken. He took the firm uncomprising line that Mansfield was right, that his children had to be his first consideration. He rebuked him gently for feeling shame. He assured him that not one member of the Liberal Party would judge him for his decision. It was easy to see that his words brought absolutely no comfort to his friend.

One thing was clearly understood. There were to be no farewell parties. The Mansfields did not wish anyone to see them off at the docks. They wished to be allowed to steal away. It is lucky that Philip Drummond knows most of the big editors well. He will ask them to publish nothing till the Mansfields have gone.

Mr. Robert Mansfield
Deserting Natal Chairman
Liberal Party

So, Robert, I read in the *Sunday Times* that you're ratting to Australia, eh? You ratted from the International Club and now you're ratting from the country.

And what about your black brothers and sisters, whose rights you fought for? You didn't even want them to have separate cups and saucers, remember? And now you're going to leave them, eh? Who's going to protect them now? What are they going to think of the white hero who promised to protect them with his last drop of blood, and now is running away? You always talk as though it is the Government who has betrayed the black man, but now the black nation is saying it is you.

And who got hurt? None of your family. First the coolie dolly who got shot in the face. And then the man who blew his head off. You've got no guts, but then I never thought you had. You're a kaffir-lover and a worm, but now it is clear that you are a worm most of all.

I bet you can't wait till you get at the abo dollies. Lubras they call them, don't they? They'll be a bit small for you, won't they? You'll have to try lubracation, ha! ha! A nice juicy time you'll have, I'm sure. They've got no decent laws there.

Goodbye, digger, and good riddance. Australia's loss is our gain.

Proud White Christian Woman

Robert Mansfield's decision to emigrate to Australia has cast a damper over the National Conference of the Liberal Party. Mansfield may have passed severe judgment on himself, but the party has certainly not done so. And why should Mansfield have passed such severe judgment on himself? When fanatics fire shots into your house and then blow up a good part of it, and when your daughter screams in the night, why should you stay? It is true of course that Mansfield has made some pretty stirring speeches in his time. Even at recruiting meetings he would tell people that the party could offer them only toil and blood and tears and sweat. Well, lots of people can face the toil and sweat, but the blood and tears are more difficult.

What moral duty has any person to stay in any particular country? Is there such a thing as an ethics of emigration? What ethics of emigration ever existed in countries like Britain, Ireland, Puerto Rico, Pakistan? If there had been a universal ethics of emigration, there would never have been a United States of America, nor any Afrikanerdom, nor any Zulus. No one thought you were a rat if you emigrated from Ireland to America. But many people in South Africa would think you were a rat if you left. And in Israel too.

Albert Einstein left Germany and emigrated to America. But Dietrich Bonhoeffer returned from America to Germany, and to almost certain death. Today these two men are held in veneration, Einstein because he deepened and widened our knowledge of the universe, Bonhoeffer because he believed there were some things for which a man should be ready to die. If Einstein had stayed in Germany, he would have died. If Bonhoeffer had stayed in America, he might still have been alive.

Not many Afrikaners leave the country. Among them the ethics of emigration is very strong. To emigrate is cowardly. It shows lack of faith in Afrikanerdom, of its ability to face adversity as it did in the Anglo–Boer War of 1899 to 1902. To emigrate is to lose the identity that God and History have given to the Afrikaner. If he goes to Australia or Canada or England, he will cease to be an Afrikaner. If his name is Labuschagne, it will become Labushane.

The ethics of emigration amongst Indian and coloured South Africans hardly exists. What moral obligation have they to stay in a country which has made them suffer under the Group Areas Act, and has taken the coloured people off the common roll, and put them on a roll of their own, so that their sacred racial identity could be preserved? Growing communities of them can be found in Australia and Canada and England.

And as for the English-speaking, except those who think they have a duty to work for a just order of society, why should they stay? But not many have gone yet. When they do go, some of them join the militant anti-apartheid groups abroad and some spend their time longing for the country they have left, and some decide to forget it all and to give their loyalty to the land of their adoption.

Robert Mansfield did not go to the national conference of course. In fact he has already resigned his Natal chairmanship and has been succeeded by Hugh Mainwaring, son of the great Henry Mainwaring, Chairman of the Natal Executive Council, and aristocrat of Natal. He has threatened more than once to disinherit his son, and perhaps he will do it now.

The rift between Molteno and Patrick Duncan is widening, especially over sport and over John Parker's underground efforts to get all-white South African teams banned from international competition. Duncan wants the Liberal Party to support John Parker openly, but Molteno regards such a course as suicidal. Duncan also wants the party to get rid of Molteno but that is a much more difficult proposition, for Molteno is the spokesman for the Cape liberal–conservative tradition.

But Philip Drummond is able to prevent a split in the party. It is some strange gift that he possesses.

I have been asked the question, 'It's all very well for you to talk about toil and blood and tears and sweat, but what about your children?' My answer has been, 'We would have two choices: to stay here and to give our children a father and mother who put some things even above their own children's safety and happiness, or to leave and to give them a father and mother who put their children's safety and happiness above all else.' Which would I choose? They are both good courses, are they not? I hope I would choose the first.
— Mr. Robert Mansfield, in a speech at Pietermaritzburg, 1957.

DOMINEE REFUSES TO CONDUCT
FUNERAL SERVICE
BIG CONGREGATION TORN IN TWO

One of the biggest funeral services ever seen in Bloemfontein came to an end yesterday before it had begun. Dominee van Rooyen announced from the pulpit that he would refuse to take the service for the late Mr. Karel Bosman because black and coloured people were present. It was against the policy of the Nederduits Gereformeerde Kerk to conduct mixed services and it was also against the policy of the Government. Further, according to the Native Laws Amendment Act of 1957 Bantu were not allowed to worship in a white area without the permission of the Minister of Native Affairs, given with the concurrence of the local authority. No such permission had been obtained and therefore, if he had conducted the service, all Bantu present would have been committing an offence under the Act. He was not prepared to expose them to such penalties. Therefore he regretted that he could not conduct the service. In any event he did not think the time was ripe for such mixed worship. It was very unfortunate that the family of the deceased man had not informed him that a large number of black and coloured people would attend.

The family of the late Mr. Bosman have announced that the funeral service will be held today in the Bloemfontein Presbyterian Church.

Mr. Karel Bosman was the superintendent of the Bochabela township. One could not describe him otherwise than as a greatly loved man. The word *paternal* has acquired a derogatory meaning in recent years, but Mr. Bosman was invariably addressed in Sotho as *Ntate*, Father. He was held in especial regard by the old men and women of Bochabela, because of the respect with which he treated them, and because of the pains to which he would go to ensure that such things as pensions and disability grants were given to those who were entitled to them. Many old and infirm men and women never receive these grants, partly because some do not know about them, and partly because old men and women cannot face a struggle with bureaucracy, and give up more easily when there are rebuffs and delays and rudeness. Sometimes the laws governing places like Bochabela can be very harsh, and Mr. Bosman used to soften this harshness whenever he was able.

'It has come as a great shock to the family,' said Dr. Michiel Bosman, one of Bloemfontein's leading surgeons. 'The people of Bochabela wanted to pay their respects to my father, and it is a scandal that there can be a law to prevent them. My father was a lifelong supporter of the National Party, but he was very critical of the harshness of many of the laws, especially those which control black movement and black housing in a place like Bochabela.' Mrs. Karel Bosman said she had been deeply shocked by Dominee van Rooyen's decision. 'I did not believe that such a thing could happen in a Christian country. It makes me wonder what is happening to us Afrikaner people.'

The congregation of the big Kerk is sharply divided between those who regard the refusal to hold the funeral service as a Christian scandal, and those who consider that the first duty of the dominee was to uphold the law of the country. There is also a third faction, those who find it intolerable that a black person should sit at any time in a white church, and even more intolerable that a white Christian should have to sit in the same pew in which yesterday or some day before black people had been sitting.

The Reverend Zaccheus Richard Mahabane, twice president-general of the African National Congress, president of the Interdenominational African Ministers' Federation, and one of the leading ministers of the Methodist Church of South Africa, expressed his grief over the refusal of Dominee van Rooyen to proceed with the funeral service of the late Mr. Karel Bosman.

Mr. Mahabane, seventy-seven years old, white-haired and venerable, who all his long life has cherished the hope that Christian ethics would finally triumph in the shaping of race policy, told of his grave anxiety to interviewing reporters.

'The people who do this kind of thing, the people who make this kind of law, they do not understand what they are doing to us. This man Karel Bosman was beloved by the people of Bochabela. Now he dies, and they weep for his family, and they want to go to this church to show their sorrow. They bring out their best clothes, they brush their old hats, they polish their old shoes, and they go quietly and reverently to the church. Some of them, even though their bones are old, will go into the church on their hands and knees. What is in their hearts? Only sorrow and love. And then they are told they are not wanted there. Their love is not wanted because there is a law that says that black people cannot show their love in a white church. Gentlemen, my heart is so full that I can hardly speak to you. This thing has dealt a heavy blow to the people of Bochabela. The old ones are grieved, but the young ones say, We told you so; you want to love white people, but white people don't want your love. These young people are angry with their elders. They say, If white people don't want black love then they can have black hate. Gentlemen, I have no more to say.'

The specialist has given his opinion that Miss Prem Boda-singh's eyes have not been damaged. As soon as Dr. Monty agrees, she will leave for New York to see Professor Eddie's surgeon friend. She will be accompanied by her father and mother. Her father is leaving his business interests in the capable hands of Mr. Jay Perumal, the husband of the saint. The news about Prem's eyes has cheered him up and if the news from New York is good, he may soon be making jokes again.

They say that M. K. Bodasingh thinks only of money. It isn't true. He values his daughter above any money. Even Prem thinks that her tongue was too sharp in the past. She has made herself a promise that it will not be so sharp in the future.

When Prem comes back from New York she is going to work for Mr. Bhoola, at FOSA, the Friends of the Sick Association, the one who said that if she became a Christian she must keep her eyes on Christ so that she would not get a chance to look at Christians. Mrs. Bodasingh went to see Mr. Bhoola while Prem was still in hospital, and asked him if he would give a job to her daughter. Mr. Bhoola, so to speak, jumped at Prem, and who wouldn't, but he wasn't going to show that to Mrs. Bodasingh, because he did not believe in kowtowing to the rich, so he said, naturally he would have to consult his committee. He said this in his very smiling way, but that only made her tongue a little sharper. She said to him very astringently,

– It would no doubt help you and your committee to come to a decision, Mr. Bhoola, if you knew that when my daughter marries FOSA, she will bring with her a dowry of five thousands pounds.

Mr. Bhoola, who was always thrown into a state of excitement by the promise of money, still continued to look smilingly doubtful, but not too doubtful, for he had no intention of losing the five thousand pounds.

– Five thousand pounds would help you to build your library, Mr. Bhoola. I hear you want a library.

– Yes, we do want a library, Mrs. M. K. But you see it is a question of procedure. The committee expects to be consulted in such matters.

– Everybody knows, Mr. Bhoola, that the committee thinks you are a kind of Mahatma, and they do exactly what you tell them to do. But do not trouble them or yourself. I shall offer Prem and her dowry to the Blind Society. Sometimes these blind people can see things that even a Mahatma cannot see.

Mr. Bhoola let out what might almost be described as a cry of pain.

– Mrs. M. K., you mustn't take offence. Prem is a girl in a thousand.

– Of course she's a girl in a thousand. And her dowry is one in a thousand too. Do you take her or leave her?

– I take her, Mrs. M. K.

– Without consulting your committee?

– They will confirm my decision, Mrs. M. K.

– Of course they will confirm it. Where will they get another director like Mr. Ahmed Bhoola? What is more, they know a dowry when they see one.

– Your tongue is as sharp as ever, Kuniamma. M. K. was a brave man to marry you.

Mrs. Bodasingh permitted herself a smile.

– Perhaps I was too sharp, Ahmed. But when I see you sitting there, smiling and doubting and playing the big director when you are being offered a girl in a thousand, it makes me sharp.

– People who are small inside like to look big outside, Kuniamma.

– Modesty doesn't suit you, Ahmed. It never did. Take this and look after it carefully. It's the dowry.

. . . Yes, my dear aunt, of course I realise that the whole event is very painful. But it has been made much more painful by the English press. If this event had not been blown up out of all proportion, the matter would have been confined to Bloemfontein instead of being broadcast to the whole nation. That is bad enough, but it has also been broadcast to the world, and you may be sure that our enemies at United Nations are preparing a fresh attack on us.

I remember that I wrote to you after the Loeriestad affair, and told you that once Clause 29(c) of the Native Laws Amendment Act came into operation, this kind of thing would not happen. Well, it should not have happened. I blame the Bosman family for this. They should have known that permission was required. And I blame Dominee van Rooyen also. He should have foreseen that a large number of people from Bochabela would want to attend. I am informed that he told his own elders that he had no idea that black people would come. It had never happened to him before, and he was totally unprepared for it. One can only suppose then that he had no idea of the esteem in which Mr. Bosman was held.

I agree with you, my dear aunt, that the whole thing is very sad. But the really sad thing is that it need not have happened. And the other sad thing is that it should have been broadcast to the world. Some time ago I decided to accept Dr. Hendrik's view that mixed worship was undesirable, but it is a great pity that funeral services were not specifically exempted. Cheer up, my dear aunt. My Minister often says to me, 'Van Onselen, you can't make omelettes without breaking eggs.' And do you remember what President Truman said? 'If you can't stand the heat, stay out of the kitchen.'

So your friend Robert Mansfield is leaving. He couldn't stand the heat. That is the trouble with these liberals. They think they can build Utopia on love and goodwill. They are always calling out for justice, but when justice is embodied in law, then they condemn the law. They have no understanding of human nature. They think that Jew and Gentile, English and Afrikaner, Zulu and Indian, white and black, will all live in peace together when the laws of separation are repealed. And when it all blows up, they will come running to the Afrikaner for protection.

This man Mansfield was a big talker, but he did not understand the realities of politics. Nor do liberals understand the revulsion and abhorrence that they and their beliefs evoke in the true Afrikaner. Nor do they understand that they expose themselves to physical danger from what one might call the extreme Right, to which this man Rohrs clearly belonged. One must condemn violence, but one must also condemn those who invite violence, and he was certainly one.

My dear aunt, I am sorry again about the Bloemfontein event. Let me say again that it should not have happened. Dr. Hendrik made provision for such events in Clause 29(c). The Minister decides after consultation with the local authority. But I agree that funeral services should have been exempted.

Mrs. Fischer keeps well, and still talks a great deal about her visit to Weltevreden.

The Reverend Isaiah Buti, pastor of the Holy Church of Zion in Bochabela, entered the room of the Acting Chief Justice, if not with awe, then certainly with deference. And certainly with respect too, for not only did Judge Olivier occupy one of the highest seats in the land, but he was held in high esteem by the black people of Bloemfontein. Was he not the man who had tried to prevent Parliament from removing coloured voters from the common roll?

The room was the biggest Mr. Buti had seen in his life. The table also was the biggest he had seen, and behind it was a grand carved chair, and behind the chair portraits of those who had been chief justices of the Union of South Africa. And now from the chair rose the impressive figure of Acting Chief Justice Olivier, with his hand held out to his visitor.

– Welcome, Mr. Buti. I got your letter, and now you are here. Sit down and tell me all about it.

– Thank you, judge. I must first collect myself. I must get used to this room.

– Take your time. It's a very big room.

– There's much power in this room, judge.

The judge laughed.

– Not so much as people think, Mr. Buti.

– Judge, I wrote to you because I am anxious. I have lived in the Orange Free State all my life. Of course we are a conquered people, but we have lived in peace with the white rulers. But things are changing, judge, and I am anxious that they should not change in the way they are changing now.

– What are you referring to, Mr. Buti? The killing of the police?

– Certainly that, judge. But not only that. I am referring to the feeling against the whites. It is the worst I have known it to be.

– And the causes?

Mr. Buti gave a humble and apologetic smile.

– You know them as well as I do, judge.

– And what is the biggest?

– The pass laws, judge, perhaps most of all. You have heard those words, *temporary sojourner*?

– Indeed.

– That's what we are, my lord, temporary sojourners. Do you know the prayer of Chief Hosea Kutako?

– I have read it, Mr. Buti, but I do not remember it. What did he say?

– His prayer ended thus: O Lord, help us who roam about. Help us who have been placed in Africa and have no dwelling place of our own. Give us back a dwelling place. O God, all power is yours in Heaven and Earth. Amen.

– Yes, I remember.

– That's what we are, judge. We have no dwelling place. The Government says I have a dwelling place in Thaba Nchu. They say my dwelling place is not here in Bochabela, where I live and work and have my wife and my children, and my church, the Holy Church of Zion. I am lucky, judge, because I am a minister. But most of the people of my church are workers. They work in white factories and white shops, they work for white builders and white carpenters. Our girls, and often our women too, work in white houses. Sometimes we feel, judge, that we have no meaning for white people except our work. My son works in a white factory and my two daughters work in white houses. But if I were to die, they would all be sent to Thaba Nchu. My wife is not allowed to rent a house, and my son is too young to rent one. Judge, you are a very busy man. Do you want to hear any more causes?

– No, Mr. Buti. The one you mention is cause enough.

– You see, judge, I am a minister. I am not likely to lose my job. But the men of my church often lose their jobs. Sometimes it is their fault, but sometimes it is not. The factory closes down, the white employer dies. The employer of Mr. Philemon Moroka died, and he could not get a job. So they told him he would have to give up his house and go back to Thaba Nchu with his wife and four children. Once you lose a house, judge, it is very hard to get another. If Mr. Moroka is offered another job in Bloemfontein he will have to leave his wife and children and come to a single men's hostel in Bochabela. Then perhaps after a year he will get another house, and he will be able to bring his wife and children back. And sometimes it happens that, just after a man gets another house, he loses his job again, or he dies. The Moroka family are luckier than most, because his mother has a nice house in Thaba Nchu. But sometimes widows and their children are sent back, and there is no house, and no work either. There is not much work in such places. That's the way we live, judge. We have been placed in Africa and we have no dwelling place of our own.

Judge Olivier listened to Mr. Buti with much pain, not only pain for the people that Mr. Buti was talking about, but pain for his own impotence. How can the ombudsman invoke the majestic power of the law when it is the law itself that is the cause of the injustice? What had Mr. Buti come to ask him? To do something that he had no power to do? He thought wryly of Mr. Buti's words that there was much power in this room. It was almost as though the black man knew that the white man was suffering, for his next words were meant to comfort.

– Judge, we have had more luck in Bochabela than in many other places. The laws have not been applied so harshly. Sometimes they have not been applied at all. You will find widows still living in Bochabela. That was the work of Mr. Karel Bosman. No one shouted at you in his offices, no one called you boy, no one called your wife Jane. They called us Bantu of course, which is a word we do not like, but we never heard the word kaffir.

Then Mr. Buti was silent for a long time.

– The funeral service was very painful, judge. We wanted the people of Bloemfontein to see that we loved this man. We went there to show our love. But it wasn't wanted. I haven't come here to attack the church, my lord. I've come to ask you to do a work of reconciliation.

– Me?

– Yes, you, my lord.

– What can I do, Mr. Buti?

– Judge, every year on the Thursday before Good Friday we have in the Holy Church of Zion the service of the Washing of the Feet. Many people from other churches come to see it, and they are satisfied. This year the minister, that is myself, is going to wash the feet of Mrs. Hannah Mofokeng, who is the oldest woman in Bochabela. And my daughter is going to wash the feet of Esther Moloi, who is a crippled child. And I am asking Judge Olivier to wash the feet of Martha Fortuin.

– Martha?

– Yes, judge.

– She has washed the feet of all my children. Why should I hesitate to wash her feet?

Mr. Buti's face was filled with joy. He stood up and opened wide his arms.

– Do you understand, judge, I want our people to see that their love is not rejected. Do you see that?

– Yes, I can see that.

– It will be simple, judge. I shall call out the name of Martha Fortuin, and she will come up and take a seat at the front of the altar. Then I shall call out the name of Jan Christiaan Olivier — you will not mind, judge, if I do not call you a judge?

– No.

– Then you come up to the altar, and I shall give you a

towel to put round yourself, and then a basin of water. I shall take off her shoes, and you will wash her feet and dry them, and go back to your seat. Then I shall put on her shoes, and she will go back to her seat.

– Does she know that I am to wash her feet?

– She knows that her feet are to be washed, but she does not know who is going to wash them.

– Will she be embarrassed?

– I do not think so, judge. She is a holy woman. She knows the meaning of it. After all, the disciples' feet were washed by the Lord, and no one was embarrassed but Peter, and he was rebuked for it.

– There's one thing more, Mr. Buti.

– Yes, judge.

– She does not know. Then who does know?

– Only myself and my elders. And of course you, judge.

– Well, that is proper. You see, Mr. Buti, a judge can do this kind of thing privately. He is as free to do it as anyone else. But a judge must not parade himself — you understand? — he must not . . .

– I understand, judge. Judge, you have made my heart glad. For me, and for many of my people, this will be a work of healing. I hope for our young people too. You know, judge, some of them think that white people do not know how to love, so why should they love them? I told them that Jesus said we must love our enemies, and one bright boy said to me that Jesus did not live in Bochabela.

On the evening of the day before Good Friday, Judge Olivier set out privately for the Holy Church of Zion in Bochabela. He parked his car near the church, and set out to walk the short distance. As he passed under one of the dim street lamps, he was recognised by a young reporter by the name of David McGillivray, who was in Bochabela following up a story, but who decided that it might be better to follow the Acting Chief Justice.

The judge was welcomed at the door by Mr. Buti and was taken to a seat at the back of the church.

– I am sorry to put you at the back, judge, but I do not want Martha to see you.

So it was that David McGillivray saw the washing of the feet.

– Brothers and sisters, this is the night of the Last Supper. And when the supper was over, Jesus rose from the table, and he put a towel round himself, as I do now in remembrance of him. Then he took a dish and poured water into it, and began to wash the feet of his disciples, and to wipe them with the towel. And when he came to Peter, Peter said to him, Lord are you going to wash my feet? And Jesus said, What I do now you do not understand, but you will understand it later. Peter said, You will never wash my feet. Jesus said, If I do not wash your feet, you will have no part in me. And Peter said, Lord, not only my feet, but also my hands and my head. Jesus said, If I wash your feet, you are clean altogether.

– Hannah Mofokeng, I ask you to come forward.

The old woman was brought forward by her son Jonathan, a white-haired man of seventy. And Mr. Buti washed her feet and dried them, and told her to go in peace. Then he called for Esther Moloi, the crippled child, who was brought forward in her chair, and for Maria Buti, his own daughter, who washed and dried Esther's feet. Then both girls were told to go in peace.

– Martha Fortuin, I ask you to come forward.

So Martha Fortuin, who thirty years earlier had gone to work in the home of the newly married Advocate Olivier of Bloemfontein, and had gone with him to Cape Town and Pretoria when he became a judge, and had returned with him to Bloemfontein when he became a Justice of the Appellate Court, now left her seat to walk to the chair before the altar. She walked with head downcast as becomes a modest and devout woman, conscious of the honour that had been done her by the Reverend Isaiah Buti. Then she heard him call out the name of Jan Christiaan Olivier and, though she was herself silent, she heard the gasp of the congregation as the great judge of Bloemfontein walked up to the altar to wash her feet.

Then Mr. Buti gave the towel to the judge, and the judge, as the word says, girded himself with it, and took the dish of water and knelt at the feet of Martha Fortuin. He took her right foot in his hands and washed it and dried it with the towel. Then he took her other foot in his hands and washed it and dried it with the towel. Then he took both her feet in his hands with gentleness, for they were no doubt tired with much serving, and he kissed them both. Then Martha Fortuin, and many others in the Holy Church of Zion, fell a-weeping in that holy place.

Then the judge gave the towel and the dish to Mr. Buti, who said to him, Go in peace. Mr. Buti put the shoes back on the woman's feet and said to her also, Go in peace. And she returned to her place, in a church silent except for those who wept. Then Mr. Buti read again.

– So after he had washed their feet, and had sat down, he said to them, Do you understand what I have done? If I, your Lord and Master have washed your feet, you ought also to wash one another's feet. For I have given you an example, that you should do as I have done to you.

But young David McGillivray does not hear these words. He has left the Holy Church of Zion, and has gone to find his editor at all costs.

Young McGillivray has got the story of the year, there can't be any doubt about that. In the whole of South Africa his paper alone carried the great story, and it enjoyed pride of place for twenty-four hours, because the afternoon papers don't publish on Good Friday. It was the front-page story, with great black headlines like those that tell of war, or the eruption of Krakatoa, or a rugby victory over New Zealand. Even on Saturday morning it was still the big story, *Acting Chief Justice Kisses Black Woman's Feet*. No fewer than three papers had those identical words, and that's not surprising, for how else can you tell that story?

Well, for better or for worse the story has gone round the nation. It's the kind of story that hardly any South African could be indifferent to. You either like it or you don't like it.

They don't like it at all in the Palace of Justice or the Union Buildings. As for the judges in Bloemfontein, most of them don't like it. Such things are not done and, if they are done, they should not be seen to be done. Some people think that Judge Olivier did it on purpose, but those who know him well don't believe that at all. In fact most judges don't believe it. Probably no one reads a news item with greater clarity than a judge, and young McGillivray's story makes it quite clear that he was in Bochabela for quite another purpose.

Perhaps it's wrong to say that the story has gone right round the nation. *Die Stem* of Pretoria has not mentioned the strange happening in Bloemfontein and, as far as the South African Broadcasting Corporation is concerned, it didn't happen at all. The English press — ah well, of course, of course, but they do blow things up, don't they?

And on Saturday two of the great papers of the world, *The Times* of London, and the *New York Times*, told the story. Stories like that place the South African ambassador in Washington in a most unsatisfactory position. In the White House such an event is regarded as a redeeming act in the history of a wayward nation, but in the embassy it is regarded as an act destructive of the tireless propaganda that goes out in praise of separate coexistence and separate education and separate worship and separate lavatorial accommodation.

— Judge.

— Yes, Mr. Buti.

— I am ashamed to look at you, judge. I didn't know that that young man was from the newspaper. You asked for it to be private, but now everybody knows it.

— That's not your fault, Mr. Buti.

— So you forgive me?

— There's nothing to forgive, but if you wish me to forgive you for nothing, I do so.

— That makes me better, judge. But apart from that, you did a great work. You helped to heal the pain of the Bosman funeral. There's nothing else that could have done it. I could preach a thousand sermons and I couldn't do it. I told you about the boy who said that Jesus taught that we should love our enemies because he did not have to live in Bochabela. He told me on the Friday that he was sorry. And, judge, the people want to give a new name to the church. It will still be the Holy Church of Zion, because all our churches are called that, but they want to call the church in Bochabela the Church of the Washing of the Feet. Some wanted to call it the Church of the Kissing of the Feet, but most of them thought we must keep to the Bible.

– Very sensible.

– And I want to ask you one more thing, judge.

– Ask it then.

– It's not an easy question, judge. But people are saying that the Government will be angry with what you have done, and that you will not become the Chief Judge of South Africa. Is that so?

– I do not know, Mr. Buti. It may be so, and it may not. But taking part in your service on Thursday is to me more important than the chief-justiceship. Think no more about it.

In view of the many misunderstandings that have arisen, the *Bloemfontein Herald* wishes to make it clear that its representative, Mr. David McGillivray, did not go to Bochabela to attend the Maundy Thursday service at the Holy Church of Zion. He went there to investigate a totally unrelated matter, and it is wholly coincidental that he was able to attend the service known as the Washing of the Feet, the full report of which appeared in our edition of yesterday.

— The Editor.

The Acting Chief Justice
Court of Appeal
Bloemfontein

My sisters and I were brought up by my mother to have great respect for judges, especially the judges of Bloemfontein. So don't think it is easy for me to write to you.

You are a disgrace to the Court of Appeal. A judge is not supposed to go looking for publicity, but when he gets his publicity by kissing the feet of a black dolly in front of a whole congregation, then he loses the respect of people like me, and believe me, there are lots of people like me.

If a man like you kisses the feet of a black dolly in public, then imagine what he does in private. I bet he kisses a lot of things besides feet. How can you stand the smell and the fuzziness? You disgust me speechless.

Sometimes I think I would like to leave my country, if it can produce a judge like you. But I'll stay around while we have men like Dr. Hendrik to stand up for the white nation. Last year Dr. Hendrik made a law to stop white and black going to the same church, and it is a scandal when a judge breaks it. I'm not an educated person, but I go mad trying to understand how a judge can break the law, and why nothing happens to him. Too big, I suppose, eh?

I'd just like to tell you one thing. In the Anglican Church, to which I belong but I don't like it, we have a service called the Washing of the Feet. There's no service called the Kissing of the Feet. You not only insult the white nation. You insult the white church too.

I sign myself
Proud White Christian Woman

– Pappie!

– Daughter, what are you doing here?

– I came to see you, pappie.

– And what about Dirk and the children?

– Dirk said I must come. We're so proud of you, pappie, for what you have done for our nation.

– Daughter, let me breathe. You mustn't choke me like that. I'm not used to it any more.

– Ma would have been proud too. It wasn't only for our country, pappie, but for our Afrikaner people. There's something going wrong with us. Our hearts are growing too hard, pappie. That's why it is so wonderful.

– It wasn't my idea, daughter. It was the idea of the Reverend Isaiah Buti, minister of the Holy Church of Zion. He wanted to reassure his people after the Bosman funeral. And I couldn't say no to him. But it was never meant to be public. There just happened to be a young newspaperman in Bochabela that evening, and he saw the Acting Chief Justice arrive in his car, and he thought he'd find out what the judge was up to.

– Well, I'm glad he did. What a shame if no one had ever known. Tell me, pappie, why did you kiss Martha's feet? Was it an impulse?

– I suppose it was. After I had dried the feet, I held them in my hands, and I thought of how far they had walked for our family. And suddenly, daughter, I saw Martha and you when you were a child, and I remembered clearly how she would kiss your feet. So I thought to myself, if she can kiss my daughter's feet, why can I not kiss her feet? No, daughter, leave me alone. I'm all dressed to go to the court, and I don't want to be messed up.

– Pappie, it was wonderful. But I don't suppose everyone thought it was wonderful.

– You can be sure about that.

– I know someone who will be very angry with you.

– Who's that?

– Long Tom. He thinks the judges belong to him.

– Don't be irreverent, child. You mustn't speak about our Ministers like that.

– Have you had messages, pappie?

– Indeed.

– Nice ones?

– Yes, nice ones. People hesitate before they send nasty messages to judges. Except this one. Read it, daughter.

He watched her face while she read it, anger and shock, and then anger.

– How can people write letters like that, pappie? How can a woman do it?

– She must be a sick woman. You should pity her, daughter. Now I must go, and you must go and see Martha.

– I've seen her, pappie. I did what you did. I kissed her. Do you know, I haven't kissed her since I was small? Do you know, pappie, you've freed me from something? It's usually children who free their parents, isn't it? Well, it's my father who freed me. I said to Martha, What have you been up to? What's all this about you in the papers? She looked very coy and said Mr. Buti had trapped her into it. But she didn't mind, she said. Now she was ready to die.

   – Did she say that?

   – Yes.

   – It's a strange country we live in, daughter, that a black woman says she is ready to die because a white man has kissed her feet in a church. Is it because she has been with him so long? Or is it because he is a judge? Or is it just because he's white? I think about these things a lot, daughter, but I don't know the answers. Oh yes, I know one answer. It is that our debt is incomputable.

   – Pappie!

   – Yes.

   – One thing more and then you can go. Does this mean that Minister Long Tom won't make you Chief Justice?

   – I suppose it does, child. But don't let it worry you, because it doesn't worry your father. Listen, how long are you going to stay with me?

   – Dirk says I can stay three days. I came just to tell you that you're top of my list of favourite men. Now you can go to court.

Yes, it is indeed a strange country we live in. Down in Durban Mr. Thomas Ndlovu is to receive a medal from the City Council in recognition of his brave action in going to the rescue of a twelve-year-old white boy, who, having climbed halfway up the more or less perpendicular face of Mitchell's Quarry, found that he could go no further, nor could he come down. When it was clear that the boy might panic, Mr. Ndlovu, showing more courage than skill, climbed up to join the small boy till the police arrived. By this time a crowd of several hundreds had gathered at the foot of the face, most of them Africans and Indians. The crowd had watched the small boy's progress with groans and sighs, but now they cheered Mr. Ndlovu on with jests and laughter, and gave him an ovation when he joined the small boy.

The arrival of the police was greeted with great good humour, and in five minutes the small white boy was on the quarry floor, lost to sight in a cheering crowd, shouting their joy and congratulations. In another few minutes Mr. Ndlovu also reached the floor, and was lost to sight also. When the police decided to take the small climber home, Mr. Ndlovu held up a detaining hand and first led the boy to the noticeboard, which read, *No Climbing, By Order*. What he said, no one heard, for it was lost in an outburst of catcalls, laughter, jeering and cheering.

Mr. Lodewyk Prinsloo, a clerk-in-charge in the employ of the South African Railways and Harbours, had risen to his present position from humble beginnings, and now owned a comfortable and unpretentious house at 14 Kensington Road, Claremont, Cape. The Prinsloos were a respectable and conventional couple, and the sitting-room was furnished with an old-fashioned sofa and armchairs, while on the walls were colour photographs of his parents and his wife's parents, of their own wedding, and their three children. The photographs portrayed his parents and hers as unsophisticated and worthy. There were also two pictures, of a mountain and lake that could well have been in Norway, except that there was some kind of balustraded terrace at the water's edge which looked as though it belonged to the Mediterranean rather than to the cold north, and this conclusion was strengthened by the presence in each picture of two beautiful women in diaphanous robes such as could only have been worn in the warm south. The two women were up early, for the sun had not yet appeared over the mountain, although its rising was clearly imminent.

It was Mr. Prinsloo's day off, and he was reading the newspaper in his sitting-room, when his wife announced that two gentlemen wished to see him. She looked apprehensive and examined his face to see if she could find some clue as to

the identity and business of the callers. When she brought
them in, he understood her apprehensiveness at once. He
could see that they were men of tremendous authority. He
had never read Kafka, but if he had he would have recognised
them. They wore black suits, and did not smile when they
greeted him, or offer to shake hands. One of them said to
Mrs. Prinsloo, Mevrou, you must excuse us, we wish to
speak privately to your husband, and she left the room more
apprehensive than ever.

Mr. Prinsloo was used to inspectors. The Railways and
Harbours employed many kinds of them. They inspected
passengers' tickets, buildings, railway lines, railway offices,
docks, tugs, public conveniences, bridges, and by their
inspections kept the great organisation, so to speak, on the
move. The inspectoral body exhibited a wide range of
characteristics and temperaments — some inspectors were
morose, some fussy, some authoritarian, some jolly and not
to be feared at all. But Mr. Prinsloo knew intuitively that his
visitors were men of awesome power, and he was filled with
fear, not a general fear but a particular one, the one that he
had lived with all his life.

He did not ask his visitors to sit down. It was they who sat
themselves down, and then intimated that he should be
seated. The first inspector opened the conversation.

– Mr. Prinsloo, let us begin our business. You are
Lodewyk Hofmeyr Prinsloo, are you not?

– Yes, inspector.

– And you were born on the second day of February 1914
in the city of Cape Town?

– Yes, inspector.

– You married Petronella Margaretha van Vollenstein on
the sixth day of June 1942 in the city of Cape Town?

– Yes, inspector.

– Mr. Prinsloo, how do you explain the fact that on your
birth certificate you are classified as coloured, but on your
marriage certificate as white?

It is not easy for a man to answer questions when he is
filled with terror, but Mr. Prinsloo knew that his terror
counted for nothing with the two inspectors.

– I put myself down as white, meneer. My whole family passed for white. My father was a white man, and my mother was a coloured woman, but she was as white as my father. That is their picture there, inspectors.

– Mr. Prinsloo, we do not have anything to do with racial classification. I am from the Department of Labour, and it is my duty to inform you that as a coloured man you are not allowed to hold the position of clerk-in-charge in the Railways and Harbours Administration.

– You mean? You mean . . .

– Yes, you are discharged as from today, but the Administration will not only honour its debt in regard to holiday leave, but will also give you an additional three months on full pay.

– Mr. Prinsloo, I am an inspector charged with the administration of the Group Areas Act, and it is my duty to inform you that you will no longer be able to live in Claremont. This is an expropriation order signed by the chairman of the Board and you will be paid an amount to be determined by the Board. The Board will allow you three months to find a property that you can buy or rent in any area designated as a group area for coloured people.

Mr. Prinsloo had given up all attempts to keep up any kind of appearances. He sat on the old-fashioned sofa with his head between his hands. The second inspector was moved to some kind of pity for him, the kind of pity that one might feel for someone who has been dealt with so pitilessly.

– There is one more thing that you must face, Mr. Prinsloo. Let me tell you at once that your marriage will not be affected. It took place in 1942 and at that time such a marriage was legal. But your children will be affected. They cannot any longer attend any school designated for white children. However, I am informed by the Cape Department of Education that your children need not be moved from their present schools until you have found a property that you can rent or purchase, and that of course you must do within three months from today.

– But my job? That is finished?

– Yes. You are discharged as from today. Have you any

private belongings in your office?

– No.

– Then we shall go. Do not trouble. We can find our way.

They had hardly gone before his wife was at his side. He lifted his head from between his hands and looked at her with some kind of inexpressible grief.

– Lodewyk, what did they want?

He wiped the tears from his eyes, but was not yet able to answer her.

– Lodewyk, I am asking you, what did they want?

– They . . . well . . . they came . . .

– Yes, why did they come?

– They came, Petronella, to bring bad news.

– Bad news? Bad news what about? Your job, Lodewyk?

– Yes, my job.

– You've lost it?

– Yes. I am discharged. From today.

– Why are you discharged?

And when he did not answer her, she said,

– Have you stolen money?

– No, I have not stolen money.

– Then why? For God's sake, speak, Lodewyk. I am your wife. I have a right to know.

– They say, Petronella, they say, they say, I am a coloured man.

She shrank from him. She too was filled with fear.

– Lodewyk, are you a coloured man?

– I was born coloured. They have examined my birth certificate. But I've always gone as white. My whole family went as white.

– But you were born coloured?

– Yes.

– And you married me knowing that you were coloured?

– Yes. I mean, I knew I was born coloured.

– How could you do such a thing?

– I loved you, Petronella.

She gave a wild, hysterical laugh that he had never heard in all their sixteen years of married life. Her face was contorted with anger, not anger at the black-suited inspectors, or at the cruelty of such laws, but at the man who had deceived her sixteen years before, and who today had destroyed the security and respectability of her life.

– You'd better go out, Lodewyk. Because you won't like the packing. Go up to Kirstenbosch and look at the flowers that bring you such peace. I never want to see you again. I never want the children to see you again. You can come back at five. We'll be gone.

When Mr. Prinsloo came back from Kirstenbosch they had gone. The house was empty. It had been emptied just as had his life, of his wife and his children and his job and what, for better or for worse, he had regarded as his happiness. In twenty minutes, less maybe, the two black-suited men had destroyed his world. The colour photographs of his three children, and of his wife's parents, had been taken away. The wedding photograph had been slashed to pieces, and these were strewn over the floor. There was only one photograph remaining on the walls, and that was of his own father and mother, of the white man who had married a coloured woman, and whose children had all passed as white, until today.

The coloured woman who worked for him came to him full of perturbation.

– Meneer, what's happened? Why have they all gone?

Why should she not be told? Was he any better than she? Was he not returning to her and her people?

– Maria, they've gone because I've lost my job. I've lost this house too. It's because I'm a coloured man.

– Those two men?

– Yes.

– Meneer, I knew they were bringing evil.

She broke out with sudden vehemence, she, the docile, patient Maria.

– May God strike them down! May God strike them all down, meneer. They are wicked men. Didn't they make us, meneer? And this is what they do to their own children. May God strike them down!

Petronella Margaretha Prinsloo is with her mother, weeping
and reviling. And her mother also is weeping and reviling.
And the children are weeping and lost, for who knows what
will happen to them? They gather round their mother, who
draws them into her protective embrace. She will protect
them against the cruelty of the world, against the cruelty of
the coloured man who fathered them. She has not yet fully
realised that her children are coloured too.

— You were walking four abreast over this bridge?
  — Yes.
  — And this black man was walking towards you from the
other side of the bridge?
  — Yes.
  — And when you reached him you threw him over?
  — Yes.
  — Did you know if he could swim?
  — No.
  — Why did you throw him over?
  — He would not give way.
  — When you walked four abreast over the bridge, was
there any room to pass you?
  — No.
  — Then how could he give way?
  — I repeat my question. How could he give way?
  — We were on the bridge first. He should not have come on
to the bridge. He should have waited. He could see there was
no room to pass.
  — There were four of you abreast. If one of you had given
way, he could have passed.
  — In our district we do not give way to kaffirs. They know
it well. This man knew it well. He was insolent. He knew
when he came onto the bridge that there was no room to pass.
  — When you threw him over, he was heard to cry out, I
can't swim, I can't swim. Did you hear that?
  — He cried out something.
  — But you did not hear what it was. Perhaps you did not
care what it was.

– We did not hear what it was.

– So you threw him over?

– Yes. He would not give way. He knew he had to give way.

– Did you realise that if he had drowned you four young men would be facing a charge of murder?

– No.

– You were lucky that he was rescued by a fisherman under the bridge. If he had not been, you would have been charged with murder.

– We did not think of murdering him. We threw him over because he would not give way.

– Have you anything further to say in your defence?

– No.

– Your worship, that closes the case for the prosecution.

– The four accused will stand up.

– I find you, number one, number two, number three and number four accused, guilty of assault with intent to commit grievous bodily harm. I accept your own evidence that you all helped to lift your victim up so that he could be thrown off the bridge. You are a disgrace to white South Africa, and I can find no extenuating or mitigating circumstances. You appear to have some perverted sense of patriotism, and imagine that actions of this kind contribute to the maintenance of Christian civilisation. You claim to be patriots, but such actions do your country incalculable harm, especially in the dangerous days through which we are now living. You claim also to be Christians, yet you showed no consideration for the rights of your victim to use the bridge, and no concern for the possibility that your action might lead to his death. I sentence each of you to one year's imprisonment, and so seriously do I regard your offence that I shall not suspend any portion of your sentence.

Many of the white residents of Soetrivier and district are up in arms over the action of the visiting magistrate in sentencing four of the young men of the region to one year's imprisonment each for throwing an African man off the footbridge that crosses the Soetrivier. The men alleged that the African would not give way to them, and that they therefore threw him off the bridge. The magistrate in passing sentence said that the four young men were a disgrace to white South Africa. An angry crowd gathered outside the court building, and police escorted the magistrate to his car.

A spokesman for the protesting residents said that they were scandalised by the severity of the sentence.

'It is a terrible thing to brand four young men as criminals because of a boyish prank. We have decided to send a deputation to the Minister of Justice, asking not only for a suspension of the sentence, but also for the removal of the magistrate to some safer area.'

The white bourgeoisie is getting itself all worked up because a white judge has kissed the feet of a black woman in a church in Bochabela. Half of the bourgeoisie is disgusted, and the other half thinks that a bit of kissing wipes out the scandals of the pass laws and the rape of the blackspots and perhaps indeed lengthens the life of white supremacy.

New Guard does not indulge in attacks on the so-called independent judiciary, but will certainly not encourage white people to entertain the delusion that what happened in Bochabela is a solution to something, or that it is an indication of the way 'things are moving'. The episode is totally meaningless and irrelevant, and it shows once more how unrelated to our realities are the bourgeois values of goodwill and sporadic benevolence in our South African situation.

The aspirations of the people of South Africa were given unforgettable expression in the clauses of the Freedom Charter. They concerned themselves with government, land, rights, wealth, industry, education, freedom of movement. They made no mention of the washing or kissing of people's feet. The Congress of the People would have exploded into incredulous laughter had anyone proposed the inclusion of such fatuities.

New Guard has one final thing to say about the farce at

Bochabela. It was an example of white condescension at its very worst. The Holy Church of Zion should be ashamed of itself for staging such a demeaning spectacle. Mrs. Martha Fortuin should never have lent herself to this act of extreme hypocrisy. The wages that she earns probably amount to three or four per cent of the judge's salary. Such gross inequalities are not removed by any amount of washing or kissing.

In this country of masters and servants, the masters think they can expiate their guilt by assuming the mock role of servants. In a society of equals it would be impossible to stage such a travesty.

—*New Guard*, 8 April 1958.

It has always been an essential part of the tradition of the Afrikaner to respect people in positions of authority. This applies especially to judges, and most of all to the justices of the Appeal Court in Bloemfontein. It goes without saying that a judge must behave in such a way as to retain this respect. Judges therefore keep out of the limelight. Their province is the courtroom, not the marketplace.

Therefore when an Acting Chief Justice, Judge J. C. Olivier, attracts to himself nation-wide attention because of his actions in a black church in Bochabela, he cannot expect to be immune from criticism.

There is no theological objection to a re-enactment of Christ's washing of the disciples' feet. Christ said specifically that his disciples should follow his example. While such ceremonies are not part of the Calvinist tradition, we cannot make theological objections if non-Calvinist churches perform them. That is not the ground of our criticism.

In the first place the judge's action at Bochabela ran counter to the racial policies of the Government, and conflicted with the spirit if not with the letter of Clause 29(c) of the Native Laws Amendment Act of 1957. Mixed worship is not compatible with racial separation, and racial separation is the mandate that was given to the Government in 1948, and renewed even more strongly in 1953.

However, the judge's action went further than a tacit repudiation of the philosophy of racial separation. To the washing of the feet he added a further highly sentimental and in our view extremely objectionable element, namely he kissed the feet of the black woman after he had washed them. Whether it was known beforehand or not that the press would be present is not the question. What we do know is that an embellishment of this kind is repugnant to most white Christian opinion, and certainly to most Afrikaner Christian opinion. The performance was melodramatic and tasteless.

We have the utmost sympathy with the judges of South Africa in the distress they must feel at this departure from their tradition of dignity and decorum. May such a thing never happen again.

—*Noordelig*, Pretoria, 8 April 1958

DECLARED UNDESIRABLE

The following list of publications declared undesirable is published in the *Government Gazette* of 11 April 1958.

New Guard, 8 April 1958 — New Guard Press, Cape Town

Hot Pants in Honolulu — Marcia Dimaggio — San Diego Publishers, Calif., U.S.A.

Black Passion — Charles Transom — Phoenix Press, Chicago, Ill., U.S.A.

59 Ways to Do It — B. J. Narayadu — Sutra Publishers, Calcutta, India

Die Dominee en die Garage — Chrissie van Schoor — Voorloperpers, Cape Town

Weg met Sensuur! — Andries Brinkman — Voorloperpers, Cape Town

Adventures of the Black Girl in Her Search for God — George Bernard Shaw — World Books

Bonjour Tristesse — Françoise Sagan — Albin Michel, Paris

. . . I think your reaction to the Bochabela incident is over-sentimental, and if I may say so without offending you, my dearest aunt, more likely to come from a woman than a man, and more likely to come from an older woman than a younger. The fact that you have known the family since the judge was a small boy, and that they brought the young woman Martha with them when they came to stay with you at Weltevreden, has also, I think, affected your judgement. I think the whole affair lamentable, and my Minister shares my opinion.

That puts it mildly. In fact he is black with anger. And so is Dr. Hendrik. They regard the judge's action as a challenge to themselves. They also regard it as the judge's calculated reaction to the decision of Dominee van Rooyen not to allow the Bosman funeral service to be held in the big Kerk. And that means of course a direct rejection of Clause 29(c) of the Native Laws Amendment Act.

Dr. Hendrik has made it known to my Minister, in a very proper way of course, that it would be very objectionable to him if Judge Olivier were made Chief Justice. I hear that Dr. Hendrik has also made his views known to the Prime Minister. But he need not have worried. The Minister spoke to me with something approaching venom, and this increased as he proceeded.

'Van Onselen, the man from Bloemfontein, or perhaps I should say, the man from Bochabela, has now crossed the Rubicon. He first put his foot into the water in March 1952, when the Appeal Court struck down our Separate Representation of Voters Act. If you want to know the exact day, Van Onselen, it was 20 March. He went in further when the Appeal Court struck down our High Court of Parliament Act in November of that same year. If you want to know the exact date, it was 14 November. You can't teach me any history about the six old men of Bloemfontein.'

It was a great spectacle, my dear aunt. The Minister had now risen to his full height of six foot six, and he was spitting out sentences like a machine gun spitting out bullets. Do you remember he once took a sjambok into Parliament when he made a speech about corporal punishment? Well, I was glad he hadn't brought it to the Palace of Justice because I'm sure I would have got a taste of it. And it's a good thing the Acting

Chief Justice wasn't there, because he would have got more than a taste.

'Van Onselen, we soon settled the hash of the six old men. We appointed five more judges of Appeal. Then we enlarged the Senate so that we could get the two-thirds majority. Then in 1956, on 27 February, Van Onselen, we revalidated the Separate Representation of Voters Act. The old men knew they were beaten, except one, the man from Bochabela. The court dismissed an appeal against the Act by ten to one. Ten judges recognised the legality of the enlarged Senate. But Mr. Justice Olivier decided that the motive behind the enlargement was to circumvent the entrenched clauses. That's not law, Van Onselen. Call it what you like, call it morality if you like, but it's not law. Now don't forget this man from Bochabela was next in line for the chief-justiceship. So I sent him a message, Van Onselen, no, don't get excited, it was only a telepathic message, and it said, One more step, Mr. Justice Olivier, and your great career is ended.'

You may remember, dear aunt, that my Minister once spent some time in Hollywood, preparing for a film career. Now I could understand it. He can act like a man possessed. I think he forgot that I was there at all, except that he kept on addressing me by name.

'Well, his great career is ended now, and tomorrow he will know that he won't become our Chief Justice. That's because, when he enacted this farce in Bochabela, he reached the other side of the Rubicon, Van Onselen. He reached the other side of the Rubicon two thousand and seven years after Julius Caesar, who crossed it in January, 49 B.C. The actual day of the month I don't remember, but our Acting Chief Justice crossed it on 3 April 1958. Caesar crossed it to victory, but Olivier crossed it to oblivion. Now remember, Van Onselen, if you mention that man's name again in my hearing, that's the end of you.'

Well, dear aunt, that's the end of the story of Bochabela. By the way, Judge Olivier did one good thing. He wrote to Mrs. Fischer after the death of her son. She asked me if she should write to him about the kissing of the feet, which she seemed to think meritorious. I said no.

Respected Judge

I am a young Indian woman from Durban, and I am in New York for an operation. Although my parents are with me, I am very homesick, and I wept with joy to read in the *New York Times* the story of Bochabela. I wept with joy because it made me proud to be a South African, and that isn't always easy in New York. You did a wonderful thing, judge. I know how difficult it is for a white person.

  With much respect

    Yours sincerely

      Prem Bodasingh

Dear Jan Christiaan

I am remembering today the solemn young boy who used to come to stay at Weltevreden. I was a newly married young woman, and I used to tease him about his solemnity. I did not know then that he would become a great judge.

Well, I have just read about his visit to the church in Bochabela, and of how he washed and kissed the feet of Martha Fortuin, who also came with the family to Weltevreden. Jan Christiaan, can a person sob with joy? Yes, a person can, because I sobbed with joy. My heart contained joy and grief simultaneously.

There is so much grief in our land that when one suddenly encounters joy it sets one to weeping. I grieve most about our own people. When I read about the Bosman funeral, and about the fate of this humble railway clerk Prinsloo, my heart could break. What has happened to us? I hear that Dr. Hendrik is to be our next Prime Minister, and I tremble at the thought and pray to God that He should not let it happen. This is a strange opinion to come from a woman who has been a member of the party for forty years. I joined it when I married Koos, and I am glad he is not alive to see what has happened to us. I was proud of the party, and General Hertzog was my idol. Do you think that he would have allowed these devils to hound poor Lodewyk Prinsloo out of his job and to drive his wife and children from him? The party was God's instrument to raise the Afrikaner from the dust and ashes of the English war, and to give him back his pride and his country, but now it has become the instrument of the Devil to treat others just as the English treated us.

It was kind of you in your busy life to write to Alida Fischer. There's another grief for you. After her son's death she came to Weltevreden, and her pleasure in the birds and the trees and the mountains and the sound of the little waterfall at night made me see my old home with new eyes. She came to me at the instance of my dear stick-in-the-mud nephew, Gabriel van Onselen, who lives for table tennis and the Department of Justice, and who, I much regret to say, cannot wait for Dr. Hendrik to become Prime Minister. Alida Fischer calls him Archangel Gabriel, because his true self came out of its shell when her son was arrested. I must say he disliked her son intensely, but when the trouble came he went at once to the rescue. I should explain that her son was promoted over Gabriel's head, although Gabriel was at least ten years his senior, and one does not recover from such a blow easily. The trouble is that Gabriel is not a Broeder-bonder. I suppose they have never thought it worthwhile to have him.

It would not surprise me if Gabriel gave up his selfish flat and went to live at Mrs. Fischer's. He has been a blessing to her but so has she been to him. The truth is he has got his mother back again, and there could not be a better arrangement.

Well, Jan Christiaan, thank you again for your great service to our people. Is there any chance that you might come again one day to Weltevreden? That would be a joy to me. Mind you, I am not lonely. It is ten years since Koos died, and the farm keeps me busy. And all night I read and read. When my time comes to die I shall have read nearly all the books in the world, except the modern ones of course, most of which are rubbish.

I send affectionate greetings to you, Jan Christiaan, and to Martha Fortuin also.

     Trina de Lange

Dear Judge

I did not think I would write a second letter to you so soon. I wept to read the story of your visit to Bochabela. So many things drive all our people apart that it gives one joy when some of them are brought together.

You know of course that it was my son's belief that only separateness would bring us peace. That was his father's belief also. Their beliefs did not bring me any happiness because I had to conceal my own. But the sad truth is that their beliefs did not bring them happiness either.

I thank you again, judge. I suppose that in the midst of all our troubles it is only a small thing. But it is a big thing for me.

  Yours respectfully
  Alida Fischer

. . . I am telling you something very confidential, my dear aunt. Mrs. Fischer has asked me to make my home with her. She has offered me the part of the house that was occupied by her son, and she says I can be as private as I wish. She says I do not need to have all my meals with her; we shall come to some arrangement.

Then she said something which I could see was painful for her to say. She told me that her son's bathroom was to be turned into a boxroom, and that the boxroom would be made into a bathroom, and that it would be connected with what would be my bedroom.

Now I must tell you something very difficult. The Minister won't like the idea at all. He hates the name of Fischer, and if I go to live there he is quite capable of taking it as an affront. What is more, the post vacated by the late Dr. Fischer has not yet been filled. The Minister has never suggested that I might get the post, but he has more than once spoken of his dependence on me. The post of course is not filled by the Minister but by the Public Service Commission. However, the Commission would pay attention to a suggestion from the Minister. So you will see that I am in a difficult position. I am sure that I would be very comfortable at Mrs. Fischer's, but that might well mean the end of my promotion.

I admire you, dear aunt, for starting a clinic at Ethembeni. But it is my duty to sound a note of warning. This man Emmanuel Nene, of whom you have such a high opinion, is under constant scrutiny by the Security Police. They suspect that behind that captivating smile of his he is a subversive character, and they have considered banning him under the Suppression of Communism Act. He is the organising secretary of the Natal African Landowners Association, and is inciting landowners in the blackspots to resist the lawful expropriation of their land. But worse than that, he has recently been appointed Natal Organiser for the Liberal Party. I think you should consider your course of action very carefully.

Emmanuel Nene is certainly organising the landowners in the blackspots to resist expropriation, and this is certainly called incitement by many white people. But if white farmers ever had cause to resist expropriation, that would be regarded as a legitimate activity. Emmanuel is followed everywhere by the Security Police, and this causes much anxiety among members of the Liberal Party, who would be desolated if he were banned under the Suppression of Communism Act.

His energy seems inexhaustible. He has given up part of his house to serve as a clinic, and Mrs. Katrina de Lange, one of the leading farmers of the district, brings out an African nurse from Newcastle twice a week. Her neighbours regard the venture as unusual, and make little jokes about it, but one does not oppose Mrs. de Lange very openly, because she has been one of the staunchest members of the National Party for many years.

Emmanuel Nene has given himself yet another task, and that is to make the Mansfields' departure to Australia as painless as possible.

– You judge yourself too harshly, Robert. You remember I said you were going to get wounded, but I didn't know how badly. We don't judge you. Now what about Prem? Did you see her before she went to New York?

– Yes, I did, Emmanuel. But I couldn't bring her here. I was afraid that our daughter Felicity would start screaming. But more than that. I couldn't have taken her into the room where — you know — where she was shot.

– How did you get on with Prem?

– You know Prem, Emmanuel. She was as natural as a girl could be. But I don't think I could ever have brought her into this room again, even though the man is dead.

– Yes, I understand that. And you have heard that the operation went well?

– Yes, I've heard it. Eddie says his surgeon friend is a genius and he seems to be.

– Now, Robert, there is one more thing. There are two people you haven't seen.

– I know.

– And you can't go without seeing them. You stood by them all the time you were in Newcastle. They feel your going very much. But what would they feel if you went without seeing them?

– I know, Emmanuel. I am ashamed of it. I must try to make it clear to you. If it had been ourselves, I think Naomi and I could have taken it. But first Prem, and then Felicity.

– You needn't explain. Now listen, Robert. I'm going back to Ethembeni tomorrow. Then the next day if you can, you come to my house at Ethembeni, and I'll take you to see Wilberforce and Elizabeth.

– I'll do it. You're a wonderful chap, Emmanuel.

Emmanuel gave his captivating smile.

– That's what my wife used to say, Robert, when we were first married. But lately she doesn't say it so often. Especially since I organised the Landowners Association, and since Philip made me into an organiser.

– Why, doesn't she want you to do these things?

– Of course she wants me to. But she doesn't like me always being away from home, where she can't see what I am doing.

– Well, Nhlapo, let me tell you, you and Elizabeth did it well.

– You think so?

– Yes, I think so. When I brought Robert to see you, I could tell that he was nervous to meet you. But you comforted him.

– Do you know what I think, Emmanuel? There are times when it is easier to be black than white.

– You are right. On this particular occasion it is so. Here is a white man who stands against these laws, and except for a few other white people he stands by himself. And look what other white people do to him. But when you and I stand against the laws, everybody is with us. No one tries to kill us.

They were both silent till Emmanuel spoke again.

– I'm sorry, Nhlapo. I'd forgotten about the assegai. Tell me, did you ever find anything?

– Nothing. Absolutely nothing. Not to this day can I think who would want to kill me. Now listen, Emmanuel, I have a big thing to tell you.

– I'm listening.

– I am going to join the Landowners Association.

– Well, well, I am listening.

– You think I shouldn't?

– I would never think such a thing. I know you couldn't join the party. But I always hoped you would join NALA.

– You never asked me.

– No, I didn't ask you. You are a Government servant. You would make the Government angry. They would put this Sergeant Magwaza onto you. He would watch you, and stop your car on the road and search it for weapons, and talk to your teachers, and even your pupils, and he would search your house. But the Government could do worse than that. They could warn you to resign from NALA, and if you did not, they could ban you from all public life. Just suppose, Nhlapo, that they said you could not enter any educational institution. That would be the end of your job, and what would you do then? How could I ask you to join NALA?

– Elizabeth and I talked about it. We knew I couldn't join

your party. But I am a landowner, and why should I not defend my land? Is a Government servant not entitled to defend his land? We decided that if I did not defend my land I would cease to be a man. We decided that ceasing to be a man was the worst thing that could happen to me, much worse even than being banned. We are a defeated race but not so defeated as that.

– Nhlapo, I like that language.

Emmanuel Nene's eyes were shining with joy, and he was full of excitement.

– But I am going to look after you, Nhlapo. You are older than I am, but I will not allow you to become prominent in NALA. Otherwise your fate, well, that is, if you are going to have a fate, will come sooner. That Sergeant Magwaza will break you if he can. Sometimes I wake in the night and ask myself how a black man can trap black men for a white Government. I have asked him that too. He looks at me with hate. If he could kill me, he would kill me. He hates me because I don't hate him, because I smile at him, because I ask him how he can trap his own brothers. You know I am a religious man, Nhlapo, but I ask myself how God can make such a man.

– You must not do that, Emmanuel. You must not think that when you do wrong, it is God that makes you do it. A man with your name! Emmanuel, God with us! It won't do.

– Well, well, you have thrashed me with your tongue. You are an older man and I respect you. But I shall not allow you to become prominent in NALA. Therefore do not be ambitious.

Robert, this is the last letter you'll get from me. You're going, and I'm going too, but not to Australia. I'm going Upstairs. The doctor says it will be from three to six months. The big pain hasn't started yet, but I know where it is going to be.

I'm not afraid of dying, Robert, but I'm not keen to go Upstairs. Even my mother told me that there you have to mix with the black nation. That's not exactly my idea of heaven. My mother always told me to make the most of it here because there's no white leadership with justice Upstairs. But I don't give up hope altogether. I remember those words, 'In my Father's house are many mansions.' That might mean no mixing.

I'm sorry to leave you, Robert. I've enjoyed our correspondence. I'm sorry never to have met you, but I'm not very keen on men. If I had listened to my mother, I'd never have married. It was a big failure. For one thing he had only one thought in his mind, and that was sex. I divorced him but my mother didn't want to take me back, so I've lived my life on my own, reading, and listening to the radio, and writing letters. And watching life from my window, ha! ha!

I'm not sorry for what I wrote to you, Robert. You wasted your time trying to bring together what God put asunder, as long ago as the Tower of Babel. He came down to confound their language so that they would not understand one another's speech. You went against that, didn't you? And look what you got.

Well, I'm not writing any more. It didn't help anyway. But I wish you luck in Australia, digger. I don't want to take any hate Upstairs.

I've got a nice surprise for you, Robert. I'll sign myself
      Humble White Christian Woman
PS. I'm only sorry for one thing. What I wrote about you and your daughter. I shouldn't have done it. But sometimes it seemed as though the Devil got into me.

PART SIX

Into the Golden Age

. . . Pretoria of course is in mourning, but underneath is a feeling of excitement and expectancy. The Lion of the North has gone and no one can say he was a great Prime Minister. He had great force of character, but Dr. Hendrik has both that and great force of intellect. He knows just where he and the country are going, and if anyone can take us safely into the future it will be he.

Of course it is not cut and dried. My own Minister will be a candidate for the premiership, and at least one other. But as soon as the choice is made, I shall write to you again. You know of course that in my view there is no other leader but Dr. Hendrik. I am not given to hero worship, but there is no doubt in my mind but that he is made in the heroic mould. I believe his will is totally unshakable. I believe he will not bow to world opinion, but will do what he thinks is right and practicable. He is said to have an unyielding personality, implacable in fact, but I think this is merely the way in which his enemies regard his indomitability.

My Minister has not discussed the succession with me. It would not be proper for him to do so, and I am glad that this is so. What would I do if he were to ask me outright who was my candidate for the premiership? It would be an impossible situation for me. I would have to decide in the twinkling of an eye, so to speak, whether to lie and demean myself, or to tell the truth and offend him. A nasty choice, my dear aunt.

You will of course have read that ex-Chief Lutuli was assaulted here in Pretoria when he was addressing an all-white study group. A group of young white men stormed the platform, and assaulted the chairman, also the secretary, who unfortunately was a woman, and got Lutuli on the floor and kicked him. The chairman and others tried to protect Lutuli, but not until he had received several blows, including one to his jaw. A spokesman for the young men declared that they considered it grossly improper for a black man to address a white gathering, especially in Pretoria, the historic capital of Afrikanerdom, and the seat of a Government which had time and time again declared that it totally disapproved of such gatherings. When the police arrived the assailants were arrested, the chairman apologised profusely to Lutuli, and Lutuli continued his address. He said later that he cherished no rancour, and that the meeting gave him great encouragement for the future. It gave him much hope that Afrikaners were beginning to question the policies of Dr. Hendrik and Mr. de Wet Nel.

Well, it was unfortunate, but I do not think the study group should have arranged such a meeting. The time is not ripe for this sort of thing, and Pretoria is certainly not ripe for it. I don't know how De Wet Nel got into the Cabinet. During last session he issued an instruction that all white officials in his Department of Bantu Affairs, when visiting black institutions, should greet black officials and others, not by shaking hands, but by putting their hands together and raising them, almost in an attitude of prayer or supplication, and saying, 'Molo, molo.' Well, I happened to be at the airport in Cape Town on the day after Parliament had risen. The place was full of M.P.s going to their constituencies, and it must have happened three or four times that, as a new arrival approached a table where other M.P.s were sitting, they would greet him and he them by raising their hands in supplication, and saying, 'Molo, molo.' Then they would all burst into ribald laughter. What Mr. de Wet Nel would have thought of it, I don't know. He takes himself very seriously, and will say very piously that he is a Minister because it is the will of God that he should be one. It helps one to understand the meaning of the saying that the ways of Providence are inscrutable. Do you remember, my dear aunt, out of your great knowledge, that that is what the eminent lawyer F. E. Smith said to the judge who asked him, 'Do you know, Mr. Smith, why I have been elevated to this position?'

DR. HENDRIK ELECTED BY CAUCUS
SUMMONED TO GOVERNMENT HOUSE
ACCEPTS THE PREMIERSHIP

Dr. Hendrik was this morning elected leader of the National Party by the party caucus. He succeeds the late Johannes Gerhardus Strijdom, who died on Sunday. Dr. Hendrik was elected unanimously, after two other Ministers withdrew their candidatures. Immediately the result was known, Dr. Hendrik was summoned to Government House, and asked by the Governor-General to lead the Government. He accepted, and will announce his Cabinet this afternoon.

Dr. Hendrik's appointment has been greeted with tremendous enthusiasm by the intellectuals of the party and of Afrikanerdom generally. His acceptance by the rank and file will take a little longer, but will certainly be total. Ordinary members of Parliament stand in awe of him, and not one of them would dare to debate with the new Prime Minister.

Quite apart from these considerations, Afrikanerdom will welcome Dr. Hendrik as the Afrikaner most fitted to lead the country in the difficult years that lie ahead. Foreign hostility to the policies of separate development has grown steadily fiercer over the last ten years. Afrikaner Nationalists believe that they have in Dr. Hendrik a man who has the ability, first to stand up to the United Nations, and second to convince the world at large that the policies of separate development are pragmatic and just.

Warm tributes were paid by the caucus to the late Prime Minister. He was also known for his courage and forthrightness, but it is widely recognised among Nationalists that his qualities of heart far outweighed those of his head.

White opposition comment is guarded. So is the comment of the black press. But underlying such comments is a deep note of pessimism. Both white and black non-Nationalists distrust the new Prime Minister's self-certitude and inflexibility, and both groups expect a deterioration in white-black relations, but will for the moment adopt a policy of wait-and-see.

ADDRESS TO THE NATION

The policy of separate development is designed for happiness, security, and the stability provided by their home language and administration, for the Bantu as well as the whites.

The different nations from which we are descended have each had a golden age, a period in which they reigned supreme among the other nations in world history. We here in South Africa have not yet had our golden age. We are as yet but the builders of a nation. But our nation will also be led to a zenith and in that climax of that golden age we shall also be of great significance to the world, still greater than now. We are already a nation, small in numbers, but yet great in our deeds . . . We have been planted here, we believe, with a destiny — destiny not for the sake of the selfishness of a nation, but for the sake of the service of a nation to the world of which it forms a part, and the service of a nation to the Deity in which it believes . . .

I have earnestly asked myself whether the advocates of total unity of the different races can bring justice and fairness to everybody. I am absolutely convinced that integration in a country like South Africa cannot possibly succeed . . . I am seeking justice for all the groups and not justice for only one group at the cost of the other three.

If meddlesome people keep their hands off us, we shall in a just way such as behoves a Christian nation work out solutions in the finest detail and carry them out. We shall provide all our races with happiness and prosperity.

—The Right Honourable the Prime Minister Dr. H. F. Hendrik.

So we are going into a golden age, led by our new Prime Minister, Dr. Hendrik. In this golden age it will be the role of the masses to dig the gold, and the role of the rulers to spend it. No one will be prevented from participating in the activities of the golden age, except of course that black people must realise that 'there is no place for the native in European society above the level of certain forms of labour'.

Dr. Hendrik holds the belief that by the year 1976, or some other equally miraculous year, the 'black tide' will turn, and will start streaming back to the 'homelands', which by that time will have an irresistible lure for those who left them for the very reason that they were poverty-stricken. The people cannot live on these fantasies. They demand a just share of the resources of the country they helped to build.

New Guard reminds its readers of those heroic words of the Freedom Charter: 'The national wealth of our country, the heritage of all South Africans, shall be restored to the people.'

These words do not refer to the wealth of the destitute 'homelands'. They refer to the gold of Johannesburg and Welkom, to the coal of Witbank and Newcastle, to the platinum and the copper and the chrome and the other mineral riches of our one undivided country; to the vineyards of the Cape and the maize of the Triangle, and the sugar of Natal; to the ports of Cape Town and Port Elizabeth and East London and Durban, not one of which could operate for an hour without the muscle of those people who are not considered good enough to sit in the Parliament that controls everything and everybody.

Dr. Hendrik is deceiving himself, his party, and his people. He hopes to deceive the masses as well, but he will not succeed. He hopes above all to deceive the 'meddlesome people who won't keep their hands off us', but he won't succeed there either.

New Guard refuses absolutely to join in the chorus of greeting to the new Prime Minister, raucous from the Nationalists, cautious from the spineless white opposition and the black lackey press.

Freedom is not yet.
— *New Guard*, 29 August 1958.

DECLARED UNDESIRABLE

The following list of publications declared undesirable is published in the *Government Gazette* of 5 September 1958.

New Guard, 29 August, 1958 — New Guard Press, Cape Town

Pret in die Pastorie — Chrissie van Schoor — Voorloperpers, Cape Town

Across the River and into the Trees — Ernest Hemingway — Charles Scribner's Sons, New York

Healthy Sexuality — J. D. Kissinger, M.D., Ph.D. — Phoenix Press, New York

Mr. and Mrs. Robert Mansfield and their son and daughter left Durban by the s.s. *Kalgoorlie* this morning on their way to Perth, Australia. Mr. Mansfield is to take up a post at the Latrobe High School. The Mansfields were seen off by a small company of friends, including Mr. Philip Drummond, national chairman of the Liberal Party, Mr. Emmanuel Nene, Natal organiser of the party, Miss Prem Bodasingh, who has recently returned from New York, and Mr. Hugh Mainwaring, the newly appointed Natal chairman of the party.

Mr. Mansfield said he had no comment to make on the reasons for his departure. The family wished to leave as quietly as possible.

A voice from the grave, eh? I'll explain, Robert. The Doctor told me I ought to write my last letters, as I soon won't be able to hold my pen because of the drugs. Well, I'm writing to you because you're really my only friend. That's a shock to you, eh? My sisters and I haven't written for years, and I'm not going to write just because I am dying.

I hope you'll be able to read it, because my hand is shaking. That's if you can take time off from throwing boomerangs at the kangaroos, ha! ha! I write ha! ha! but I don't laugh any more. Don't think I'm crying. I'm preparing for my journey. I'm being prepared by Father Don, who is the hospital chaplain. He's a holy man, and he's making me a bit holy too.

I know that you pray, Robert, and I want you to pray for me till I die. When I die, the doctor will let you know. He knows somebody who knows your address. He's a Jew, but I don't seem to worry any more about the nations.

Do you know I have repented of my sins? I'd write them down for you, but I haven't enough paper, ha! ha!

I must soon put my pen down. It's a Parker 69, and the

doctor is going to send it to you when I die. I told him he wasn't to say who sent it. He promised, but I could see he thought I was crazy.

Father Don says I wrote wrong things to you. Well, I'm sorry. I send best wishes to you, digger, and your wife and family. And to that Indian girl when you write to her.

I sign myself,

Humble Christian Woman

PS. Look, I'm going to put my pen down now. I'm going to put it down slowly, because I'll never pick it up again.

Last PS. I told you I'd never be touched by the black nation, but now they are talking of black nurses. It would serve me right, ha! ha!

. . . Well, my dearest wish has come true, and Dr. Hendrik is our Prime Minister. I shall myself go into the future with greater confidence. He says we are entering a golden age, and I believe it.

My Minister withdrew his candidature as soon as it became clear that the caucus wanted Dr. Hendrik. I don't think he had set his heart on it. He looks as cheerful as he has always looked. I do admire him. I admire him all the more after watching him handle the deputation from Soetrivier who came on behalf of the four young men who threw a black man off a bridge. The deputation asked the Minister for a suspension of the sentence of one year's imprisonment passed on each of the young men. They also asked the Minister to remove the magistrate to some other district.

My Minister told the deputation that he had studied the records of the case, and he saw no reason to interfere with the sentence. He appointed magistrates to administer justice, and in no circumstances would he alter their sentences or instruct them in their duties. Only a higher court could do that. He understood that the four young men were appealing against their sentences, and it was for the higher court and not for him to alter the sentences if it so decided.

The Minister then stood up, to his full height of six foot six inches.

'Gentlemen, this is the Palace of Justice, and only justice will come out from it. The magistrate said that these four young men were a disgrace to white South Africa, and I share his opinion. Young men must not be encouraged to think that because they are Afrikaners, they can throw black men off bridges. In regard to the possible transfer of the magistrate, that is no business of yours. It is a private matter that I shall discuss with him personally, so that I can ascertain his own wishes in the matter. Gentlemen, good day.'

The members of the deputation left the Minister's office in subdued fashion. Their faces showed a diversity of emotions, anger, resentment, humiliation. I forgot myself so far that I said, 'That was well done, Minister,' to which he gave a slight nod. A sudden thought went through my mind, and I wondered if it went through his also. I thought, how many votes will the party lose in Soetrivier?

More odd still, I suddenly remembered the lines of Clough:

> And not by eastern windows only,
>   When daylight comes, comes in the light,
> In front, the sun climbs slow, how slowly,
>   But westward, look, the land is bright!

Not very appropriate, I agree, but I wasn't thinking of Soetrivier at all. I was thinking of our new Prime Minister and of the golden age that lies before our country.

> Black man, we are going to shut you off
> We are going to set you apart, now and forever.
> We mean nothing evil towards you.
> A fresh new wind shall blow through your territory.
> Under your hands freed from our commandment
> You shall build what shall astonish you.
> The ravished land shall take on virginity
> The rocks and shales of the desolate country
> Shall acquire the fertility of the fruitful earth.
> Chance-gotten children shall return to the womb
> To re-emerge with sanctions and lead pattern lives

Of due obedience to authority and age.
Morality shall be recovered, the grave
And fearless bearing, the strange innocence
Of the tribal eyes, and all the sorrows
Of these hundred years shall pass away.
This is our reparation, our repayment
Of the incomputable debt.
We mean nothing evil towards you.

ABOUT THE AUTHOR

ALAN PATON was born in 1903 in Pietermaritzburg, in the province of Natal, South Africa. After attending Pietermaritzburg College and Natal University, he taught school for three years in the rural village of Ixopo, the setting for *Cry, the Beloved Country*. In 1935, he was made principal of the Diepkloof Reformatory near Johannesburg, a school for delinquent boys, where he instituted numerous reforms. Toward the end of World War II, Paton decided to make a study of prisons and reformatories, and traveled to Sweden, England, Canada, and the United States. It was on a visit to Norway that he began to write *Cry, the Beloved Country*, which he finished three months later in San Francisco. Paton retired from Diepkloof Reformatory shortly thereafter, and went to live on the south coast of Natal where he wrote many articles on South African affairs, and helped form the liberal Association of South Africa, which later emerged as a political party. Written with simplicity and restraint, eloquence and compassion, his other works of fiction include two novels, *Too Late the Phalarope* (1953) and *Ah, But Your Land Is Beautiful* (1982), and a collection of short stories, *Tales from a Troubled Land* (1961). Among his nonfiction works are: *South Africa in Transition* (1956), *Hope for South Africa* (1958), a volume of essays edited by Edward Callan, *The Long View* (1968), a memoir and tribute to his wife, *For You Departed* (1969), and the first volume of an autobiography, *Towards the Mountain*. He died in 1992.